# FUSE

E. L. TODD

**Fuse**

Copyright © 2020 by E. L. Todd

All rights reserved.

No part of this book may be reproduced in any form or by any electronic or mechanical means, including information storage and retrieval systems, without written permission from the author, except for the use of brief quotations in a book review.

CONTENTS

| | |
|---|---|
| Chapter 1 | 1 |
| Chapter 2 | 7 |
| Chapter 3 | 15 |
| Chapter 4 | 21 |
| Chapter 5 | 31 |
| Chapter 6 | 45 |
| Chapter 7 | 77 |
| Chapter 8 | 95 |
| Chapter 9 | 109 |
| Chapter 10 | 121 |
| Chapter 11 | 129 |
| Chapter 12 | 137 |
| Chapter 13 | 149 |
| Chapter 14 | 165 |
| Chapter 15 | 177 |
| Chapter 16 | 183 |
| Chapter 17 | 189 |
| Chapter 18 | 209 |
| Chapter 19 | 221 |
| Chapter 20 | 229 |
| Chapter 21 | 237 |
| Chapter 22 | 243 |
| Chapter 23 | 255 |
| Chapter 24 | 273 |
| Chapter 25 | 291 |
| Chapter 26 | 305 |
| Afterword | 319 |

# ONE

The balance of the dagger was unparalleled. No matter how it was gripped, the weight remained uniform, spinning around a center of gravity that was placed directly between the edge of the hilt and the blade itself. Naturally, the blade could roll off the wrist and slice through the air without being seen by the naked eye.

It was a masterpiece.

Cora set it on the counter and admired her handiwork. The metal gleamed under the candlelight and shone like the sun first thing in the morning. As she was the village's most skilled blacksmith, her weapons were simply the best.

The door flew open, and heavy boots thudded on the floorboards.

Cora already knew exactly who it was, judging by the lazy way he shifted his gait as he walked. She had the misfortune of dealing with everyone in the village, including the slime bags she could hardly tolerate. "I just made a new crossbow. Would you like to see it?"

Seth approached the counter then rested his thick arms on the surface. His brown eyes examined the blade before he turned his look to her, the corner of his mouth lifting in a smug smile. "I'd rather see you."

Bile rose up her throat. "The feeling isn't mutual, Seth. Now tell me what you want so you can be on your way."

"Come on, sugar."

Her insides burned with molten fire. "I'm not sugar. I was given a name for a reason, so use it."

That stupid look on his face never disappeared. "Going to the bonfire tonight?"

"Not if you're there."

The smile slowly dissipated. Apparently, he'd had enough insults to finally be offended. "You're colder than metal, you know that?"

"Maybe I just don't like you." She turned away to grab her hammer but was forced to a halt.

Seth grabbed her by the wrist and yanked her toward him. "You better start. Because you're going to be my sugar whether you like it or not."

The feel of his hand was more repugnant than burning lava. Every fiber of her being screamed in agony from the unsolicited touch. Without thinking twice, she snatched the dagger and prepared to stab him right through the palm.

"Cora." Dorian's voice sounded from the doorway. The power in the word alone was enough to stop her.

Seth pulled his hand away and stepped back, fear emanating from his eyes. He massaged his hand as if Cora had landed the blow. His arrogance no longer rang like a loud bell.

Dorian slowly walked into the shop, discontent obvious in the hard lines of his face. "Seth, leave. I can control Cora for only so long."

Seth cast a dark look at Cora that clearly said, "This isn't over." Then he walked out, his heavy boots sounding against the floorboards once more. When the door shut behind him, Cora and Dorian were finally alone.

Dorian approached the counter, disappointment clear in his eyes. He hadn't said a word, but it was obvious what he was about to say.

Cora returned the dagger to the counter. "It's the finest one I've ever made."

"It's impressive." He rested his elbows on the counter, his eyes glued to her face.

She wouldn't meet his gaze because she knew what was coming.

"Stop fighting it. You need to pick a husband."

"Why?" Anger rose out of her throat like fire. "I'm perfectly happy with the way things are."

"You need someone to look after you."

"I look after myself," she snapped.

"You can't be a blacksmith forever. People in town say—"

"I don't care what they say. I'm the finest blacksmith for leagues. No one questions that. If they really want to have dull weapons in the line of duty or in the midst of a hunt just because of what's between my legs, then they are idiots."

Dorian ran his fingers through his thick, dark hair, pulling it over his eyes before he pushed it away again. "I can't look after you forever. I have my own family to think of."

After she had been abandoned in the street, Dorian took Cora in as an orphan. He fed her, gave her housing, and taught her the craft. But he'd stopped taking care of her a long time ago. "You don't look after me. I support myself with my weapons. Frankly, you'll never find a better blacksmith or cheaper help. I'm the one who's doing you a favor."

He shook his head slightly. "But how long will that last? No one minded your skill in the beginning. But you're a lady now, Cora. You've been one for a long time. It's proper to take a husband and start a family."

"But what if I don't want a husband and a family?" Cora had no interest in any of the boys in town. They were exactly that—*boys*.

"That's too bad," he said coldly. "That's the way things are."

"Says who?" she questioned. "Society's rules aren't actual rules. They're opinions. And I have my own."

He looked down at the counter and sighed like this conversation was giving him a headache. "Cora, you're a smart woman. Maybe you disagree with what I'm saying, but that doesn't make my counsel wrong. The road ahead will be nothing but difficult if you continue to resist. I suggest you pick a husband while there are still good ones to choose from."

"Please don't tell me you think Seth is a good choice." He was an arrogant bastard. Cora wouldn't consider him if he were the last man on the face of the earth.

"I think he's better than some. His family owns the cotton fields. You would be well taken care of."

Cora couldn't stop herself from rolling her eyes.

"Cora." His deep voice sounded again. "I admire your independence, but don't be childish. You're smart enough to understand how the world works. If you don't marry, you'll be sold to the brothel."

"I'd rather die." She'd slit her own throat if she had to.

"Then marry Seth. Or pick someone else. It doesn't really matter. But you can't stay like this forever."

She picked up the blade again and admired it under the dim light. Weaponry was the only thing she had any passion for. Concentrating on molding the metal and getting the forges to the exact right temperature was what made her feel alive. Romance, marriage, and babies… They simply weren't her thing.

"Cora."

She slowly looked up at him, hiding her thoughts deep behind her eyes.

"I wish my sons were half as tough as you are." Dorian looked after her when he didn't have to, and even though his family didn't have much, they somehow managed to feed another mouth. While he wasn't particularly affectionate with her, he was never cruel. "Maybe the rest of the village doesn't admire you, but I do. I taught you the trade, but somehow, you outshine me. You don't take bullshit from anyone, and you hold your head high in pride, not arrogance. And you're beautiful without being vain. But those qualities don't mean much if you throw them away. Marry a good man and make the sacrifice. You can continue to do all the things you love without the grief. I know you've trusted my counsel in the past, so trust it now."

Marriage was repulsive. Being legally bound to a man she didn't love would be torture. But she was running out of options. Dorian always had her best interests at heart, and he treated her like another son. If there was anyone she trusted, it was him. "I'll think about it."

## TWO

Miss Fitz always told the best stories.

Whether they were true or false, it didn't matter. The tales were riveting and entertaining. The young and the old gathered around the roaring fire just to hear Miss Fitz talk about ancient history and prophecies of the distant future.

Cora always came, despite the stares directed her way. Disapproval rang in the air, and the girls whispered to one another while giving her cold looks. She was the talk of the town because she was one of the last few to take a husband.

She didn't care what they thought.

Cora took a seat against a tree log and admired the flames in the center of the clearing. They burned with a rhythmic pattern, the flames dancing to the music of the stars, crackling and popping to make their own songs.

She became lost in thought when Miss Fitz started to speak.

"Tonight, we will speak of the dragons."

Some people at the campfire sighed in disappointment. The legend of the dragons had been told for ages. But others stiffened in interest, wanting to hear the tale as many times as they could.

It happened to be Cora's favorite.

Miss Fitz adopted her storytelling voice, making it echo and bellow throughout the clearing. Everyone snuggled together under their sheep blankets and kept warm. "At the beginning of time, dragons ruled Anastille. They lived high in the mountains and low in the valleys. They were the kings of the land, ruling over every living thing.

"But all of that changed when man first set foot onto Anastille thousands of years ago. Unable to stay in their homeland after the highest mountain exploded in fire, they retreated to the first landmass they could find. Unfortunately, they didn't know who ruled it."

Cora hung on every word, even though she'd heard the story at least a dozen times. The idea of winged beasts ruling over man was eminently interesting.

"Dragons are wise and powerful. They didn't blindly trust the humans who came to their land. They watched over them closely, making sure there wasn't a threat of any kind." Miss Fitz looked at everyone in the crowd, watching their faces for a reaction. "After hundreds of years, the humans grew tired of the constant watch. They were allocated a small amount of land near the sea. As their population regrew, their resources dwindled. So, they asked the leader of the dragons for full freedom, to coexist in the land the dragons had claimed for their own."

Cora fiddled with the ring on her forefinger. It was brown and constructed of birchwood. Nestled inside was a beautiful emerald. Dorian had given it to her years ago, but she never knew where he'd obtained it. Although she was a blacksmith, she understood the jewelry wasn't cheap.

"Reluctantly, the dragons obliged. For hundreds of years, the humans had remained quiet and isolated. They never complained or turned hostile. And they seemed to appreciate the dragons' beauty, particularly their scales. It's common knowledge that the one flaw dragons possess is vanity. If ever met with a hostile dragon, compliment the brightness of their scales. That might be the one thing that can save you.

"The dragons could have simply killed the humans and ended their infiltration into the land, but as earthly creations, they understood the ground, soil, and grass couldn't belong to a single species. In fact, everyone was simply borrowing it before his own body returned to the soil. While dragons are always wise, they didn't realize just how poor this decision was."

Tension rose in the campfire. Children pulled blankets tighter around their shoulders, and the fire crackled in silent protest at the story. The stars in the sky shone on, listening just as intently. Cora pulled her knees to her chest and wrapped her arms around her legs, forming a small ball.

"The leader of the people, King Lux, protested for equal freedom in Anastille. No longer would they be guests in this distant land. They would be delegated their own land and their own laws. Simply allocating more land wasn't enough. So, he asked the dragons for a gift, a symbol of true bonding. After a full year of deliberations, since dragons take their time with everything, they finally decided to grant the wish. We call this the First Fuse."

Quiet whispers erupted around the campsite. New visitors to the campfire asked their companions endless questions rather than just letting Miss Fitz explain it herself.

Miss Fitz raised her hands to silence everyone. Not once did she have to speak to gather everyone's cooperation. Even in her silence, she possessed authority. "The First Fuse is the greatest moment in all of history, for it's the moment when the dragon voluntarily agreed to fuse with a human, to become a hybrid, for man and dragon to exist as a single person."

When Cora first heard this story, she could hardly believe her ears. To be combined with a dragon, to have the ability of flight and fire-breathing, was something that kept her up long into the night. Sometimes, she dreamed of spreading her wings and soaring high over the tallest crags of the mountains in the north. Sometimes, she dreamed of having scales of armor that glimmered under the light of the sun. And sometimes, she wished her dreams were a reality.

"When a dragon chooses to fuse with a human, it's the greatest gesture a dragon can make. People say they can communicate with just their thoughts, and sometimes with only emotions and not even words. The joined being is comprised of two hearts, and at any time, the human version can reveal himself as he once was before molding back into the form of the dragon.

"When a human fuses with a dragon, he's blessed with an unnaturally long life. He becomes almost immortal, only susceptible to death by mortal wound. Such a gift isn't taken lightly." Miss Fitz examined the faces of the crowd, and when she had the effect she desired, she continued on. "That was the beginning of the new age, where dragons, humans, dwarves, and elves lived among one another as equals."

Cora didn't know much about the elves or the dwarves. She knew they existed at one point, but that was the extent of her knowledge. After only seeing humans all her life, it was hard to imagine anything else.

"But this didn't last long. King Lux was corrupt and greedy for power. He began a campaign to fuse with as many dragons as possible and annihilated the ones who refused to cooperate. Over the span of one hundred years, he accomplished his goal and wiped out the race of dragons completely."

While she'd never known a dragon or even witnessed a picture, this part of the story always made her sad. The humans came to their land as refugees, and the dragons graciously gave them asylum. And that was how the human race repaid them? It made her sick.

"There was an uprising with the elves and dwarves. They never approved of the humans in the first place, and once this enslavement began, they considered it an act of war. This led to what we know as the Great War."

Cora had heard about this too, and it was definitely bloody.

"While outnumbered, the humans defeated their enemies with cruelty. General Rush, King Lux's son, was the vilest soldier in their army. He killed more elves and dwarves than most soldiers combined. He was considered their secret weapon because his blood lust could never be satiated. Powered by political greed, he was instrumental in the winning of the war."

Cora would never understand how tensions could lead to such a bloody battle. Humans were innately greedy, but understanding the extent made her despise her own species.

"Now, the dragons are no more than a fairy tale." Miss Fitz's voice drifted off in sadness. "They're just a folktale we exchange when the town's gossip has run dry. Now, we live in a cruel world ruled by men."

Cora fingered her ring again, her mind deep in thought.

A boy at the edge of the campfire spoke out. "Can the dragons ever come back?"

"Unlikely," Miss Fitz answered. "Very unlikely."

"Is King Lux still fused?" a young girl asked.

"That, I'm not sure," Miss Fitz answered. "But since he's lived for so long, I can only assume."

Cora's skin prickled at the thought. So, there could be a dragon left in Anastille. But he was a prisoner to Lux, a cruel king.

"How does a human get a dragon to fuse?" the first boy asked.

"That's a mystery to me," Miss Fitz said. "But I can only assume by some dark torment. No dragon would voluntarily serve a man who wiped out his entire race."

King Lux already robbed them every quarter when his men came to collect rent. Some families were left to starve just so the king's pockets would be a little heavier. The soldiers insisted the tax was required to keep them safe from attack or invasion.

But from what?

Humans were the only beings left in Anastille. What exactly were they being protected from? It was all an excuse to wipe the commoners of every coin they possessed.

It was bullshit.

Miss Fitz surveyed the eager minds before she spoke again. "The dragons never should have trusted us so completely. Opening their hearts to us was their downfall. And I'm ashamed of my species for doing such a grotesque thing."

Amen to that.

"Miss Fitz, why are there three kings?" a young girl asked.

Miss Fitz straightened like that was a question with a long-winded answer. "No one knows for sure, but I suspect—"

The watchman jogged up the dirt road with a torch in his hand. Everyone turned in his direction because it was uncommon to see anyone run anywhere—unless something dire had happened. He stopped by the campfire and turned to Miss Fitz. He was covered in sweat, and fear was in his eyes. The light of the campfire highlighted every feature on his face. The man of the guard, covered in armor and weapons, was actually scared. And that didn't bode well for the rest of them. "The Shamans approach the gate."

## THREE

The Shamans had only come to town on one other occasion, and it was to interrogate a man who served in the king's guard. Rumors had spread of their foulness. They were covered in black clothing, every inch of their skin hidden from sight. They had the form of a man but the stench of something dead. When they moved their heads, it was with peculiar slowness, as if they were birds searching for their next meal in the soil. Just their presence chased away all hope.

Cora had only seen them from a distance, and that was close enough. Despite her brave heart and fearless edge, she knew they were unbreakable opponents. Not a single weapon forged in her finery could match their power.

They didn't even carry weapons.

She could only assume they were mages, possessing great magical power that couldn't be matched with a blunt ax or a crossbow. Their defenses were deep inside their brains, and the fact that no one was certain what their powers were made them all the more frightening.

Dorian pulled Cora inside the home he shared with his family. "You'll stay here tonight."

She didn't want to burden him with her presence. The house was small, and they already had three boys to look after. She was another mouth to feed, another person to occupy a bed. "I'll be fine above the shop." She'd taken up residence in the small space. It had a bed, a bathroom, and a kitchen. It wasn't much, but it was more than enough for her.

"No." Dorian locked the front door and hooked his broadsword to his hip. "No one knows why they're here or what they want. We stick together." Dorian never showed fear, but it was clear he was worried about the safety of his family. "Lie low. Keep the shop closed tomorrow."

"That's our business." She tried to keep the hysteria out of her voice. Without income, they would have no way of buying meat from the butcher or getting eggs from the farmlands. "It has to stay open."

"Nothing is worth our lives, Cora." His brown eyes bored into hers, somehow convincing her with just a look. He had the unnatural ability to manipulate her with simple concern. "Stay inside and be quiet. End of story."

A day had come and gone, but the Shamans were still in town. Without leaving the house, Cora knew they were there just from the heavy feeling in the air. Fear was around every corner. The springtime joys had quickly dissipated the second the Shamans arrived.

Dorian walked through the front door with meat and potatoes. "This should hold us over for a while."

Cora immediately moved to him. "What are people saying?" She followed him all the way to the kitchen and watched him salt and prepare the meat. Warning was in her heart that something devastating would happen now that the Shamans had arrived. What did they want? Or, whom did they want?

Dorian rested both hands on the counter. "I don't know."

"You don't know?" Cora found that hard to believe.

"No one's talking," Dorian said as he worked with the meat. "Everyone's lips are sealed. All I can gather is they are questioning people about something."

"What?"

"I don't know," he said with a shrug. "The Shamans must have made a good threat to keep everyone from talking. Whatever it is they are interested in, it must be important."

Very.

Dorian covered the meat and let it sit on the counter. "Don't worry, Cora. If we can't figure out why they're here, then that's probably a good thing. The less we know, the better."

"Are they interrogating everyone?"

"That I don't know," Dorian said. "Hopefully, they'll get what they want and leave."

"Yeah…hopefully."

Dorian sent her a look of encouragement before he gripped her by the shoulder and gave her an affectionate squeeze. "We're a tough gang, Cora. We always make it through."

Several days had come and gone, but the Shamans still hadn't left. They weren't always seen, but their presence was felt. The darkness that accompanied them everywhere seemed to follow them like a heavy cloud.

Cora was bored out of her mind.

Dorian told her to stay inside and forget about the shop, but when she wasn't doing something with her hands, she went a little crazy. She'd just finished a new crossbow, but she hadn't had the opportunity to even test it.

She needed to get out.

Dorian was helping his brother in the fields, and everyone else was in their bedrooms. If she slipped out then returned later, no one would notice. And if the Shamans came to the shop, she would simply hide upstairs.

After she made up her mind, she left the house then walked down the dirt road. The village was completely empty. No one was coming or going. The usual buoyant atmosphere was absent, as if it never existed at all. All the doors were locked, and the curtains were drawn over the windows.

It was a ghost town.

Cora was halfway to the shop when she heard a blood-curdling scream. It made her bones tense. Her heart went from a steady and slow rhythm to an explosive pace. That scream echoed in her ears, and she couldn't shake it off. It wasn't the sound of kids playing together in the dirt. It was a shout of absolute terror.

Cora turned down the alleyway between the butcher's shop and the wax emporium. All she had was a short blade hanging from her hip. With the Shamans' presence, it would be smart to keep walking, but Cora couldn't ignore what she heard.

Someone needed help.

When she reached the end of the buildings, she turned left and spotted Tommy, the butcher's eight-year-old son, hunched against the back wall. Tears were streaming down his face, and he was cowering over in fright.

A Shaman was there.

He was leaning over the child, making weird movements with his fingertips. He was wafting something toward him, the air or a specific smell. The scene looked too eerie. A smart person would have turned and run.

Cora pulled out her dagger and prepared to attack. "Stop whatever the hell you're doing, Shaman."

A high-pitched scream erupted from inside the dark hood. The creature immediately turned to Cora, his fingers still outstretched. His face couldn't be seen inside the hood. It was just a sea of black. The creature was unnaturally still while he watched her. Then, he crooked his head to the left.

And that sent chills up her spine.

A low hiss erupted from inside the hood, formidable even though it lacked any words.

"Tommy, run." Cora refused to take her eyes off the Shaman. To do so was instant death.

"No…" The carnal voice came out almost as a whisper. He turned back to the child and resumed whatever foul thing he was up to. His fingers started to work the air again, and he resumed his attempt to suck the life out of Tommy.

Anger exploded inside Cora's heart, and she lunged forward with her blade at the ready. Without thinking twice about it, she stabbed her blade deep into his side and was repulsed to feel how soft it was. It wasn't hard with muscle and bone. In fact, it felt like there was nothing there at all.

The Shaman turned quicker than the eye could follow, and without touching her, he threw up his open palm and sent her high into the air and across the dirt ten feet away.

She crashed hard onto the ground, immediately making her body ache from the collision. She knew she couldn't stay down, no matter how much it hurt. If she didn't get up, she would die.

Cora rose to her feet then pulled out the small dagger she kept in her boot. She took a defensive stance and eyed the Shaman without blinking. Now the creature adopted his own defensive stance like he was about to charge her.

That's when she noticed Tommy was gone. He must have run off during the fight.

Thank goodness.

Cora knew she couldn't outmatch this thing—whatever the hell it was. Her only option was to run. Even though her dagger was special, the first one she ever made, she grabbed it by the hilt and threw it as hard as she could, penetrating him right where the eye should be. The hilt extended past his hood, embedded into whatever flesh the fiend was composed of.

The Shaman shrieked and reached for the dagger.

And that was when Cora ran like hell.

## FOUR

"Where the hell were you?" Dorian gripped her by both shoulders and shook her as though that would make her answer faster. "Why do you always disobey me? Is it out of principle?"

She was still catching her breath after running as fast as possible. "Actually, yes. But that's beside the point."

"Why are you covered in sweat and dust?" He looked down at her filthy shirt and pants. "Rolling around with the pigs?"

She didn't have time for their regular banter. "I stabbed a Shaman in the side and again in the eye. Now I'm running for my life."

Dorian's hands slowly lowered from her shoulders, and the paleness that swept over his face was remarkably similar to the whiteness of the moon on a clear night. "You did what now?"

"I stabbed a Shaman. Not sure how I got away."

Now that he realized she'd said what she truly meant to say, his pot started to boil. "You went looking for trouble?"

"No." Although, that sounded like something she would do. "I was walking to the shop when I heard a boy screaming. When I went to investigate, the Shaman was leaning over the boy and doing something strange…sucking out his life or something."

Dorian's hand moved up his cheek and into his hair. He fisted it uncontrollably, trying to hold on to his last drop of sanity. She'd just announced his death sentence, and he wasn't handling it well.

"The Shaman was doing some kind of dangerous magic. That boy would have died if I hadn't intervened."

"Then you should have let him die." He lowered his hand to his side and stared at her with the coldest expression she'd ever seen. It was practically winter in his eyes.

"How can you say that?" Dorian was compassionate and strong. He took her in when he didn't have to. Everyone else turned away at the thought of raising an infant little girl, but he took on the challenge.

"When it comes down to you or someone else, always choose you." He viewed the situation in black and white, but if he had been there, he would have seen the episode in full color. Despite what he said, Dorian would have helped the boy if he'd witnessed the same thing Cora did. "You've just put a bounty on your head."

"I know…"

He stepped away and rubbed his temple. "Did you kill him?"

Cora couldn't help but release a sarcastic laugh. "I wish."

"It's only a matter of time before he traces you back here. We'll deny being close to you, but we can't hide you. You need to leave."

Now that Cora saw the fear in his eyes, she loathed herself. Dorian feared for his own family, his three sons and his wife. Cora was the reason they were in jeopardy. "Where should I go?"

"Into the wild. You know the terrain, and you're skilled with a bow. Hide out for a while until the coast is clear."

"How long?"

"Until I come get you."

"But how will you find me?"

Dorian crossed his arms over his chest and considered the question. "Remember when I taught you the way of the bow? Do you remember where that was?"

She would never forget it. She had been young at the time, but that didn't make it any less clear in her mind's eye. Dorian gave her all the skills she needed to provide for herself. Without him, she would have had to resort to much more drastic measures. He was the closest thing she'd ever had to a father. "Yes."

"That's where we'll meet."

"Okay." She swallowed the lump in her throat, finally feeling the fear wash over her skin. She wasn't afraid of what might happen to her. Death wasn't something she feared. But she feared losing the only people who gave a damn about her.

Dorian retrieved weapons from the back of the house and handed them over. "You have enough arrows for hunting and defense. And here's your other dagger and short blade."

She took everything with weak hands and an even heavier heart.

"Take the back exit out of the village. And don't look back." Dorian guided her to the rear of the house, where the door was located. He held it open and looked at her one more time.

Would this be the last time they ever saw each other? Was this the end?

Dorian grabbed her by the shoulder and gave her a gentle squeeze. "Cora, you're a smart girl. Everything will be alright."

"I'm so sorry…" She couldn't finish the words because the remorse killed her. "I'm sorry for putting you in this position."

He didn't give in to the sadness, nor did he show any fear. "Sweetheart."

Cora's eyes watered slightly at the affectionate name. He hardly ever called her that, maybe three times in the span of her entire life.

"You know me. I always take care of the people I love. Right now, you just need to worry about yourself. Do you understand me?"

She nodded.

"Cora." He stared at her hard, forcing her to speak. He taught her long ago that simple nods and shrugs weren't real answers. Only the spoken word meant something.

"I do."

He kissed her forehead, the scruff from his jaw rubbing against her skin, and then pulled away slowly. "Until we meet again." Affection was in his eyes, a fatherly love.

Cora didn't give in to the emotion because it would break her. She'd never had to say goodbye before, and now she realized just how hard it was. "Until we meet again."

The village of Vax was located in a brush valley. The soil was perfect for farming, and the distant mountains acted as the perfect scenery. Just a league away from the village was a stream that supplied clean water in the summer and winter. It was peaceful, hidden away from the rest of Anastille. It was all Cora had ever known, with the exception of visiting nearby villages for metal ores. But those were several days away by the crow's flight, so she only traveled once in a great while.

She hiked away from the trail and headed to the crags near the river. It was important to stay hidden from unfriendly eyes, and she knew it was only a matter of time before the Shamans realized she'd left Vax. They would search for her endlessly, and when they found her, they would slaughter her with some terrible magic.

She ended the thought and kept going.

Dorian and his family were left behind, and she hoped no ill would come to them because of her foolishness. When she'd stabbed the Shaman, she'd aimed to kill. When her blade felt nothing but smoothness, that was when she panicked. They definitely weren't human.

They were something else entirely.

Now, she had a bounty on her head. A part of her considered surrendering just to end the situation. If she had to do it to save Dorian and the others, she wouldn't hesitate.

She'd slit her own throat.

How much did she expect to accomplish out there past the grapevine? Would she really be able to evade them? How long would she stay out there? What if Dorian never came? What if—

*Come to me.*

Cora tumbled to the ground as her skull felt as if it had caved in. Agony washed over her entire body. It was as if hot coals had been dumped on her head, and no matter how she moved, she couldn't escape the burn. An invisible rope had wound around her neck and controlled her effortlessly. The words had no physical form, but they overpowered her. She gripped her skull as she lay on the grass, unable to think or stand.

*Come to me.*

Just as before, it ripped her skull in two. The voice echoed endlessly in her brain, causing an aftershock of static. The sound wasn't audible, but it was so strong it practically made her deaf.

Then an image came into her mind, a picture of the dead white tree near the ancient boulders. Everyone in Vax knew about the tree because of its history. It was the only tree in the entire world that thrived in the winter and went dead in the summer and spring. And the fruit it yielded was the sweetest.

*Shit, I'm coming.*

She thought the words to herself, unsure if she could communicate with the voice in the same way.

*Hurry.*

*If you shut the hell up, I can.*

The voice finally fell silent.

After the pressure left her brain, she slowly rose to her feet and wiped away the blades of grass. A ladybug was on her shoe, and she gently flicked it off. As soon as the voice was gone, she felt better. It was like nothing had happened at all. Fortunately, she was in a field of flowers. If she'd been near a cliffside, she probably would have tipped over and fallen to her death.

Cora hiked through the field and headed to the winter tree. She was obeying a voice without knowing to whom it belonged, but she didn't see any alternative. If it had the power to communicate with her like that, it probably had other powers.

Was it the Shamans?

She stopped dead in her tracks at the thought.

She pulled out her bow and fit an arrow to the string. It probably wouldn't pierce their soft flesh, but it might be enough to take out another eye. If they found her this quickly, then she had no chance of escape to begin with. They may bring her to death, but she could do everything possible to take them with her.

Her bow was aimed the entire way, prepared for whatever fight she was about to face. Distantly, she felt comforted by the possibility of the Shamans.

If they were there, then they weren't torturing Dorian.

She made it over the slight rise then approached the white tree from behind a boulder. She pulled an extra arrow onto the string for added impact. It wasn't smart to waste an arrow that way, but she suspected she wouldn't need the rest anyway.

Cora grounded herself and took a few breaths before she stood upright and pointed her bow to kill. Her fingers held on to the arrow and the string, feeling the tension shoot completely up her arm. Her shoulder no longer ached from the strain like it did when she'd first trained with the bow.

She searched for the hooded Shamans, the fiends that didn't seem to originate from this world. The black leather that covered their bodies gave them the definition of humans, the same biceps in the arms and the same muscles in the legs. But she knew there was something completely different under the apparel.

Cora scanned the clearing, her eyes glancing over the winter tree, and landed on something she hadn't been expecting whatsoever. Instead of seeing the Shamans, she saw something much more terrifying.

Blood-red scales shone under the afternoon sun. When they caught the light in just the right way, they mimicked fire. The colors changed from deep red to light yellow, making a fresco that was constantly changing.

Each piece was textured like glass, reflecting everything that came near the armored skin. Gentle cracks connected each one together, like riverbeds on the world map.

With every slight movement, the muscles underneath the scales became more prominent. The behemoth of strength was unmistakable. The sheer size of the creature dwarfed everything in its vicinity.

Claws that were inches long dug into the earth. Each spike was gracefully curved to an extremely tapered point. It was sharp enough to slice Cora in half with a single swipe.

Cora's eyes drifted up the curved back of the creature, taking in every image of something so deadly but also beautiful. Her eyes settled on the folded wings, thin in material but strong enough to lift its heavy weight. And that was when she noticed the red blood oozing from the wound.

Her gaze traveled farther up its slender neck and to the face that made up every child's nightmares. Eyes the same color as sunflowers burned into her with imminent hostility. Not once did they blink. They took her in, absorbing all of her features.

The creature's mouth was the most interesting part. It was closed, and there were no lips. But it was clear that behind the snout were endless rows of razor-sharp teeth that could slice a boulder in half.

Cora's heart stopped beating, and her lungs forgot how to breathe. In stark astonishment, she slowly lowered her bow and felt her entire body go weak. She'd been expecting the deadly creatures from the village. But what she came face-to-face with was much worse.

A dragon.

# FIVE

Fearless, Cora didn't back down from any fight. Defeat was never an option, and she gave everything she had until there was nothing left. But she wasn't stupid either.

This was a fight she couldn't win.

She set the bow on the ground along with her arrows. Her eyes were glued to the dragon the entire time, not letting it leave her sight. "I always pictured dragons to be the kinds of predators that got off their asses and hunted down their food, not commanded their dinner to come to them."

The dragon took in a slow breath, and its throat rumbled with disapproval. Steam billowed up at the end of its snout, a clear threat of being burned alive. *Looks like this meal is suicidal.* More steam erupted from the end of its snout.

Instead of shaking in her boots and feeling the adrenaline just before death, she felt oddly calm. Knowing there was nothing she could do to win this battle gave her an odd sense of calm. "If you're going to eat me, let's get on with it." She wasn't sure what was worse, being eaten by a dragon or being tortured by the Shamans.

They both sucked.

*You aren't appetizing to me. No offense.*

Cora felt her eyebrow rise as far as it would go. "None taken." She noted the deep baritone of the dragon's speech. She didn't know anything about their species, but she was certain this dragon was a male. "Then why did you command me here like a slave?"

*Why did you come, if you aren't a slave?*

Cora narrowed her eyes in irritation, surprised by how argumentative the creature was. She was even more impressed with its intelligence. It communicated with her flawlessly, as if having a human conversation was completely ordinary. "I wasn't given much of a choice."

The dragon looked over the distance before its eyes returned to her face. *You always have a choice.*

Cora didn't pull her eyes away from the creature, unsure exactly what was happening. Now, she wished she'd done more research on dragons when she had the chance. But then again, why would she if they were considered extinct? "Why have you summoned me here?"

*Sorry, do you have somewhere else to be?*

The sarcasm in his voice told Cora he knew exactly what she was doing. But how he knew was a mystery to her. "You're an ass, you know that?"

He breathed the fire deep in his belly, and this time, smoke erupted from his nostrils.

"Is that supposed to scare me?"

*If being burned alive doesn't alarm you, then you need some serious help.*

She eyed his broken wing and returned her gaze to his face. "You clearly want me alive."

*For now.* The threat lingered in her mind after the words faded away. *Fix my broken wing.*

Cora crossed her arms over her chest. "Do I look like a healer to you?"

*You look like you know enough.*

"Well, I'm not the kind of girl you boss around. Just because you're bigger than me, and breathe fire and whatnot, doesn't mean I'll do anything for you."

*I'm a dragon.* He said it like the fact was reason enough.

"Your point?"

*You should want to help me.*

"Why?" she demanded. "You disrupted my journey and forced me here. Then you insulted me. And now, you're asking for my help? The only thing I feel toward you is irritation."

He tilted his massive head slightly, his eyes narrowing to slits. *You're peculiar.*

"I'll take that as a compliment."

*Fix my wing, or I really will burn you alive.*

Cora gave him a blank look and shifted her weight to one leg. "I don't respond to coercion."

*Then what do you respond to? Jewels? Coin? A dragon claw?*

"No," she said quickly. "Just some old-fashioned respect."

Now the dragon had a blank look on his face.

She sighed and lowered her arms. "Just ask nicely. All you've done up to this point is boss me around. I'm guessing you're new to this human interaction thing, so let me enlighten you. Ask politely."

Frozen to the spot, the dragon just stared.

"Come on." Cora tapped her foot impatiently. "Have some manners and ask politely. If you'd done that from the beginning, you would have saved a lot of time."

He blew out more smoke like this conversation was extremely irritating.

Cora had nowhere to go nor anyone to see, so she waited.

The dragon rose to its full height and looked her squarely in the eye. *Will you please fix my broken wing?*

Cora didn't hide the smile that spread across her lips. "Since you asked so nicely, of course." She approached the dragon without any fear of being swiped with a claw or becoming his dinner. "You'll need to lie on the ground because I can't reach."

The dragon slowly lowered itself to the dirt, but its wing was still seven feet from the ground. Cora would never be able to reach it, not unless she climbed on his back. "May I climb up?"

He stared straight ahead, looking across the meadow and toward the village of Vax. *You may.*

She crawled up his arm and shoulder until she reached the back of his neck. Then she made her way to the injured wing that was folded in. When she looked down, she realized just how high up she was. And she also had a startling revelation.

She was standing on a dragon.

"I need you to stretch out your wing so I can get a better look."

The dragon released a deep growl before he complied. The wing slowly expanded, and the wound was exposed.

Cora examined the injured flesh and realized he hadn't been stabbed or shot with an arrow. He'd been burned. "Did you breathe fire on yourself?" Was that even possible?

*No.*

"Then what happened?"

The dragon was quiet for so long it wasn't clear if he would answer. *I was shot with fire.*

Cora spread the wound apart and inspected the burned flesh. The wound looked fresh, perhaps only a few days old. "What does that mean?"

His back recoiled slightly, the memory chafing again against his scales. *Shamans used their magic. Tarnished my beautiful scales.* His skin began to burn with heat, his anger emerging to the surface.

Cora froze when she heard the words echo in her mind. Shamans chased down this dragon and used their powers against him, and then Shamans came to Vax. Was that truly a coincidence? "Why did they do this to you?"

*I'm a dragon.* He said nothing more, those few words sufficient to explain the whole picture.

"Are they trying to capture you? Or kill you?"

The dragon fell silent once again, his back rising and falling with his heavy breathing. *Does it matter?*

"Actually, it does." She stared at the back of his neck, noting the large spikes protruding. They were a darker shade of red, almost brown. "Because two Shamans came to my village. They tried to hurt a child, and I intervened. I stabbed one in the side and the eye, but it didn't seem to affect him at all. That's when I left the city and fled into the highlands."

The dragon turned his head so he could stare at her over his shoulder. His colossal yellow eye bored into hers. *I knew you were running from something. But from what, I did not know.*

"It sounds like we have the same enemy."

*No. They are everyone's enemy.*

"Why do they want you?"

The dragon faced forward again. *Just because you're forward with your information doesn't mean you should expect others to be in return.*

"Why be secretive?" She moved the wing slightly, making sure important tendons hadn't been damaged. "If you trust me with your wing, then you know I'm not your enemy."

*You don't understand the definition of trust, clearly.*

She tried not to be insulted by his coldness. Dragons were strange creatures. Very much so. "For argument's sake, they are chasing both of us. I say we stick together and lie low. You can't travel with a wound like this."

*Yes, I can.*

"You shouldn't. You need to heal."

*I can walk.*

"But walking isn't resting."

*I need—*

"Are all dragons this stubborn?"

A growl erupted from deep in his belly. *I'm not stubborn. I'm just wiser than you.*

"I don't know about that…" She folded the wing to his back then slid down to the grass. "Isn't it important to keep your scales pristine and clean? If this wound doesn't heal right, you may have a scar." Miss Fitz said dragons were full of vanity. If there was one thing they cared about, it was their looks.

The dragon tensed at her words, his eyes scanning the horizon.

Cora knew she'd made an impact.

*If I do as you say, you'll make sure I don't have a scar?*

Cora hid her smile. "Yes. No one will know the difference."

Cora had an ulterior motive. She needed to get to the top of the crags where she'd agreed to meet Dorian. He was her only source of news, and if she missed his passing, she wouldn't have a clue what was going on in Vax.

The dragon didn't need to know that.

They slowly made their way up the mountain, taking the longer route since the dragon couldn't move around so easily, not with its large girth. Even if he could fly, that wasn't an option. With his bright red scales, he would be spotted in a second.

"What's your name, anyway?" Cora walked in front, her bow slung over her back along with her quiver of arrows. Her dagger remained in her boot, and her short blade was attached to her belt. The weight didn't hunch her shoulders or work her back. She was used to exerting herself on a daily basis when she forged her weapons over the burning fires.

The dragon always used long pauses before responding. He was either extremely thoughtful in his answers, or he dragged them out on purpose. *Flare.*

"That's your name?"

The irritation was clear in his projected thoughts. *That's what I said, is it not?*

"It's just…that doesn't sound like a dragon name." She hiked up the hill and concentrated on getting the soles of her boots in the right areas.

*Why would I want my name to sound like all the others?*

Cora shrugged and kept walking.

*And yours?*

"Cora."

His deep voice slowly enunciated the word. *Cora.*

"Pretty, huh?"

*Eh. Not as pretty as my scales. Even in the moonlight, they sparkle like diamonds.*

Cora raised an eyebrow as she walked, confused by that response. She was told dragons were particular about their looks, but she didn't realize how excessive it was.

*When I breathe fire, it looks like a dance of flames.*

She tried not to laugh. Listening to him talk about his beauty was entertaining.

*How much longer?*

"Not too long."

The dragon fell quiet behind her, his massive claws thudding into the dirt with every step he took. The ground beneath them shook as they scaled the mountain. When they approached a tree nested with birds, the winged creatures took flight the moment they sensed the vibrations from the dragon's approach.

"Can I ask you something?"

*Was that the question?*

She ignored the sarcasm in his voice. "I thought the dragons were annihilated."

The dragon fell quiet.

She glanced over her shoulder. "Hello?"

*I'm still waiting for the question.*

She faced forward again and hid her irritation. "Are you the only dragon left in the world?"

*No.*

"Really?" She stopped in her tracks and turned around. "There are others?" The idea of these winged creatures roaming the skies once more was incredible. If there were enough of them, they could take back the land from King Lux, and those disgusting Shamans could be returned to wherever the hell they came from.

*Yes.* Flare tilted his head and examined her closely, his eyes narrowing slightly. He studied her like she was swaying grass in the breeze or dancing flames in a hearth. Nothing was happening, but he couldn't look away. *But you already knew that.*

"What?" She put her hands on her hips. "Does it look like I already knew that?"

*How can you not? Your elven brethren must have told you everything by now, despite your childish age.*

She raised her hand in irritation. "Whoa, hold on. My childish age? What does that mean?"

*It means you're a child. Or are you not old enough to understand the vocabulary?*

Even though her opponent was a dragon, she really wanted to go head-to-head with him. It was so easy for him to insult her. He did it fluidly, like he truly enjoyed it. "I'm not a child. I'm a woman."

He leaned in farther, getting a close look at her features. *You've never killed a man before.*

"What does that have to do with anything?"

*Everything.* He pulled his head away.

"Maybe I haven't killed anyone, but I'm considered old in the village. I've seen twenty-one years. I'm practically ancient."

Flare snorted, and a small amount of fire erupted. Cora was far enough away to barely feel the sting of the flames. *Twenty-one years is merely a second.*

"Then how old are you?"

Flare looked away, dismissing the question. *That's a very rude question to ask.*

"You asked me."

*No. I assumed.*

Cora wanted to stomp her foot in protest, but that would just confirm his assumption that she really was a child. Flare had said something far more important than her age, so she focused on that. "What did you mean by my elven brethren?"

*You're an elf. Therefore, you must know what they know.* Flare peered at the sky before he turned back to her.

"I'm not an elf."

Flare tilted his head slightly, and his yellow eyes scanned her face. *You are.*

"No, I'm not. I may be young in your eyes, but I'm definitely not an elf." She'd never even seen an elf, so how could she be one herself? No one had ever made that assumption before. Everyone in the village accepted her as one of their own.

*I see the world with my eyes, nose, and claws. I know an elf when I see one, smell one, and touch one.*

"But I'm not," she argued. "I'm a human."

*You're half human, half elf. Hybrid.*

Cora felt the sweat form under her brow and on her palms. A dragon was looking her in the eye and telling her she belonged to another race. "With all due respect, you're wrong."

*Your features are softer than those of humans. The curves of your eyes are exaggerated, shaped like the almonds you find in your forest. Your upper lip reminds me of a bow. The fair skin of your neck and face is unnaturally smooth and soft. Not a single mark has adorned your face because your skin there is impenetrable. You're petite, much smaller than the average woman of the human race. You're strong, able to run long distances and lift heavy objects because your body is mainly composed of lean muscle, not fat. But I see the human aspects as well, such as your wide shoulders and ungraceful movements. Not to mention your limited intelligence.*

At first, his words were complimentary, but that quickly changed toward the end. "I am intelligent. I'm saving your wing, aren't I?"

*You thought you could kill a Shaman with a dagger.* If he could roll his eyes, he would have.

"That doesn't mean I'm stupid. It means I'm brave."

*You're confusing bravery with recklessness.*

The constant insults were making her hot under the collar. She'd never been so insulted in all her life, and the fact that her aggressor was a magical dragon wasn't helping matters. "You know what…" She put her hands on her hips and tried to think of something harsh. "Your scales aren't even that pretty."

Flare immediately tensed under the insult, every muscle in his arms recoiling for a fight. His neck straightened, and he looked down at her like she was firewood about to be lit with his flames. A growl erupted from deep in his belly, echoing along the mountainside.

Maybe she shouldn't have said that.

*Do you want to die, hybrid?*

Whenever she was scared, she acted braver. "Do you want to lose your wing?"

He snorted gently, and smoke rose from the end of his nose.

"Then maybe you should keep the insults to yourself."

*They aren't insults. They are honesty.*

"Well, I'm being honest too."

*No, you aren't. You're asking to be turned into lunch.*

"If you were going to kill me, you would have done it by now." She turned her back on him and kept walking forward. She hid her fear well, and she suspected that made the dragon respect her more. Or maybe she was completely wrong, and he would burn her alive.

## SIX

THEY STOPPED AT NIGHTFALL.

Cora couldn't see where she was going without a torch. Without light, she would be walking aimlessly in the dark. Progressing through the rough mountain terrain wouldn't be smart if she didn't know where she was stepping.

Flare never seemed fatigued, but he didn't complain when she decided to stop for the night. They found a grassy area near a cliff face. The fog had settled in, giving them an extra blanket of invisibility. It would be impossible to track Cora under those circumstances.

She had a thin blanket to keep her warm, and she used her pack as a pillow. She lay on her side and stared at the dragon sitting a few feet away. He was curled into a ball with his head resting on the tip of his tail. His eyes were open, watching her just as she was watching him.

She'd been thinking about what he'd said for the entire day. Could he be right? Could she really be a hybrid? She'd always been different from everyone else in the village. Could that be why?

*What troubles you?*

Her eyes moved to his. "What makes you think anything is troubling me?"

*You furrow your brow when you're stressed.*

Could he really read her that well? They'd only been together for an afternoon. "I was thinking about what you said. About me being elvish."

*What about it?*

"I've always felt different from everyone else. Like I don't completely fit in."

*Your brash personality probably turns them away.*

She gave him a cold look. "Would you stop insulting me?"

*Just being honest.*

"Well, be a little less honest."

*I can try.*

"Anyway...I don't know where I come from, so I guess it's possible."

*Clarify your meaning.*

"My guardian said he found me abandoned at the gate. He took me in and raised me as his own. He doesn't know who my parents are or where I came from. All he knew was my name because it was left in a letter."

*What else did the letter say?*

"Nothing."

Flare adjusted his position against the rock wall, his eyes still on her. *It's unlikely an elf would ever abandon her child. It's very rare for them to have children at all, let alone toss them aside like an overproduced commodity.*

"Then why would my parents leave me?" As much as it shamed her to admit it, it still bothered her that her parents didn't want her. Dorian took her in and was a wonderful guardian, but he wasn't her father. Every gathering in the village was full of families, and it pained her to know she'd never had one of her own.

*I don't have the answer you seek.*

Cora looked up at the stars because she couldn't stand his yellow eyes any longer.

*But it wasn't because they didn't love you.*

She slowly turned back to him, caught off guard by the gentleness of his words. "What?"

*An elf would never abandon their child unless they had no other choice. They were trying to protect you from something. What, I do not know.*

That hope was enough to make her heart swell in longing. In her dreams, she pictured the loving eyes of her parents staring fondly at her. They were reunited as a family, and everything was finally as it should be. "You really believe that?"

*I do.* Flare continued to stare at her, his colossal eyes glued to her face. *But I also believe they are no longer on this earth. They would have come back for you by now if they were living and breathing. The fact that they haven't after all this time can only mean one thing.*

The painful truth of his words hit her right in the chest. It was a fear she'd been prepared for. Her parents didn't want to come back for her, or they weren't alive to come back for her. Either possibility was devastating. "You're probably right." She turned on her side and faced the opposite way from the dragon, hiding the tears that began to leak from the corners of her eyes. She kept her silence and allowed them to fall down her cheeks and to the soil beneath her. Crying wasn't in her nature, and she certainly didn't do it in front of anyone else.

As a dragon, Flare could sense vibrations in the atmosphere. Without even looking at her, he could sense her agony. It hummed in the air surrounding her, and it was loud enough to press painfully on his ears. He could feel every tear as it fell down her cheek.

He could feel everything.

"How's your wing?" Cora gripped the edges of the rock and climbed over the wall. It took most of her concentration to scale the mountain and get to the top of the rise.

Flare climbed over it in just a few seconds, his body packed with the muscle to move mountains. *It's fine.*

"We're almost there. It'll be better soon."

A slight tone of panic colored his voice. *Will my scales still be glorious?*

Sometimes it felt like she was talking to two different people. There was the calm and collected version of the dragon, and then there was the rude and vain version of the same beast. "Yes, they'll be fine."

*Will I have a scar? I can't have a scar.*

"I'll make sure you don't have a scar. Don't worry."

Flare released a deep breath that sounded like a sigh.

Cora made it to the top of the cliff then brushed the dirt off her pants. "So, can you read my mind all the time?"

*No. I can't read minds.*

"But you're doing it now."

*No. I'm speaking into your mind. You're responding verbally.*

"So, could I communicate with you the way you're communicating with me? Just by thinking in my mind?"

*Yes. But I don't suggest it.*

"Why?"

*Unless you're skilled with mind craft, I can hear your other thoughts, thoughts you may not want to share.*

"So, you *can* read minds."

Flare's facial expressions didn't change much as a dragon, but he could manipulate the air around him, change the tone. Right now, he was clearly irritated. *No. It's how I converse with humans and other dragons. Humans can choose to communicate internally, but most of them don't know how. They just respond out loud.*

"They don't know how? Then how come I know?"

Flare shook his head slightly. *I don't have an answer to that.*

Cora grabbed her water sack from her bag and took a drink. "Would you like some?"

Flare glanced at it. *No. That's a mere drop for me.*

She returned it to her pack. "Suit yourself."

*I can sense people's thoughts and emotions but only if they are willing. And I can't look into their minds and see anything I want, such as the past. I can only feel whatever that person is thinking in that moment of time.*

"Couldn't you force yourself into a mind and manipulate it?"

*Yes. But I never would.*

"Why not?"

*It's rude.*

"The whole thing sounds complicated."

*Not really. Sharing your mind with someone else is the most personal thing two beings can do. It belies a level of trust that can't be explained in words. When two beings agree to that level of communication, they usually possess a profound relationship.*

"So…could I penetrate your mind?"

He snorted. *Not unless I allowed you to. My mind is much stronger than yours.*

Cora shot him a glare.

*I don't mean that as an insult. Dragons are distinct. The level of security around our minds is impenetrable. Our anatomy is simply different. The only opponent who could break me would be another dragon. But of course, a dragon would never do such a thing. It's our only rule.*

"Your only rule?"

*The only rule our society abides by.*

"So, that means you could kill each other?"

*Yes.*

"And that's something you do?" Killing was illegal among humans. It surprised her that ferocious beasts didn't practice the same law. Bloodshed must have been common during the days of the dragons' reign.

*Never.*

"Then why isn't it a law?"

*Why have a law for something that never happens?*

"Just a precaution."

*Not worth our time.*

"Do you have any other powers?"

Flare stepped forward and continued their journey, dismissing the question. *You ask a lot of questions.*

"I'm curious. Before yesterday, I didn't know dragons still existed."

*We are remarkable creatures.*

She rolled her eyes.

*I saw that.*

"Like I care."

He swatted her playfully with his tail and made her trip.

Cora caught herself before she hit the ground. "Jerk."

*Child.*

She jumped to her feet then brushed the dirt off her hands. "You're lucky I'm still willing to fix your wing."

*And you're lucky I'm still willing not to burn you alive.*

She adjusted her pack before she resumed their path to the river. She had a hole in the knee of her pants from climbing the rock face. When she'd left Vax, she didn't have time to grab everything she might need. Hopefully, Dorian would bring extra supplies. "When a dragon and a human fuse together, do they have that level of communication?"

*Yes.*

"Have you ever fused with a human?"

Flare flinched slightly, clearly offended by the inquiry. *Again, you ask a lot of questions.*

"I'm just curious. I learned that it used to be common between dragons and humans…before we went maniacal."

*If I wanted you to know that information, I would have presented it long ago.*

Cora didn't understand that response at all, but she assumed it was a complicated no. "For what it's worth, everyone in my village hates the king for what he did to the dragons, including me."

Flare didn't respond outwardly to that information.

"I'm sorry." Cora knew Flare must feel alone. Even if there were other dragons in the world, there couldn't be many. She couldn't imagine that type of loneliness, to be one of the last remaining people of her species.

*No need to apologize.*

"If there were ever an uprising against the king, you would have the support of many humans."

*I know.*

"And you would have my support as well." Flare was abrasive and harsh at times, but she was beginning to realize he was harmless. What happened to his race was a crime, and he deserved justice for it.

*I appreciate that.*

She faced forward again and heard the faint sound of a stream in the distance. "We're almost there."

*Good. I need a bath.*

They reached the stream and lay under the large willow tree that provided plenty of shade as well as cover from unfriendly eyes. Flare extended his wing out so Cora would have access to the wound located at the base.

"I'm going to clean it, so it doesn't get infected."

*My scales prevent such diseases.*

"Well, let's clean it just to be on the safe side." She grabbed a fresh piece of cloth from her bag then soaked it in the river. After she squeezed out the extra water, she attended to the pierce in his hide.

Flare didn't flinch as she treated him. He stared across the water and watched the sun move in the sky.

Cora wiped away the dried blood and scabs and examined the wound more closely. Most of the area was singed from the fire that struck his scales. It was black and reeked of burned flesh.

*It's bad, isn't it?*

"It's not as simple as I thought."

Flare took a deep breath in disappointment.

"But I think I can fix it. I just need a special plant."

*What?*

"Root tip. It's good for burns."

*Maybe for humans. But not for dragons.*

"It's worth a shot." She set the cloth down then headed deep into the trees. She knew basic information about plant lore from the town's workshops. While her main occupation was a blacksmith, she was interested in all realms of academia.

When she located the root, she yanked it from the ground then returned to where Flare lay. "I found it."

*That was fast.*

"Looks like I'm intelligent after all." She pulled the root from the leaves then ground it into dust with a rock. Once the particles looked like grains of sand, she wiped them across the wound, letting the burned flesh absorb it.

*Is it supposed to burn?*

"Yes."

Flare continued resting his chin on his claws.

She let the root tip absorb into the wound then grabbed the long, slender leaves she removed. "Now I'm going to stitch it up."

*What does that mean?*

"I'm going to force the wound to close. It'll heal faster, and there won't be a scar."

*I've never heard of that.*

"It's something I figured out on my own." She began to work, piercing either side of the wound and tying it together, closing the wound so nothing could get inside. The root tip would remove the ash from the scales and promote the healthy regrowth of new scales. She'd never worked on a dragon before, but she could only assume his physiology was similar to her own. "All done."

Flare turned his head so he could examine it himself. *It looks the same.*

"You need to give it time to heal on its own."

*How long until my scales are more beautiful than the world itself?* He flipped again, changing his personality almost immediately.

"At least a few weeks. This is a nasty cut."

He snorted in disappointment then faced forward again.

"Just be patient, Flare. It'll be back to normal in no time." She rubbed his massive flank and felt the muscle through the hard scales.

Still upset, Flare remained silent.

She packed up her supplies and saved the remaining root tip for a later time. It was a good plant to have on hand. "I'm going to take a bath." She hadn't bathed in a few days, and she was beginning to feel the grease in her hair and the dirt under her fingernails.

Flare didn't acknowledge her words, still in a sour mood.

Cora walked to the edge of the water then began to undress. She stripped off her shirt and undergarment then moved to her pants. She removed everything, including her final undergarment. Since Flare was just a dragon, she didn't see the harm. He was technically a male, but that was irrelevant if he was a different species.

She walked into the water then turned around to look at Flare. "The water feels nice."

Flare stared at her hard, unblinking. He took in every inch of her, looking her up and down. The look he gave her was different, far more intimate than ever before. Then he quickly jerked his head in the opposite direction like he was ashamed for looking at all.

After she dried off and combed her hair, she changed into a new set of clothes and washed the old ones in the river. Flare was still facing the opposite direction, looking into the trees.

The tension rose with every passing minute, and Cora realized she'd made a deadly mistake. Somehow, she'd offended him without meaning to. She hung her clothes in a tree to dry, then approached him. "Flare."

He didn't turn her way. *Yes?*

"I'm sorry about before…with the bathing."

Still like a bird about to swoop down on its prey, he didn't move.

"I didn't mean to make you uncomfortable."

*You didn't make me uncomfortable.*

She didn't? "It just seemed like…"

*You're a beautiful woman, Cora. Surely, your limited intelligence hasn't stopped you from realizing that.*

The first compliment made her forget about the second insult. "What does that matter? I'm a hybrid, and you're a dragon."

*It matters.*

"But why? I see you naked all the time."

*It just does. Now, can we end this conversation?* He claimed he wasn't uncomfortable with her nakedness, but he was clearly uncomfortable talking about it.

"I just wanted to apologize."

*Apology accepted.*

Cora didn't press it further because it was clear he didn't want to listen. She walked back to her pack then pulled out a bag of seeds. "I have some nuts. Would you like some?"

*I don't eat nuts.*

"What do you eat?"

*Meat.*

"Are you hungry?"

*I haven't eaten in over a week. Since I can't fly, I can't hunt.*

"I can get you something."

Flare released another sarcastic snort, which Cora realized was his version of a laugh. *I eat bears, goats, deer, and mountain lions. No, you can't get that for me.*

The offense burned in her blood. His assumption that she had a bow but didn't know how to use it irritated her to her very core. She tossed the nuts on the ground and rose to her feet. "Wait and see."

Flare eyed her with his magnetic orbs. *Now isn't the time to do something rash.*

"It's not rash. I've done it before."

*You won't prove anything if you die in the attempt.*

"Do you ever shut up?" She pulled her bow off her back and held it at her side.

Smoke rose from his nostrils.

She pulled an arrow from her quiver then marched into the trees. "I'll see you at lunchtime."

Half an hour later, Cora returned to the campsite with a black bear in tow. She pulled it along on a blanket, using her strong legs for power. She kept her back straight as she pulled, dragging it across the dirt until she stopped in front of Flare.

She faced him head on and crossed her arms over her chest, victory in her eyes.

Flare stared at the bear, seeing the arrow pierced right through its skull. Only a skilled archer could have pulled off that accuracy. The ability to launch an arrow at that velocity was commendable.

Cora waited for something, a compliment or an apology.

Flare slowly turned his eyes on her, his look unreadable.

"So…?" Cora tapped her foot in expectation.

Flare was still silent.

"I think you owe me an apology."

*Why?*

"Because you assumed I couldn't accomplish this."

*I made that assumption based on the information I had at the time. I'm sorry you took offense to it.*

"How would you feel if I assumed you couldn't fly?"

*You would be right. I can't fly.*

"You know what I mean."

*All I'll say is, I'm impressed.*

Cora knew that was all she would get out of him. And based on all the insults he directed at her, it really was a compliment of the highest degree. "Thank you."

Flare leaned forward and pulled the arrow out with his teeth. He tossed it at Cora's feet. *You may not want to watch this.*

"Why?"

*It's not exactly pretty.*

"Do you want me to build a fire so you can cook it?"

His eyes lit up in a smile. *I eat my meat raw. And if I want to cook it, I can do it myself.*

"Well, are you going to eat the skin? The fur?"

*Yes. Why?*

"I could skin the bear to make a coat. I'm not sure how long I'll be out here on my own."

He stared at her without blinking, his eyes unreadable once again. *That's probably best.*

She pulled out her knife then got to work, feeling the dragon's eyes on her the entire time.

A full week passed.

Cora was more comfortable around Flare after being around him every hour of the day. And Flare seemed to feel the same way in return. A quiet companionship formed between them.

Whenever Flare was hungry, Cora would hunt for him. And whenever Cora decided to bathe, Flare walked farther into the trees and faced the opposite direction.

Camping near the quiet stream was peaceful despite the danger they were both in. The Shamans never came for them, but Dorian didn't make an appearance either. Flare and Cora could travel somewhere else together, but it was difficult for Flare to travel by land with his massive size. He was meant to soar over the trees.

"Do you think they'll find us?" Cora sharpened her dagger in front of the fire.

*Eventually.*

Alarm shot through her heart. "Do you think we should keep moving, then?"

*We're fine. There are many hiding places to search.*

"Do you fear them?"

*Yes and no.*

"Which is it?"

*There's no such thing as a simple answer.*

Just when she thought she'd gotten used to his odd statements, he threw her off. "Do you care to elaborate?"

*I'm not afraid of them because I'm stronger than them. My scales are thick, and my muscles are strong. In battle, I can prevail. But I am afraid of them because they can't be killed.*

"They can't be killed?"

*At least, I haven't figured out a way.*

"How is that possible?"

*They possess dark magic. It's unclear where they came from or how they got their powers, but it's certain they aren't indigenous to Anastille.*

"Then how did they get here?"

*King Lux must have found them. Where, I don't know.*

"When I stabbed one in the side…it was soft. Like stabbing a pillow."

*I know the feeling. I've bitten one before.*

"They creep me out…"

*I think that's the point.*

"So, they serve the king?"

*Yes and no.*

It took all her strength not to roll her eyes. "Meaning?"

*They aren't the type of beings that serve a ruler. They want something in return for their servitude.*

"And what do they want?"

*I don't know the answer to that either. But I'm sure it's something valuable.*

This knowledge was making her skin crawl. She felt sick to her stomach and even a little light-headed. It wasn't easy for her to admit she was afraid, but in this instance, she didn't feel ashamed. She'd never encountered something more foul or fierce.

Flare seemed to pick up on her mood. *I may not be able to fly, but I can protect you.*

Cora turned her green eyes on him, surprised by the gesture. Until that point, it didn't seem like he cared whether she lived or died. "I don't need someone to protect me, but I appreciate the thought."

Flare chuckled. *I've never heard someone refuse the protection of a dragon before.*

"You aren't my slave. You don't owe me anything."

*You fixed my wing.*

"That was a courtesy anyone should have given you."

He shook his head slightly. *Most people would have preyed on my vulnerability and chained me down. They would have removed my wings permanently and sold them to the highest bidder. Then they would move in for my claws.*

She fought the bile rising in her throat. "No one would do that."

*Your ignorance scares me.*

"No one in my village would have done that."

*It was a common practice three hundred years ago. Any injured dragon was stripped for parts and sold to the highest bidder. The skulls were worth the most.*

"Well, that was then, and this is now."

*And some things never change.* Flare looked across the water, his yellow eyes remembering another time.

"How old are you?"

*Last time you asked that question, I didn't answer. And you can expect the same response.*

"Why is it a hard answer to give? Whether you're one hundred or three hundred, what does it matter?"

*Age is a very private thing. The older you are, the more insane you become. If someone ever confides that information to you, understand it is a gift and an honor.*

"Why are you more insane the older you are?"

Flare was quiet as he considered his response. *The more things you see, the more people you lose, the more you lose who you are.* He said nothing else, as if that statement explained everything.

"I don't understand."

*I knew you wouldn't. But you're an elf. One day, you'll understand exactly what I mean.*

"Do elves have long life-spans?" She didn't know anything about them other than the fact that they'd existed at one point. She wasn't even sure where they were located in Anastille. They were pretty much a myth.

*Very.*

"How long?"

*So long, they are practically immortal.*

"That's not a good thing?" The idea of living forever sounded great to her.

*No. After a thousand years of living, most elves take their own lives.*

"What?" She blurted out without thinking. "That's insane."

*Not really. The elves have a ceremony. Gathered among remaining friends and family, an elf will be laid to rest, never to wake up again. It's actually a very beautiful thing.*

She didn't understand it, and she probably never would.

*The only exception to that is elves who find a partner. As long as their partner is alive, they stay alive as well. But once that person is gone, they don't usually last long afterward—unless they have children.*

"How do you know so much about the elves?"

*It's common knowledge. The dragons were close to them before the Great War.*

"What happened after that? They weren't close anymore?"

*The elves exiled the dragons and humans from their land. We aren't welcome there and are considered enemies.*

"But why?"

*The dragons' ill decision to allow the humans to infiltrate the land was not approved by the elves. And once the humans took over and slaughtered the dragons, the elves hid away in their mountains and forests, choosing to live in solitude. They'll never forgive the dragons for allowing this to come to pass. They lost a lot of their land, their magical beasts, and their own kin. Because elves live for so long, it's hard for them to forgive. Decades can pass before they even consider granting another chance. Time means something different to them than it does to you.*

Cora struggled to process all of this. It was unbelievable that she'd lived in Anastille for so long but knew so little about it.

At one point, she'd thought the dragons were a myth too. "Since I'm a hybrid, does that change anything?"

*I've never known a hybrid, so I can't answer that question.*

"But surely this has happened to someone in the past."

*It hasn't.*

Was that possible? "You're telling me I'm the first?"

Flare nodded. *The elves hate the humans as much as the dragons. It's frowned upon to have any kind of relationship with a human, no matter how noble or innocent they are.*

"Then how did my parents meet?"

*That's unknown.*

What did that mean for her? Was her life-span half as long? Or was it not extended at all? "I'm surprised people in Vax didn't realize I was a hybrid."

*Why would they? They've never seen an elf before.*

"I suppose."

*Your features blend well together, human and elf. The result is a beautiful woman with soft features. You're delicate like a flower but have the sting of a bee. You're strong and hearty like an elf but calculating like a human. I suspect most of the men in the village fancied you.*

For the first time, Cora smiled. "Wow."

Flare regarded her in confusion. *What?*

"You just gave me a compliment. Actually, quite a few of them."

*Is it really a compliment when it's so obvious?* Flare looked into the trees like he was uninterested in the conversation entirely.

"A compliment is still a compliment. And coming from a dragon, it means even more."

*So, it would mean less if it weren't from a dragon?*

Cora didn't understand the question. "Sorry?"

Flare stared at the water and remained still.

Now she was even more confused. "I just—"

"Cora?" Dorian's deep voice erupted from the trees to the left. His voice was unmistakable to Cora. She'd recognize it anywhere since she'd been listening to it her whole life.

"Dorian?" She'd been so involved with Flare she'd forgotten what she was waiting for.

Flare jumped to his feet quicker than Cora could watch with the naked eye. He was aggressive for the first time, flaring his nostrils and arching his tail defensively. His massive shoulder shoved Cora aside, blocking her from view with his massive scales. A mighty roar erupted from his mouth along with a jet stream of fire.

Dorian dodged out of the way before the fire could strike him. "Cora!"

Cora recovered from being slammed onto the ground then smashed her fists against Flare's thick scales. "Flare, stop! He's okay. He's not here to harm us."

Flare ceased the flames coming from his nostrils but kept his body tense for battle. *Who is he?*

"My guardian."

*How did he know where to find us?*

"I agreed to meet him here."

Flare looked down at her, disapproval in his eyes. *And you didn't tell me this?*

"I was afraid you would overreact—exactly what you're doing now."

He growled, and smoke rose from the tip of his nose.

"Oh, don't blow your nose at me." Cora marched around him then approached the trees. "Dorian, it's okay. Flare won't hurt you."

Dorian walked out from the safety of the trunks, his eyes on Flare the entire time. His shoulders were tense in fear, prepared to dodge out of the way from another round of fire. But his eyes showed his evident awe of the creature. He couldn't look away from Flare's shiny scales and intimidating claws. "Cora, are you alright?"

"I'm fine. Flare is harmless."

Flare released a mighty growl that shook the ground beneath their feet.

Cora felt the vibrations all around her. Even though she didn't fear him, her hair stood on end.

Dorian wasn't scared of anything, but this was an exception. He put his arm around Cora's shoulders, trying to protect her from something neither one of them could defeat.

"Okay, he's not harmless," Cora said. "But he won't hurt us."

Flare lowered his head so he could get a good look at Dorian. A quiet growl escaped his lips as he regarded him with a shrewd eye. *This is your guardian?*

"Yes." Cora stepped between them to keep them both comfortable. "He came here to check on me."

Flare didn't look at Cora. He was only interested in Dorian. *He'll tell the others I'm here.*

"No, he won't say a word."

Flare growled again.

"Just give me a moment to speak to him." She grabbed Dorian by the hand and pulled him into the trees. Dorian kept looking over his shoulder, unable to believe a dragon was just feet away. "Sorry about that. I would have given you some warning, but I didn't have a chance."

Dorian finally fixed his gaze on Cora, still in shock. He rubbed his forehead and took a moment to make sense of things. "Cora, how the hell did you find a dragon and befriend him?"

"It's a long story."

"Well, you better get talking."

Cora recounted how she met Flare and what they'd been doing since. "I repaired his wing, and he's kept me company while I've been waiting for you. Since we're running from the same enemies, it just kind of worked out."

"This explains why the Shamans came to the village." Dorian put his hands on his hips, two packs hanging from his back. "They were looking for him."

"Well, now they're looking for both of us."

"Now I understand why the Shamans wouldn't explain why they were there. How could they tell us that they were hunting the last dragon on the face of the earth?"

"He's not the last dragon," she blurted.

Dorian's normally calm face immediately contorted into one of sheer surprise. "He's not?"

"He says there are others, but he hasn't given me anything specific."

"Has he fused?"

"No. He's just a dragon."

He nodded in understanding. "I'm not sure if you're better off with him or worse off."

"What do you mean?" She crossed her arms over her chest and lowered her voice so Flare couldn't listen to their conversation.

"I'm assuming they want his head more than yours. If you stick with him, you'll always be hunted."

Cora had just met Flare, and while he was rude to her most of the time, she was comforted by his presence. He'd become an ally and a friend. Perhaps she got along with beasts better than she did with humans. "Does that mean the Shamans are still looking for me?"

He sighed and closed his eyes. "They want you dead, Cora." He didn't dull the blade of the ax. He came down hard and struck her right on the neck. "And they aren't going to stop until they find you."

She'd expected those words to hurt more than they did. Perhaps she already expected that outcome the second she stabbed the Shaman in the side. "Did they hurt you? The others?"

"No," Dorian said. "They interrogated us, but no harm was done."

She breathed a sigh of relief, eternally grateful nothing had happened to them because of her stupidity. "I'm so glad."

"We're all worried about you," Dorian said. "I'm not sure what we can do. We can present the charge to the king and say it was self-defense—"

"No. I don't want this to go any further." Dorian and the others would be dragged down, and that could present worse problems. If they pissed off the king, they could be flogged then hanged.

"But we can't do nothing." Dorian's voice was low but full of terror. "We can't just leave you to your fate."

"Dorian, there's nothing else you can do. I don't want any of you to stick your neck out for me. I'm not worth it."

He shook his head slightly, his eyes downcast. "Then what is your plan? To live on the run? To look over your shoulder for the rest of your life?"

"I don't know." She really didn't have a plan. She'd never planned for this eventuality because the thought never crossed her mind. "But I'll figure something out. Perhaps I'll stay with Flare. I'm more likely to survive with a dragon than alone."

"If he doesn't eat you."

"He's harmless." Cora didn't know Flare well enough to make such assumptions, but she somehow knew he would never hurt her. Despite his ferocity and bad temper, he was thoughtful and protective. "He wouldn't lay a hand on me. Or, should I say, claw…"

Dorian rubbed the back of his neck then began to pace like he was brainstorming. "Perhaps in a few years, you can come back to the village. Surely, they have more important things to focus on than some woman who stabbed them."

"I'm sure I will." She would say whatever Dorian needed to hear. "It'll blow over in no time. I'm not done growing, so I'm sure I'll look different in a few years. I won't have to hide."

"Yeah…maybe."

If the Shamans were still in Vax, they might have followed Dorian to the top of the crags. It hadn't crossed her mind until that moment. "Were you followed?"

"No. I took the caves. If they followed me, they'll get lost when they come out."

"Okay."

"But you two shouldn't stay here any longer. It's only a matter of time before they figure it out."

"I know." They had to keep moving. Once Flare's wing was healed, he should be able to fly. Perhaps he would let her ride him. The thought sent a thrill down her spine.

Dorian pulled one of the packs off his back. "Extra weapons and clothes."

She peered inside and saw most of her belongings. She also spotted a sack of gold. "Dorian, what's this?" She peered inside and noticed the sum. It definitely wasn't hers.

"I want you to have it. You'll need it."

It was his entire savings. He kept it hidden behind the stove. "Dorian…I can't take this." She shoved it to his chest. "I really appreciate it. Truly. But…I can't."

"Cora, I want you to have it." He handed it back.

Dorian had already done enough for her as it was. On top of that, he'd risked his own safety hiking up the mountain just to speak to her. There was no way she could let him do this as well. "This is your savings, Dorian. You should give it to your sons."

He stared at the sack resting in his palm then slowly looked up at her. His brown eyes never changed, intense and emotional. He gave her a look she'd never received before, not by any living person. "You're my daughter. You're my family."

Her heart convulsed in painful waves. She was unsure how to hold the emotion inside without breaking down, and it escaped in the form of a tear. Growing up with three boys squashed all emotion out of her body. She wasn't allowed to cry or show weakness.

But now, she couldn't hold it back.

"Please take it." He placed it hard in her palm. "I can always earn more money. But you… You need this." He closed her fingers around it and forced her to grasp it.

"I don't know what to say…"

"You don't need to say anything." He lowered his hands to his sides. The look of sadness never left his face. Unable to do anything to save her from this fate, he felt helpless. "I wish I could do more."

"You've done enough, Dorian. You raised me…" She had more to say but couldn't get it out. There were no words to describe everything he'd done for her. He'd taken her in with no strings attached, and not once did he ever expect anything in return.

"You're the one who's given so much. You've taught my boys to be real men." He gave her a smile to cheer her up.

She released a chuckle then blinked to combat the wetness. "They struggled there for a moment."

"The first time I gave Marcus a hammer, he almost nailed his hand to the counter."

She'd never forget the memory.

"Then you showed him how it's done." He smiled with his lips but not his eyes. They were saying farewell without actually saying it, knowing this could be the last time they ever saw each other. The reality was too hard to handle, so they did what they could.

Cora placed the coin purse in the pack then shouldered it. Time was ticking, and she knew Dorian needed to return to the village before nightfall. She wasn't ready to say goodbye, but she couldn't admit that out loud. If she didn't remain strong, he would worry about her.

Dorian's eyes showed the same thought. "I don't want to leave."

"I know."

As she stared at the ground, an idea came to her. "Every year, on this day, I will come here. If you're able to get away from the village, stop by and see me."

His eyes lit up, the thought delighting him beyond reason. "I'll be here."

"And if I don't come…it's because I can't." She swallowed the lump in her throat because she knew what that would mean.

"I'll come anyway in the hope we'll see each other again." He glanced toward Flare, who was sitting on the bank, staring into the water. "Can I trust him?"

"Yes."

"Are you absolutely certain?"

There was no doubt. "I think he's just as lost as I am. I don't know what he's running from or where he's going, but I suspect we're going to end up in the same place. I've always sided with the dragons from the first time I heard their story. The dragons believed in us even when they had no reason to. And now, I will believe in them."

Dorian nodded at that answer.

"Can I ask something before I go?"

"Anything." His restraint was crumbling. Emotion spread on his face, knowing the farewell was looming high over his head.

"Do you know where I come from? Who my parents are? Do you know anything?" She was pulling at a thread, but she needed to ask anyway.

Dorian didn't react at all. It was as if he'd known the question was coming. He bit his bottom lip gently like he was deciding something. He broke eye contact and stared at the ground, keeping his thoughts to himself.

She patiently waited to hear something new.

"No. I'm sorry."

"Because Flare says I'm half elven." She hoped that piece of information might change something, jog his memory. The night Dorian found her, it had been dark and rainy. There might have been something there he couldn't see at the time.

"Why does he think that?"

"He says I look it."

Dorian returned his gaze to her and closed his eyes longer than a typical blink. "I know the elves are beautiful. Perhaps that's what he means." He was dancing around the question, but it wasn't clear why.

"No. He was very specific."

"I'm sorry, Cora. All I know is that I found you on the muddy road. You were wrapped in a deep green blanket, and despite the rainfall, you smiled when you looked up at me. And I'll never forget it."

The warning in her heart told her he was hiding something. He wasn't being completely truthful. But she trusted Dorian more than anyone in the world. If there were something to tell, he would speak up. "I just thought I'd ask."

"It's natural to want to know where you come from."

The sky was beginning to grow darker as the sun moved farther down the horizon. The trees swayed in the light breeze, and some of their leaves came loose. "You should get going."

"I know." He looked up at the trees before he stared at her again. Then he closed the gap between them and embraced her with a warm hug. He locked his arms around her and rested his chin on her head. "Please take care of yourself, Cora."

"I will." She didn't want to cry again. That wasn't an option. "Look after the others."

"You know I will." He pulled away and looked down at her, the sorrow heavy in his features. "I'll see you next year."

She nodded. "Until next year."

He cupped her face then pressed a kiss to her forehead. When he pulled away, his face was contorted in pain. He was struggling to hold on as much as she was. It looked as though he might speak again, but his lips remained closed. He stepped away and walked in the opposite direction, never saying goodbye or farewell. His feet crunched against the fallen leaves and blades of grass. Every step echoed in the clearing, sounding as loud as her own heartbeat. Every second felt like an eternity. Time had slowed down so she could memorize every sight and sound. The farther he went, the duller her heartbeat became. Fear gripped her by the throat, making it difficult to breathe. But she stood there, still and shaking at the same time. She watched him go, hoping he would turn around one last time.

But he never did.

## SEVEN

Cora braided her hair then placed it over one shoulder. The strands had grown long in the past year, and she hadn't had a chance to cut it. Now she wasn't sure when she'd be given the opportunity.

Flare sat by the water, but his eye was on her the entire time. *Are you ready to talk?*

Cora had ignored him the night before. She'd made her own campsite a small distance away and turned her back to him, shutting him out completely. Flare had respected her privacy and didn't pry.

But now that the sun had risen, things were different.

"No."

Flare had the unnatural ability not to blink. He could stare for an hour straight without needing to close his eyes. It was something Cora had noticed the moment they met. *I'm here to listen if you change your mind.*

"Thanks." She didn't feel like opening up to anyone, especially a dragon. "Where do we go now?"

*We?*

"Yes. We."

*I don't remember agreeing to that.*

"We're both on the run from the same hunters. Doesn't it make sense to stick together?"

*I have a much higher bounty on my head than you do. Honestly, you're safer without me.*

"Maybe. Maybe not."

*There is no maybe.* He stood up to his full height then expanded his chest as he took a deep breath.

"Why are they hunting you?"

Flare purposely ignored her.

"Maybe if you told me your cause, it would change things."

*What makes you think I have a cause?*

Cora didn't have all the facts, but she was smart enough to piece things together. "Two of the king's men are hunting you. You must be a slave on the run. You mentioned there were other dragons, so they must be in the king's possession. And if that's the case, we must free them. And then we must overthrow the king and give the land back to the creatures it truly belongs to."

He regarded her coolly, not giving anything away. *You think I want to overthrow the king?*

"In a nutshell."

*And you want to help me?*

"I have nothing else to do."

He shook his large head. *Boredom isn't a good reason.*

"It's not the reason. I need to figure out how to kill the fiends that haunt me. If I don't, they'll hunt me forever. And since I can't kill them, the only way I can get rid of them is by getting rid of their master. So, you and I have the same interest."

*And the safety of the dragons means nothing to you?*

"Of course it does. Now that I've met one in the flesh, I realize just how incredible they are."

If dragons could smile, Flare would be showing all of his teeth.

"So, what do you say?"

Flare left the riverbank then walked to her place under the tree. *What are your skills?*

"I'm an archer. I'm a fighter. And I'm a blacksmith."

*You forge weapons?*

"I've been doing it for years."

*That's interesting.*

"I'm smart and athletic."

*True.*

"And contrary to your belief, I'm very intelligent."

*Not so sure about that one.*

"I'm a great ally. I think we could work well together."

Flare shifted his body, his bright scales reflecting every wave of light. Despite his ferocity, he was beautiful in a deadly way. *The road will be dangerous.*

"I know."

*And I can't guarantee your safety.*

"I know that too."

*Then we have a deal.*

"Perfect. But I have one condition."

*Oh really?*

"You need to trust me."

*That is something that only comes with time, not demand.*

"You need to tell me where you were, how you escaped, and everything else that's relevant. You can't expect me to help you and keep me in the dark at the same time." That should be enough to convince him to open up. They both had their own secrets that they needed to guard, but they couldn't hide from each other forever.

Flare arched his back like he was stretching. His mass of muscle moved fluidly, like waves in the ocean. He possessed enormous power and strength, but he also carried elegance like a crane in a meadow. The dragon was more than just a formidable beast. He was a living work of art. *You're right.*

"That's a sentence you'll be saying a lot more often."

He gave a playful snort. *Don't push it.*

They headed east, going the opposite direction of where Vax was located.

Cora walked beside the dragon, moving through the meadow and approaching the first line of trees. "Will you be able to make it through the forest?"

*Yes.*

"The branches won't scratch you?"

His heavy feet pounded against the earth with every step. *My scales are not only brilliant, but also impervious.* He held his head high in pride, keeping his body perfectly rigid as if he were modeling for an unseen painter.

Cora was always taken aback by Flare's responses. Most of the time, he was cool and collected, but anytime his scales were mentioned, he insisted on their beauty and brilliance. Sometimes it seemed like he was two different people; one was vain and the other humble. "So…you're going to head into the forest?"

*Yes.*

They reached the line of trees then migrated through the trunks under the canopy. The trees were tall, but Flare still had to keep his head down as he traversed the brush. "So, how did you come here? Did you escape from High Castle?" Flare had agreed to answer her questions, but she was still unsure if he actually would.

*Yes. I escaped from High Castle.* He remained behind her, following her lead.

"How did you escape?"

*I waited until the watchmen were asleep. Then I walked out.*

Could a dragon just walk out of a castle? "And then what?"

*King Lux sent the Shamans to retrieve me. I flew to the mountains, but they remained close on my tail. When they unleashed that fireball, it damaged my wing and forced me to crash. That's when we crossed paths.*

"How did the Shamans keep up with you to begin with?" She'd never seen a dragon fly, but she could only assume they were incredibly quick.

*They flew as well.*

"What? They rode their own dragons?"

*No. They have flying steeds of their own. They're like horses but…sinister.*

That disgusted her more than the creatures themselves. "Gross…"

*Unnatural.*

"That was why they came to my village. They wanted to know if anyone had seen you nearby."

*Probably.*

"What's High Castle like?"

*Exactly how you would imagine. It's guarded by high walls, the guards all look the same in their armor and weapons, and the inside is drab like a winter afternoon. Slaves wait on the higher officials, and prostitutes are passed around like a communal bottle of wine. It's depressing, to say the least.*

One thing caught her attention specifically. "They have slaves?"

*Yes.*

"A lot of slaves?"

*The biggest commodity of Anastille is free labor. They're shuttled around between King Lux and the two stewards.*

"Are the prostitutes slaves as well?" That disturbed her most of all.

*Yes.*

She looked at the forest floor and watched her boots crunch against the dirt.

Flare glanced at her in his peripheral vision. *I'm sorry if that disturbs you, but you'll have to get over it.*

"I'm not disturbed."

*You're clearly affected by it.*

"Are you saying my compassion and empathy make me weak?"

*No. I'm saying your fear does.*

"Fear doesn't make someone weak. Without fear, there's no such thing as bravery. What you do when you're scared defines you. It gives your actions meaning. So, don't sit there and judge me with your dragon eyes."

*I don't judge anyone.*

"It sure seems like it."

When Flare fell silent, she knew she'd bested him. She didn't gloat, but it gave her satisfaction. "Did you leave a lover behind?"

Flare faced her while he continued to walk forward. *I don't understand your question.*

"It's pretty simple. Did you leave someone you love behind? Another dragon?"

He faced the trail once more. *No. I don't have a lover.*

"Are you close to the other dragons?"

*No, not necessarily. But that doesn't make a difference. They shouldn't be used for King Lux's gain. Did you leave a lover behind?*

Cora struggled to follow his sudden change in subject. "No. In fact, I was trying to get rid of them most of the time. I didn't participate in any of the marriage lotteries, and now that I'm one of the last women to remain unmarried in the village, the pressure has increased tenfold. Dorian even pressured me into it."

*Marriage lottery?*

"It's a stupid tradition. Women place a number on their chest, and the men draw numbers from a hat. Whatever number they pull, they dance with that woman. At the end of the lottery, the men choose a wife from the selection of women they danced with. It's the most barbaric thing I've ever heard of."

Flare didn't have facial reactions like a human, but his eyes shifted and moved, depending on what he was thinking. *It's strange, indeed.*

"It's idiotic. Why can't two people just fall in love and decide to get married? They force women into the lottery at such a young age that they have no idea what they're doing."

*How young?*

"Sixteen."

*Then you managed to avoid the lottery for a long time.*

"I refused to participate, but the town gossip started to increase. People called me manly because I was an unmarried blacksmith. It's just not natural to them. I almost considered it because Dorian wanted me to. A part of me is glad the Shamans are after me. It's better than being forced into a marriage."

*What's so bad about it?*

"What's so bad about it? Are you kidding—"

*The question wasn't meant as a challenge. I'm only curious.*

She held her tongue and calmed down before she spoke. "I would be tied to this man forever, and he would boss me around like a dog. He would make all decisions for me and force me to stay home all day and have ten of his children. And I would be married to a man I didn't love. That would be the worst part."

*And that's important to you?*

"Absolutely. Isn't that the point of marriage?"

*Yes and no.*

"Okay, you need to stop saying that. That's not a real answer."

*Actually, it's a very accurate answer. Marriage is a tool to unite two families together, combining their assets and titles. Marrying someone you actually like is simply a bonus.*

"You don't really believe that, right?"

*Do I believe in it? No. But I don't deny how the world really works.*

"How do the dragons do it?"

*Marriage doesn't exist. Dragons stay together as long as they wish, sometimes having hatchlings, and when the love runs its course, they go their separate ways.*

"Dragons don't stay together forever?"

*Sometimes. But it's extremely rare.*

"Why?"

*Remember, dragons are immortal. To spend eternity with someone is an enormous commitment.*

Cora never thought about it that way. "Have you ever been in love?"

His face was blank all over again. *You ask a lot of personal questions.*

"I'm just curious. You don't have to answer."

*Perhaps in Vax it's okay to ask whatever you wish, but outside that village, it's very rude to ask such things. You should learn that now.*

"I didn't mean to be rude. I thought we were friends."

Flare fell silent, his eyes scanning the trees in front of them.

"I apologize." She didn't want to make her relationship with Flare tense. After all, he was the only friend she had at the moment.

*No.*

Now things had become worse. "You don't accept my apology?"

*No. I've never been in love.*

She smiled. "Thanks for sharing."

*What about you?*

"Never. The boys in my village aren't exactly my type."

*What is your type?*

She shrugged. "I don't know. But I'll know when I see him."

They rested against the trunks of two tall trees. The forest had grown dark, and every once in a while, an owl would hoot into the night. Flare rested on the dirt, his chin sitting on his claws. Cora leaned against the trunk of a tree, a blanket covering her.

"What was it like before the humans came?"

Flare opened one eye, and the luminescence of the color glowed in the darkness. *You ask that like I was there.*

"Weren't you?"

He closed his eye again. *Why are you so determined to discover my age?*

"Because it's fascinating. The idea of living for so long, experiencing so many generations, is incredible."

*Perhaps I take it for granted, but it's not that fascinating.*

"So, what was it like?"

He chuckled slightly. *The history of the dragons is common knowledge, so I'll share that with you. That doesn't mean I was alive at that point.*

"I'll take it."

*The dragons didn't have rules or laws like the humans do. We simply didn't infiltrate each other's minds without explicit permission. While we value treasure, gold, and jewels, there was no such thing as steal-*

*ing. If a dragon has to resort to such measures, then he's not a true dragon.*

"How so?"

*Dragons are hunters. We find our own treasures, not steal them. That is our way.*

Cora nodded in interest.

*They lived freely among one another, either in the mountains or the forests. When the humans came, everything changed. They had to congregate and decide what to do with the new species.*

"Why didn't they just send them away?"

*At that time, dragons weren't the ferocious beasts they're considered to be now. They were trusting and ignorant. Since they were peaceful, they assumed other species were the same way. They'd been coexisting with the elves and the dwarves for so long, they didn't see why it would be different with humans. But they were wrong.*

She hugged her knees to her chest.

*The king of the elves, Tiberius Riverglade, told the dragons it was a bad idea to allow the humans to infiltrate the land. Unfortunately, the dragons did it anyway. And then their race was completely annihilated. The only dragons that survived were the ones who fused.*

"Combined with a human?"

*Yes.*

"What happened to the other dragons?"

*The ones who refused to fuse were killed.*

She swallowed the lump in her throat. Pain burned deep inside her. The dragons opened their lands to strangers, and the second they turned their backs, they were stabbed in the dark. It was enough to make anyone sick. "The other dragons voluntarily fused?"

*No. King Lux broke in to their minds and gained control. Basically, he forced them to do it. Once the dragon was a prisoner, they were forced to do the same to others, breaking down their own kin to be enslaved by the human race. Death was preferable to the torture, but they weren't even given that option. It was the worst possible existence anyone could ever imagine.*

"Oh…"

Flare opened his eyes and stared into the distant trees. He took a deep breath, his entire body rising with the effort. The sadness in the simple action was paramount to every living thing in the glade.

"I'm sorry." She couldn't begin to understand the sorrow in Flare's heart.

He took another deep breath, combating his emotions.

Cora wished she could say something to cheer him up.

His breathing continued until a gleam formed in his eyes. A glossy haze spread over his irises until it was a heavy drop. The weight of the water became too burdensome then dripped down his scaly cheeks.

The sight broke her heart. "Flare…" She crossed the glade then went to his side. She brushed her hand down the bridge of his nose, comforting him in the only way she knew how. It wasn't clear if he could feel her ministrations through the hard scales, but she did it anyway. "I'm sorry." She had already uttered those words, but she wanted to say them again.

*Don't apologize.*

"I wish I could fix this." Seeing an enormous beast give in to his grief was heartbreaking.

*Nothing can repair the evil inflicted on the dragons. Even eternity isn't long enough for the humans to make up for what they did. All we can do is free those that are left and hope that will be enough.*

"What do we do first?" They left the forest and ventured down the opposite side of the mountain. They were approaching Polox, the circular city located at the coastline. The local harbor was full of ships with tall, white sails. The second they crested the top of the horizon, they could sense the sea salt in the air.

*I need to speak to someone.*

"Who?"

*I have a friend in the neighboring city.*

"A dragon?" She couldn't keep the excitement out of her voice. Now that she knew one dragon, she'd become obsessed with the species.

*No.*

"Oh." She didn't hide her disappointment. "Then why are we at Polox?"

*You need a sword.*

"I have a short blade."

*That's not good enough.*

"Well, I'm not trained in the sword, so it'll be pretty useless to give me one."

*I assumed you were intelligent enough to figure it out.* He gave her a pointed stare.

"I am. I just don't think it's necessary to risk getting caught for a sword."

*It won't be any normal sword. In fact, the sword will be unlike any other.*

That caught her attention. Blacksmithing was her biggest passion in life. She was always working on the next big weapon to sell. The more creative she got, the higher the price. "Go on."

*I will give you three of my scales to forge your weapon. Mixed with platinum ore, your sword will be sharper than anything known to man. It'll also be lighter than air and easy to wield. Enemies before you will flee, and the ones who stay won't have a chance against your power.*

Her jaw immediately hung loose. "Whoa…what?"

Flare stared at her without blinking.

"You're going to give me your scales?"

*There's no other element in the world as strong.*

"But…I can't take your scales." That was absurd. Dragons prized their scales, claws, and teeth more than anything else according to the stories she'd heard. To let them be mutilated from their hide was unthinkable. "Absolutely not."

*You aren't taking them. I'm giving them to you.*

"Even then…I can't do it."

*You don't want a powerful weapon?*

"Of course, but not at that cost. I'll have to cut them from your hide and injure you. It would be a crime."

*Not when I'm allowing you to do it.*

The gesture wasn't lost on her. The fact that he was even considering this indicated he trusted her to a certain degree. Dragons prized their vanity above everything else, and the fact that he was willing to damage his was extraordinary. "Why?"

*If we're going to continue this journey together, you need some real protection. Your flimsy arrows and dagger aren't going to accomplish anything. I would give you enough scales to make armor, but I can't spare that much at the moment.*

"Dragon armor?" She couldn't wrap her head around that one.

*Yes.*

She took a step back and rubbed her temple. She was getting too much information at once. "Your wing isn't even healed yet."

*So?*

"And then you're going to walk around with more wounds? Am I the only one who thinks this is preposterous?"

*Don't forget how powerful dragons are. Pain doesn't affect me the way it affects you.*

"Even then…"

He released an irritated snort. *We're losing time. Do as I command, and let's move on.*

He'd just said the wrong thing. "Back up, buddy. Just because you want something doesn't mean you get it. I get that you're a powerful dragon and everything, but that doesn't mean you are allowed to boss me around."

Irritation burned in his eyes. *You're the most peculiar human I've come across. If I made this offer to anyone else, they would take it without thinking twice about it.*

"Because they're assholes."

He cocked his head slightly.

"I don't want to mutilate you and strip you for parts. I actually care about you."

His eyes softened in a way they never had before.

"Can we do this some other way? Will your scales naturally fall off when new ones grow?"

*Yes, but that could take a hundred years.*

"Oh…"

*If you remove my scales, you can heal the wounds with the plant you harvested and eliminate the scars. The pain is irrelevant to me. I only care about the appearance.*

Of course that's all he cares about. "I'm still unsure…"

*I insist. The better weapon you have, the more likely you are to stay alive. And I need you to stay alive.*

"Wait…are you actually admitting you need me?"

His ears folded in hostility. *Are we going to do this or not?*

Over the course of a few weeks, the number of insults directed at her had decreased substantially. Instead of putting her down or making derisive comments, he complimented her. Perhaps she'd proved herself a worthy companion to a magical dragon, and if so, it was an astounding accomplishment. "Let's do it."

# EIGHT

She pulled her hood over her face and walked through the gate alongside a wagon. The guards didn't give her a second glance despite the late hour. Torches glowed along the wooden fence and illuminated the entryway.

The dragon scales were wrapped in cloth in her pack. Cutting them from the dragon's hide took hours. She had to use all the force she could muster to saw through the armored scales. By the time she got them off, blood had started to ooze everywhere.

And she felt like shit.

She did what she could to stop the bleeding, but there was only so much she could do. Flare didn't seem bothered by the cut. He didn't react at all, like she was giving him a massage rather than cutting him open.

Then she had to saw off the other two.

She focused her thoughts in her head just the way Flare taught her. *I'm inside.* The words echoed loudly in her mind, like she screamed them rather than whispered.

*Head to the left, near the coast. The blacksmith is next to a potions shop.*

It was strange to communicate this way. She wobbled on her feet slightly as she listened to him, wondering if he could read her mind and feel her emotions. Or were they not connected in that way? His explanation was very confusing.

She walked down the cobbled streets and past the dark buildings. Candlelight flickered in most of them, glowing gently against the black sky. She tightened her jacket around her body and kept walking, keeping her face hidden as much as possible.

She'd been there once before, but she had been just a child. Dorian took her along with his three boys. They traded their weapons in exchange for hay since the harvest had been bad that year. They had nothing to feed their livestock. At the time, Polox didn't seem so scary. But now that she was alone, it had a different feel to it.

She went to the place Flare had instructed. Once she spotted the potions shop, she noticed the blacksmith shop right next to it. The lights were out in both shops, and they seemed to be vacated.

Her mission was to break in to the blacksmith store to forge a powerful weapon made of dragon scales, but the potions shop caught her attention as well. More than likely, there was a healing potion she could use on Flare. It would speed up the process and alleviate the guilt in her heart. *I'm here.*

*Stay in the alleyway for a few hours. When the street clears, make your move.*

*Won't that look suspicious?*

*Not if you stay hidden.*

The hours passed with a dreadful slowness. People gradually left the street and returned to their homes. The guards that patrolled the area changed positions and moved to the outer wall once the city was asleep. There were no movements in either of the shops. The lights remained off, and they were empty. *It's clear.*

*Go around to the side of the shop. There's a wooden door there. It's usually unlocked.*

*How do you know that?* How could an enormous dragon ever visit any city without getting caught? And even if he didn't travel there, had someone else gone and given him the information later? That seemed even more unlikely.

*Stop asking questions. You waste so much time.*

*Just answer them. That would save time.* The words reverberated loud in her own ears.

*Stop yelling.*

*I'm not trying to.*

*Just talk normally.*

*Sorry, I've never done this before.* Her voice became even louder with the sarcasm.

*We'll work on it later. Now, go to the side of the shop.*

*Ugh.* She did as he instructed and located the flimsy wooden door. The owner didn't seem to care about protecting his shop very much. She turned the knob then gave a gentle push. Immediately, the door swung inward. *I'm in.*

*Close the curtains so no one can see the light from the flames.*

*Okay.* She migrated to the windows and shut all the drapes. Once the outside world was completely hidden from view, she got to work. *Where does the smoke go?*

*There should be a skylight in the ceiling.*

She looked up and didn't see anything in the wood. But when she got closer to the fire pit, she noticed the detachable door. She undid the hinge then pulled it open. *Found it.*

*Get to work. Be quick about it.*

*What about the smoke? Someone will see it.*

*That's a risk you're going to have to take.*

She set down her supplies then got to work. First, she had to get the fire going until it reached the right temperature. Once that was in place, she located the blacksmith's tools. They were a little different from hers back in Vax, but they would do.

*What's going on?* Flare's voice came into her ear.

*Just got the fire going. Now I'm going to start.*

*I said be quick.*

*I'd be much quicker if you'd shut up.*

Somehow, he released a growl into her ear. *Fine. Tell me when you're finished.*

She washed the blood from the red scales then patted them dry. Once they were ready to go, she began her work over the fire. She'd never used dragon scales before. Until a few weeks ago, she'd never even seen them. Now she had to figure out how to manipulate them into what she needed.

After thinking for several minutes, she figured out exactly what she had to do. Rolling up her sleeves and placing a mask over her head, she bent over the stone brick and began her work.

With a shaky hand, she pulled the sword out of the fire. The platinum hilt reflected the light from the fire like a perfect mirror. The flames danced in the metal, and she could see her own awed expression staring back at her.

Her thumbs moved along the metal, feeling every single groove and design she'd embedded in it. The image of a powerful dragon was carved into the platinum, strikingly similar to Flare's features. She thought it was fitting to honor the dragon that voluntarily handed over his most prized possession.

Her eyes moved to the blade, examining the deep red color. When she gently moved it in the air, the scales somehow released a distant hum, as if they were slicing through the air and making it scream.

She rotated her wrist, showing both sides of the blade. It was the distinct color of blood, exactly the same as Flare's original scales. Toward the very tip, the color turned a light orange. Despite its density, it was light. Cora moved the blade around her wrist and didn't feel the sting of the weight.

She'd never wielded a sword, but there was no doubt how strong this one was. Its power radiated up her arm and made her feel alive. It gave her strength, even though it possessed no magical ability.

She was in awe.

*Is it done?* Flare's impatient voice broke in to her mind.

*Just finished.*

*Get the hell out of there. The guards are still on the tower, but the sun will be rising soon.*

*Okay.* She rose to her feet and held the sword at her side. It was difficult to put it away when she loved touching it so much. *Now I just need to learn how to use it.*

*I'll teach you.*

How would that work? *How do you plan to do that?*

*You'll see.*

She returned everything exactly where she found it and closed the skylight vent. She pulled open the drapes before she stepped out of the shop. She didn't need to worry about locking the door behind her because it hadn't been locked to begin with.

She knew she should hide out until the gate opened, but she kept thinking about the potions shop. There was bound to be something useful in there. She had enough coin to pay for it rather than stealing it.

Since she had a few hours until morning, she decided to do it. Flare didn't need to know until she was done. He would probably give her hell for it, but that was a small price to pay if she healed his scales much quicker than it would normally take.

Instead of going through the door, she went to the side of the shop and found a window she could crawl through. She pressed her palm to the window and gave it a gentle shove, hoping the owner was just as careless as the blacksmith next door.

And they were.

The window opened with a gentle squeak. Cora was having unnaturally good luck that evening, and that gave her an extra high. The sword was hooked to her belt, and her pack was over her shoulder as she climbed inside and landed with a hard thud on the floorboards.

It was dark inside just like the other shop, but there wasn't a fire for light. Locating the right potion would be impossible without some visibility. She explored the desk at the front of the store and found a set of matches stored inside. After a quick swipe of the match against the hilt of her sword, she lit the lantern sitting in the corner. The smoke from the extinguished matchstick drifted to the ceiling, and she rubbed it against her tongue to extinguish it completely before she tossed it aside.

Flare's deep voice came into her mind. *Are you hidden?*

It went against her nature to lie, but she didn't see the harm this time. *Yes.*

*Wait until I give you the signal.*

*Sure.* She browsed the shelves and examined each potion. There were labels underneath, along with a few sentences for the description. She came across an assortment of things. One potion gave a person the ability to grow an extra arm for a full day. Apparently, it increased productivity. Another one allowed the recipient to grow eyes in the back of their head temporarily.

Cora didn't know that kind of magic existed.

She finally came across what she needed. It was a healing potion specifically made for beasts such as dogs, horses, and other creatures. She wasn't sure if that applied to dragons, but it was her best option.

She dug into her purse and collected enough coins for the payment. Then she exchanged the potion for the money. The liquid was inside an airtight glass tube with a cork stopper. She placed it in her bag because it would look too odd walking around with it in her hands. She was just about to head back to the window when something caught her attention.

Inside a black cage was a purple potion. Although there were no flames or applied heat, the liquid was bubbling, boiling of its own accord. It was thick, reminding her of molten lava endlessly flowing.

Her legs took her in front of the cage, and she stood there, just watching. There was something hypnotic about its contents. The way it constantly churned and boiled was creepy as well as mesmerizing.

She couldn't look away.

*Love of the Beast.*

She read the description below. *Dragon Tears—the ultimate power of healing.* She read the sentence again, searing it permanently into her brain. Was she looking at the product of dark magic? Or was it something beyond that? Was the liquid literally composed of dragon tears? Or was that just the name?

The lights suddenly turned on, making the room glow like the sun was shining through the windows.

"What the hell are you doing?" A loud shriek came from the stairway in the corner. A woman covered in multicolored beads, wearing a pair of glasses with only one lens, stared her down. "A thief!"

Cora panicked and didn't bother leaving through the window. She headed straight for the door. "I'm sorry. I didn't steal. There's money on the counter."

The woman grabbed a rope dangling from the ceiling and gave it a hard tug. A loud bell rang and reverberated across the walls and outside the shop. It was loud enough to burn Cora's ears.

It was an alarm.

Cora burst out of the door and ran as fast as she could.

The woman's shrieks followed her. "Thief!"

Cora ran across the street and headed to the gate as quickly as possible. She had to get out of there before the guards homed in on her.

The dragon's voice erupted loud in her ears, practically a scream. *What happened?*

*I got caught.*

*How? By whom?*

*I'm running for my life right now. We'll talk about it later.*

He released a growl.

Cora remembered the way back to the gate, but she took every side street possible. The sound of bells erupted from every corner of the city. She knew they were all searching for her. Even if she made it to the gate, there was no guarantee she'd make it through.

She kept running, heading down the small alleyways and ignoring the looks from the bums who slept there. If she had to kill someone to make it out, she wouldn't hesitate. If she were captured, they would hand her over to the Shamans.

And she'd rather die trying to escape than let that happen.

She broke from the buildings and headed straight to the gate. To her horror, it was closing. "You've got to be kidding me." *Flare? I don't know what to do. They're closing the gate.*

"There! In the brown cloak!" The leading guard pointed her out to his comrades. "Capture or kill."

*Flare?*

Why wasn't he responding?

*Flare, do you know another way out of the city?*

There still wasn't a response.

He must have taken off and abandoned her to her fate. There wasn't time to be hurt by the betrayal, but she couldn't deny the pain in her heart. But what else did she expect him to do?

She had to get out of this on her own. She pulled the sword from her belt then held it at the ready. She didn't have a clue how to wield it, but she would figure it out.

The guards stopped in their tracks the second they saw the sword.

"What is it?" one guard said.

"I don't know," the watchman said. "Dark magic, clearly."

This was working out in her favor. She spun the blade in her wrist, trying to be more intimidating than she really was. Her hood covered her face, so they probably assumed she was a man.

Hopefully.

More guards charged from the left. While they stopped at the sight of the sword, they didn't seem as scared now that she was completely surrounded.

"Surrender," the watchmen demanded.

She gripped the hilt tighter. She had no intention of releasing the sword. She would take down as many of the guards as possible on her way to the grave.

The guard who had demanded her surrender silently communicated with his comrades, and they moved in.

Here goes nothing.

Cora swung the blade at the watchmen with a speed she hadn't expected. The blade was lighter than she anticipated, and it sliced through the air, making a distinctive whistle.

She slashed the watchman across the chest, slicing through his uniform and his skin. He immediately fell back into the dirt, his open wounds bleeding out.

The rest of the guards hesitated at the sight of their fallen leader.

Cora didn't have time to process what just happened. All she could think about was survival.

Their fear was quickly replaced by anger, and they rushed in from all sides. Cora ducked out of the way of a blade and avoided another ax. Her only advantage in that situation was her speed. She could dodge quicker than they could attack. But that wouldn't last forever. With nowhere to hide and no plan of escape, she would tire out eventually and be captured.

She parried a blow coming her way then sliced a guard down the arm. He screamed and fell back, gripping his gaping wound. She quickly turned to stop the next blow when she felt the point of a blade pierce her side.

She didn't scream or cry out.

She was in shock.

It didn't hurt, surprisingly. Her body numbed all the pain, and the added adrenaline masked every sensation. Her heartbeat suddenly became loud in her ears, telling her it didn't have enough blood to pump.

Instead of falling to her knees, she kept fighting. "Who was that?" She turned around and held up her blade. "Because they're about to regret it." She charged the first man she came across and stabbed him hard in the gut, returning the blow he'd given to her. Then she kicked him to the ground.

She turned on her heel and faced the rest of the guardsmen. Now there were twenty of them, moving in from all sides. Blood seeped into her shirt, and she was growing weaker by the second.

She gripped the hilt tighter and prepared for her inevitable fate.

The guard closest to her left moved in, aiming right for her neck.

She stiffened her body in preparation, knowing she probably wouldn't be able to block it in her weakened state.

The man swung his sword with incredible speed, ready to put her down for good. But his sword never hit its mark. Knocked from his hands, it landed in the dirt at her feet.

A man dressed in all black decapitated the guard with a single clean swipe, severing his head from his body. It rolled to the ground and lay motionless, the same look of horror still on the guard's face.

Cora immediately stepped back, feeling the bile rise in her throat.

Alone and outnumbered, the man moved through the sea of guards and took them out one by one. Blood spilled into the air like a geyser, and the cries of dying men echoed throughout the city. Some called out for mercy, while others simply screamed until their bodies gave out. Severed limbs littered the ground, and a pool of blood soaked into the dirt, turning it into red mud.

One guard remained, and he stood shaking on the spot. He held out his sword with no intention of using it. His face was pale as the moon, and his lips were bloodless. "I have a family…" He shrank under the gaze of the attacker.

The man stared him down before making his move. He slammed the hilt of his sword into the guard's skull and sent him crashing to the ground. The guard lay motionless with his eyes closed, his chest still rising and falling with deep breaths.

The man in black wiped the blood off his sword with the guard's uniform before he tucked it into his belt. He stared into the city and watched the torches grow one by one as they set the alarm. More troops were headed to the entrance.

He approached Cora, his face visible for the first time. He was over a foot taller than her, and his shoulders screamed with strength. His arms were the size of her head, and the deadly look in his crystal-blue eyes was more terrifying than the soldiers he'd just massacred. "Let's go." His voice was oddly familiar. It rang in her ears in a way she'd heard before.

"Who are you?" She wasn't walking out with a stranger, even if he did just save her life.

"Shut up and let's go." He gripped her by the elbow and began to drag her.

Unable to walk, she collapsed on the ground. Her hand immediately went to the wound in her side, and her fingers felt the blood drip down her hands. "I can't…" She'd never said those words in her life, but now they escaped her lips effortlessly. Her vision began to blur, and her heart thudded painfully. She'd never experienced death, but she suspected this was it.

He released a familiar growl then picked her up. "Don't ever say that again."

Her head bobbed as he carried her out of the gate. She looked up into the sky and saw the sunlight breach the horizon. Splashes of pink, purple, and gold began to permeate the land. Even though her body was failing and the darkness began to descend, tranquility washed over her, giving her a sweet and peaceful death.

# NINE

He slapped her hard across the face, leaving a mark that would remain for several days. "Wake up." He gripped her by the shoulders and shook her viciously. "If you keep those eyes shut, I'll do something far worse than slap you."

Her eyes fluttered open, and the leaves of the tree were directly in her line of sight. She saw them sway in the wind, rustling with the distant breeze. Judging by the light, it was late morning.

"There she is." The man gripped her by the neck then forced her lips apart. He poured something directly into her throat and forced her to take it. "That's the rest of it."

She swallowed everything then coughed when it went down the wrong tube. Her chest burned with every movement she made, and her side would scream if it had lips. The sudden pain cleared her vision, and she focused on the man hovering above her.

She'd never seen him before in her life.

He had dark hair that was almost black, much darker than her brown strands. It was short and cleanly cut, like he visited the barber often, unlike most men in her village. His chin and cheeks were covered with a thin line of scruff that was the same color as the hair on his head.

His eyes were terrifying. They were unnaturally blue and beautiful, but their intensity was frightening. They possessed unbridled rage that could unleash at any given moment. His hard jaw was just as unforgiving. For a handsome man, he didn't look very happy.

After gazing at his face, she noticed something about his eyes. The way they were shaped was familiar and reminded her of another pair of eyes she'd stared at for long periods of time. His voice was unmistakable. She'd heard it insult her time and time again. "Flare?" But it couldn't be. It simply wasn't possible.

Approval came into his eyes. "Perhaps you're smarter than I give you credit for." He patted her on the shoulder before he forced her to sit up. "How do you feel?"

She coughed again, feeling the burn in her throat. "Like shit. How do you think?"

He rested one arm on his knee as he crouched down beside her. "You're alive, right?"

"What did you make me drink?"

"That health potion you stole—like a damn idiot."

"It's for animals."

"And what do you think you are?" Somehow, he was harsher as a human than a dragon.

"But I got it for you."

"Well, you shouldn't have gotten yourself stabbed, then."

"Look, I almost died, so can you stop being an ass for just a second?"

"Let me think about that." He rubbed his chin and looked into the trees. "No. You lied to me and did something reckless. I'm going to be an ass to you for a very long time."

She felt the wound in her side and noticed thick gauze had been wrapped around it. It was so tight she could hardly breathe. "I thought I was going to die."

"You'd only die if I let you." He rose to his feet, and that was when she noticed the blood soaked into his black shirt.

"Is that yours?"

"Yes." He grabbed his canteen of water and returned to her, holding it out so she could take a drink. "It's the area where you removed my scales."

"What?" She was horrified at the meaning in his words.

"Human or dragon, the affliction is the same." He shook the canteen in his hand, commanding her to take a drink.

"Are you okay?"

He gave her a smartass look, partially smiling while giving her an irritated glare. "I carried you ten miles. Yes, I'm fine."

"You could bleed to death."

"But I won't."

She rubbed her hairline and noticed the dried blood that crusted there. "Or we might both bleed to death…"

"That would be poetic, wouldn't it?" He shoved the canteen into her chest. "Drink this. I'm tired of holding it."

She snatched it from his hand and gave him a sour look. Then she took a drink and washed away the tart taste of the potion he just shoved down her throat. "There was a potion inside the shop called *Love of the Beast*. It said it was dragon tears or something like that. Apparently, it can heal almost any illness. I should have gotten that for you."

"It was in the shop?" His eyebrow was raised like he was genuinely surprised.

"Yeah. It was inside a solid black cage, and I didn't have time to open it."

"I'm surprised anyone would sell it."

"What is it?" She'd read the name and the description, but that didn't give her enough information.

"As you said, dragon tears."

"Yes—but what does that mean?"

He sighed in frustration. "Sometimes I forget how naïve you are."

Instead of snapping, she remained quiet because she was eager for him to continue.

"Dragon tears are both magical and powerful. They can save a person from the brink of death, heal any injury, and can even bring someone back from the dead if they're given at just the right time. As you can imagine, anyone would pay top dollar for them."

"So…does it really come from a dragon? Or do they just call it that?"

"The name is literal. Only when a dragon cries can the tears be harvested, and since there are no more free dragons, the potion is extremely rare."

Cora remembered when Flare cried earlier on their journey. He was so distraught over the annihilation of his species that he gave in to his grief. If she'd harvested them at the time, she could have used them to heal his scars. If only she'd known at the time.

"And even if dragons were still around, it would still be nearly impossible to gather dragon tears."

"Why?"

"Dragons are emotionless. They understand anger, jealousy, and betrayal but not sadness like humans. You can torture a dragon endlessly, and no amount of pain will make them cry. You can strip their treasures away and enslave them for years, and they still won't break down. They will only shed a tear for one reason."

"What reason?"

"Love. When a dragon truly, deeply loves someone, they release dragon tears, either because they lost someone they loved or because their loved one is in pain. There is no other instance."

She took this information quietly, understanding the significance of the potion. Now she understood why it was locked up, unlike the other potions in the store. "So, you have fused with a human?"

"Is that a question?" The same irritated look was on his face.

"You lied to me before."

"I never lied. I just danced around the question."

"So…what does that mean?"

"It means…we need to keep moving before those guards hunt us down. They'll be crawling over these hills by nightfall. We need to get to Solstice before their messenger does."

"Why?"

"I told you." He rose to his feet then extended his hand to help her up. "I need to speak to someone there. It's very important that I do."

She used his weight as an anchor then pulled herself up. The pain was excruciating, but she refused to admit it. His afflictions were far worse than hers, so she had no right to complain. If he was able to continue, so was she. "Then let's head out."

"You're doing alright back there?" Flare glanced over his shoulder.

"I'm fine." She breathed hard and gripped her side when it throbbed. Scaling hills and valleys was uncomfortable on her entire body, but particularly her torso. The weight of her pack wasn't helping either.

"You don't sound fine." Effortlessly, he hiked up ahead. If she didn't know he was injured, she wouldn't have figured it out.

"Well, I am."

"Want me to carry you?"

Over her dead body. "No."

"Then pick up the pace."

She kicked it into gear and moved faster, ignoring the pain shooting up and down her body. Mind over matter. That's what she had to keep telling herself. She was the reason the affliction had come to pass, so she had no one to blame but herself.

She caught up to him and kept up the same pace.

He eyed her up and down, making sure she could really handle the trek. "If you need help, just let me know."

"I don't need any help." And if she did, she would take that secret to the grave.

"Good. You look heavy."

"Excuse me?" She turned her fiery eyes on him, ready to smack him upside the head.

He smiled like he enjoyed her anger. "I was referring to your pack. But it's nice to know you're just as vain as I am." He laughed and kept walking.

"I prefer you as a dragon."

"Why? I'm the same person."

"Not really. You talk a lot more."

"Annoying, isn't it?" He surveyed their landscape, his eyes constantly searching for enemies.

"What's your name?" Flare must belong to the dragon, so the man had to have a different name.

"Flare. Or is your memory that terrible?"

"You can't have the same name." He must have been a different man before he fused with the dragon. At least, that's what she knew about the history of the dragons and humans.

"Flare is fine. Two names can get confusing."

Anger bubbled underneath the surface then spilled over like a boiling pot. "Why won't you just tell me?"

"I don't want to."

"You save my life, but you still don't trust me?"

"You didn't tell me about Dorian, so why should I tell you anything?" He turned his terrifying blue eyes on her. They were unmistakably hostile. "I may owe you my life, but that debt was repaid when I went into that town and risked my neck to save yours. We're officially even."

"I didn't realize we were keeping score." She turned vicious instantly, probably because her wound still hurt, and she had a blinding headache.

"Just don't ask me questions I don't feel like answering. If there's something I want you to know, I'll tell you."

"I've told you stuff about me."

"Like what?" He pulled out his canteen and took a drink.

"My village. My family. My beliefs. Maybe that doesn't seem like much to you, but that's everything to me."

He sighed then stowed away his canteen. "I don't do well with emotions, so…don't do the girlie thing."

"Girlie thing?"

"Where we insist on exchanging feelings and emotions…crap like that. We're on a mission, and we have to complete it. Let's just focus on that."

He irritated her more than anyone else in her life, including Seth. "I feel sorry for you."

"Sorry? Why?"

"You're closed off and won't let anyone in. Clearly, I'm harmless, but you keep me at arm's length. Why?"

"I guess I just don't trust people."

"Well, I'm not people. I'm different."

"Yes. You're stubborn, arrogant, and you talk too much. You're very different."

She stomped her foot in protest. "What happened to confiding things to me? You agreed to that then completely changed your mind."

"I never agreed to reveal my true nature to you. I was forced to by your childish behavior. If you hadn't gotten into trouble, I never would have been compelled to change form and rescue you. You coerced my hand when I wasn't ready to reveal my cards. I'm ticked off, Cora. If you don't like the way I use my tongue, you shouldn't talk to me."

"Maybe I won't."

He moved quicker and put a few feet between them. "That works for me."

After two days of nonstop travel, Cora could barely hold on. She was falling asleep while walking. Her vision was growing blurry. Sometimes, she wasn't even sure what she was seeing. She didn't want to admit she needed to rest, but if she didn't stop soon, she would collapse. "Flare."

They hadn't spoken in two days, and the silence was tenser than the ruthless conversation. "What?"

"I need a break…" She sat down on a rock and bowed her head, ashamed she had to hold him back.

"I was wondering when you would tire out."

"What?"

"I was curious to know how far I could push you. Honestly, I'm a little impressed." He squatted down in front of her then lifted up her shirt to examine her wound. "It looks good. No infection."

"Wait…you were testing me?"

"Yes. And you passed." He waggled his eyebrows then stood up again. "There's a cove close by. Get cleaned up and get some sleep. I'll keep watch."

The mention of the river brought back the memory of when she bathed in front of him. He stared at her without blinking before he eventually looked away. Now, she understood his reaction.

And she was mortified.

She automatically covered her face in embarrassment. Her cheeks reddened, and her head started to pound.

Flare seemed to know what she was thinking. "For what it's worth, I liked what I saw." He winked before he walked into the trees.

"Kill. Me. Now."


Flare kept his back to her as she bathed in the river. She cleaned the cut and washed away the dried blood. Surprisingly, there was already a scab where the open wound had once been.

The potion worked.

She washed her hair and removed all the grime she'd gathered over the past few days. After she cleaned herself, she felt a million times better. She was still exhausted, but sleep would be much better now that she was refreshed.

She left the water and dried off before she changed. Flare kept his back to her the entire time and never turned around. He didn't say a word either, letting her have her privacy and her silence. "I'm done." She pulled her hair over one shoulder and braided it. She didn't have time to do her hair like she normally would, and she didn't have a mirror.

"Get some sleep." He rose from the rock he was sitting on then ventured to the water's edge.

"Do you need help with your wounds?" She knew he must have one on his upper back where his broken wing would be located. She was still annoyed with him, but she offered her help anyway.

"I got it." He threw aside a pack he must have acquired in Polox then pulled off his shirt.

"Uh, what are you doing?" She was caught off guard by his nakedness. She'd never seen a shirtless man in her entire life. His chest was hard with strong pectoral muscles, and his waist was thin with chiseled lines of strength. His arms could pull a tree right out of the ground. She kept staring and wished she would stop.

"What? I need to bathe too."

"Well, I'll turn around. You just need to give me some warning." She quickly stepped away and stared at her pack, unable to forget the image that would be ingrained in her mind forever.

"I'm not shy." His clothes hit the sand of the shore before he walked into the water. "And I thought it would be fair since I've seen you."

She pulled out her blanket and lay on the hard ground. "I'll pass." She faced the opposite way so he wouldn't be in her line of sight before she closed her eyes. Her mind was fatigued from the lack of sleep. She assumed she would fall asleep instantly, but now she was thinking about the lines of Flare's body. Is that what all men looked like? Were they all that strong? That powerful? Or was that the dragon's doing?

After a few minutes of pondering, her mind swept her off into a deep sleep. Her dreams took her to a faraway place. She rode the back of a red dragon with her blade buckled to her hip. She defeated the armies of High Castle and rescued the dragons in captivity. And then suddenly, a pair of pitch-black eyes stared into hers. Unblinking and unchanging, they didn't look away. Whether they belonged to a friend or foe, she didn't know.

But she knew she was scared.

## TEN

When Flare shook her awake, it seemed like only five minutes had passed.

"Lemme sleep…" She pushed him off and kept her eyes closed.

"I've already let you sleep for too long. Now, get up." He shook her again. "Don't make me ask you twice."

She opened her eyes and forced herself to sit up. When she looked around, the sun was still high in the sky. She'd been asleep for nearly twenty-four hours, but it still didn't feel like enough. "I can't believe I'm still exhausted."

"It's only been an hour." Flare grabbed her pack and stuffed the blanket inside. "I'd be surprised if you were rejuvenated."

"It's only been an hour?" She rubbed her temple and recognized the distant migraine she'd had for nearly a day. "Are you a maniac? Let me sleep."

"Sorry, Cora. I can't." He pulled her to her feet then placed the pack in her arms. "We've got to keep moving. I only let you sleep because I knew your body would shut down if I didn't."

"Ugh…" She didn't mean to be a poor sport, but she'd reached her limit. Perhaps she wasn't as strong as she once thought. All those afternoons in the fields and the shop were nothing compared to this.

"We'll get plenty of sleep eventually. But for now, we need to keep moving." Flare shouldered his pack then took off at a quick pace. He didn't seem tired at all, even though he hadn't slept. Being fused with a dragon must have its perks.

"So, how does it work? Who's in charge? You or the dragon?" He probably wouldn't answer her questions because he was so secretive, but she thought she would give it a try.

"It depends on who's dominant. Right now, I am. So, I'm making most of the calls."

"Because you're in human form?"

"Yes."

"When I was talking to you as a dragon, who was I talking to exactly?"

"Both of us." Flare pulled back a branch in the way of their path so she could get through.

"At the same time?"

"Yes."

That made sense. Cora thought she noticed an anomaly when he spoke. Sometimes it seemed like there were two different people in Flare's head. "To whom am I talking now?"

"Me—the man. The dragon is sleeping at the moment."

"How does his body…fit inside you?"

"I don't have the answer to that." His sword hung at his hip and shook as he walked. "We both exist at the same time—just in different forms."

"When do you decide to be a dragon?"

"It doesn't matter when. We can change back and forth as often as we wish."

"Wow…" She couldn't wrap her head around that. "You speak to each other all the time?"

"Pretty much."

"But…don't you get tired of each other?"

"We can disconnect when we need to."

Was she supposed to know the meaning of that term? "What does disconnect mean?"

"We close off from each other." Flare seemed to be in a better mood now than he had been a few hours ago. Maybe he did doze for a few minutes. "Right now, I'm disconnected from him. He isn't witness to this conversation."

"Why do you disconnect?"

"We need our privacy. Sometimes you just want to be alone, you know?"

"To go to the bathroom?" You would need privacy for that.

He chuckled. "Not really for that. He and I have never struggled with that type of intimacy."

"Then what do you need privacy for?"

A smug grin appeared on his face. "You really can't figure it out?"

Figure out what? "Sorry, I've never fused with a dragon before. Or did I not mention that?"

"I don't think that's the problem. Your ignorance is the culprit."

Again with the insults. "Do you enjoy picking on me?"

"Actually, I do."

"I hope that wears off soon."

"Doubtful." He stopped when he reached a large rock then licked his finger before he held it in the air. He was feeling for the wind. Suddenly, he changed course and headed to the left.

Cora followed him without asking any questions. "So, are you going to answer me?"

"I guess I'll have to spell it out for you. When I'm with a woman, I don't want him there. And when he's doing his thing, I don't want to be there. Make sense now?"

The thought hadn't crossed her mind. She was grateful he was ahead of her so he couldn't see the redness of her cheeks. "Gotcha."

"It's a nice setup."

"Do you guys ever fight?"

"We argue like everyone else."

She couldn't imagine being with the same person constantly. She'd never been close enough to anyone to want that kind of intimacy. "Do you enjoy being together?"

His voice came out quiet, sounding sincere for the first time since she met him. "Yes. My dragon is my closest friend. Without him, I would be lost."

His words touched her heart. "That's sweet."

"I guess."

"How long have you been fused?"

Flare let the silence linger.

She realized the error of her question. "Sorry. I wasn't trying to figure out your age, honestly."

"I believe you."

"Do you guys sleep at the same time?"

"Most of the time. Right now, he's sleeping because he's exhausted. He's been running around with you for weeks without much rest."

"I miss him." The dragon was aggressive like the man but not in the same way. He was gentler.

"He's definitely the better being of the two of us," he said with a chuckle. "You interest him."

"I interest him?"

"Yes. He likes the fact that you're small but strong. And he says you're the bravest woman he's ever come across. That's saying something since Flare has been around much longer than I have."

"Aw…that's sweet."

"So, at least one of us likes you."

She grabbed a stick from the ground and threw it at the back of his head.

It bounced off his skull, and he rubbed the spot without breaking his stride. "Real mature."

"You provoked me."

"Well, you're going to have to learn to ignore it." He stopped walking and looked up at the sky, seeing where the sun was positioned. "We're making good time." He marched forward again, keeping the same pace.

She thought about the way Flare took down all of those guards single-handedly. She hadn't seen combat like that in her life, but she knew Flare was particularly skilled with the sword. "Where did you learn to fight like that?"

"Training. Experience."

"That was vague."

He chuckled. "It's true. I was trained in the sword, and I got better with time. Practice makes perfect, right?"

"But you're really good. Like, really."

He glanced over his shoulder and gave her a cold look. "I would be flattered if you'd worded it better than that."

"Just take the compliment, and don't be an ass about it."

He faced forward. "Don't throw another stick at me."

"I can't promise anything." With a swordsman like Flare, she could learn a lot from him. If he took her under his wing, he could forge her into the finest human weapon. "So…will you teach me?" She didn't want to ask him for anything, not when he would hold it over her head. But she was more desperate to learn than not to ask at all.

"Are you asking me to teach you?" He didn't look back at her as he spoke.

"Yes." Her red blade hung at her hip, feeling weightless. "Please…"

A quiet chuckle escaped from his lips. "I'll teach you—when you're better. For what it's worth, you did a decent job with those guards. I was surprised you weren't already dead by the time I got there."

She wanted to make a smartass comment back, but she decided to accept the compliment instead. "Thank you."

"See? I'm a nice guy—when you don't annoy me."

Another smartass comment came to mind, but she swallowed it back too. "I guess you are."

## ELEVEN

The traveling companions kept their hoods up as they entered the gate. The guards glanced them over but didn't consider either one to be suspicious. They passed through without any trouble.

Once they were away from the gate, Cora pulled her hood down. "Looks like Solstice doesn't know what happened in Polox."

"Let's hope it stays that way. I killed all the guards who saw your face, but that may not be enough."

"The owner of the potion shop saw me."

He clenched his jaw in irritation. "Great. Mathilda never forgets a face."

"Mathilda?"

"That's her name. She's a witch."

"A witch? I didn't know they were real."

"She doesn't advertise it." He scanned the crowd and made sure no one was paying too much attention to them. "If people found out, they would burn her alive."

"Ouch…"

"Then you understand her need for secrecy."

Cora walked beside him as they passed the buildings and the shops that were open along the street. Merchants were selling wooden plates and eating utensils, jewels, pots and pans, and various fruits and dried meat. She noticed no one was selling weapons, which was odd to her. "Why didn't you want me to go in alone?"

"I've already shown my face, so they know I'm here. Besides, you clearly can't do anything without almost getting killed."

She ignored his insult because the previous statement intrigued her. "Why would they recognize you?"

He gave her a cold look. "You're nosy, you know that?"

"Just curious."

"You know that phrase, 'Curiosity killed the cat'?"

She rolled her eyes and didn't bother hiding it.

"If I had a stick, I'd throw it at you."

"You would miss."

"Ha. We'll see about that."

He guided her past the merchant tables and farther into the city. He wore all black, and it suited his personality perfectly.

"When you transform into a man, are you wearing clothes?"

"I'm wearing whatever I was wearing before I made the change."

"And all your gear?"

"It comes with me."

"I still don't understand how it works…"

"You want to know a secret?" He leaned close to her ear. "I don't either."

They reached the rear of the city where a few isolated shops stood. None of the citizens of the town hung out in the street or outside the stores. In fact, it didn't seem like anyone was inside them either. "What's here?"

"You'll see." He walked to the small shop in the corner and knocked on the door.

"Do you think anyone will be here at this time of night?"

"Yes." He stood there with an expectant look on his face, like he knew someone would answer it.

"Will we be sleeping here?"

"Maybe."

She would love nothing more than to sleep in a real bed with blankets. She realized how much she took that luxury for granted now that she no longer had it. Living in Vax was boring most of the time, but now she realized what a gem it was. People disapproved of her unorthodox lifestyle, but no one had ever tried to kill her because of it.

The door cracked, and a face covered in shadow stared at them.

Flare immediately pulled down his hood and revealed himself to whomever it was that was staring at him.

The door flew open. "Holy—"

"Shh." Flare covered his lips with his forefinger. "Save whatever outburst you have until we're inside."

"Come in, come in." He ushered them inside with a wave of his hand.

Cora walked in behind Flare and stared at their host. He was a man who looked the same age as Flare. They appeared to be only a few years older than her. He had light brown hair similar to hers, and there was kindness in his eyes.

"I can't believe it's you." The man gripped both sides of his skull as he stared Flare down. "I just… I'm sorry. I don't even know what to say."

"Say nothing." Flare extended his hands. "Let's do what we do best."

The man pulled him in for a hug and clapped him on the back.

Cora couldn't help but smile at the exchange. It wasn't clear how they knew each other, but she suspected they were very close friends. The fact that Flare had a friend beside his dragon was surprising, and it gave her hope that he wasn't as cold as he claimed.

Flare pulled away then turned to Cora. "Let me introduce my friend Cora. Cora, this is a very good friend of mine, Bridge."

Bridge looked her up and down and let out a long whistle. "Day-yum."

Both of Cora's eyebrows shot up. "Uh, hi?"

Flare's expression immediately changed. He was happy just a second ago, and now he was out for blood. His brooding silence filled the air and infected everything around them.

Bridge didn't seem to notice. "Welcome." He extended his hand and shook hers vigorously. "It's a pleasure to meet you. I'm Bridge." His smile faltered when he realized his mistake. "He already said that, didn't he? I mean, any friend of—"

"Flare." Flare gave him a look that silently said everything his lips didn't.

Bridge picked up on it. "Any friend of Flare's is a friend of mine."

She tried not to be offended by Flare's distrust. She clearly had to work harder to enter his inner circle. The fact that he already had one hurt her even more since she'd lost her only family. "Thank you for making me feel welcome."

Bridge placed his complete focus on Cora. "Are you hungry? Thirsty? Is there anything I can get you?"

"Actually, both. We've been traveling for days."

Bridge nodded toward Flare. "I know he's a bit intense sometimes. Been there, done that."

She chuckled. "I'm glad someone understands."

"Come into the kitchen, and I'll fetch you something." He put his arm around her shoulders and guided her toward the hallway.

"No." Flare grabbed Cora's other shoulder and pulled her in the opposite direction. "She can stay here. I wish to speak to you in private."

She was being shut out again, and she didn't like it one bit. She'd been nothing but loyal since the moment they met. If she really were an enemy, she wouldn't have healed his wing. Actually, she would have told the Shaman Flare's location in negotiation for her own freedom.

But that didn't seem to mean anything to him.

They disappeared down the hallway and into the kitchen. Their voices trailed until they evaporated altogether.

Cora tried to stand still, but she couldn't. If Flare wouldn't confide in her, that didn't mean she couldn't eavesdrop on her own. He wouldn't know the difference. She crept down the hall and avoided the cracks in the floorboards. She didn't make a sound as she approached. When their voices were loud enough for her to hear, she stood still and listened.

"Where did you find her?" Bridge's voice held his delight. "She's one hell of a woman. Those legs are—"

"Say another word about her, and I'll cut your throat." Flare's voice remained quiet, but it contained all the menace to make an entire army stand down. The threat was unmistakable. Even though Cora wasn't in the room, she felt the tension. "She's. Off. Limits."

Bridge was quiet for a long time, probably just as shocked as Cora was. "I didn't realize you two were involved. Man, you know I meant no offense. I'm just a big flirt."

"We aren't involved." Flare's voice still contained his rage. "She's annoying and doesn't know when to shut up. But that doesn't change anything. Give her a hard time, and I'll cut your head off. She's not like the other girls. This one is different. Do we understand each other?"

"Different how?"

Flare was quiet before he found his response. "She's pretty damn smart. She can shoot an arrow, and she always hits her mark. When I couldn't hunt, she killed a full-size bear and dragged it to me. She stabbed a Shaman in the stomach and the eye and still made it out alive. Then she was ambushed by twenty guards and held her own, even though she'd never held a sword in her life. On top of that, she's half elf. I don't know what her purpose is, but she's special. Damn special."

Cora leaned against the wall and absorbed the words that filled the air. The endless compliments moved over her skin in a comforting way, and the corners of her lips rose in a small smile. Perhaps Flare didn't think she was so stupid after all. He respected her even though he refused to admit it to her face. He kept his secrets locked up tightly behind his lips because he feared her, not because he distrusted her.

And that made all the difference in the world.

## TWELVE

Cora scarfed down the roast chicken and potatoes without using any manners. Her elbows were on the table, and she ignored her dinner companions, focused solely on eating everything placed before her.

She'd been living off berries and nuts for weeks. They weren't allowed to build a fire in the evenings because the smoke would attract unwanted guests, so she always went to bed hungry.

Her water canteen had been empty most of the time, so she'd had to share with Flare, and that small bottle wasn't enough for a grown woman and man. She finished the chicken leg then wiped her mouth with the cloth napkin. It was once white, but now, it was covered with juice and crumbs.

Bridge stared at her openly, fascinated by the way she devoured everything in seconds. His arms were across his chest, and he was leaning back in his chair, relaxed and poised at the same time. Unlike Flare's, his chin lacked any hair, and he had a distinct vigor of youth in his features. "Hungry?"

She was too satisfied to be ashamed. "I haven't had a real meal in a long time."

Flare ate his food quietly, having superior manners. It didn't seem like he was starving the way she was. After all, he was eating entire bears and deer along their journey. "She stuck to nuts and berries."

"No meat?" Bridge asked.

"No fire," Flare answered.

Bridge refilled his wine and took a deep drink. "So, what brings you two here?"

"We're both hunted by the Shamans." Flare left half of his plate untouched like he couldn't eat another bite, but he downed the wine like it was water.

"How did that happen?" Bridge started to pour another glass of wine, but the bottle was empty. He shook it like that would make more come out.

"Cora was living in her village when she picked a fight with one of them." Flare had a distinct aristocracy to him. He always held himself with a certain stature, and his calm and collected air was strikingly different from everyone else's. His confidence was clear in the way he moved.

"I didn't pick a fight." Cora tried not to rise to Flare's taunts. He purposely teased her to provoke a reaction. She needed to learn to seize control and prevent that from happening. "The Shaman cornered a boy in the alley and was doing something…strange to him. He was sucking the life out of him, for lack of a better word."

"The Soul Suck." Flare was looking at Bridge as he said it. "Probably low on magic."

Cora eyed the two men. "They suck souls to refuel their magic?"

"Yep." Bridge left his chair then opened a cabinet behind him. He pulled out a glass of amber-red scotch. "And I think we need something stronger if we're going to discuss this." He plopped down into the chair and poured two glasses, one for himself and one for Flare.

"That's…" Cora couldn't think of an accurate reaction to that disturbing news. "What happens to the person whose soul has been sucked?"

"What do you think?" Flare pushed his plate away, officially full. "They die."

"But…what about the afterlife?" Death was bad enough, but losing your entire soul was worse.

"They probably don't go there." Flare took a long drink of the scotch then sucked his inner lip when he felt the burn. "But then again, a lot of people don't go there anyway."

"What does that mean?" Every time Cora learned something new, she realized there was a mountain of information she was ignorant to.

"It means what it means." Flare shook the glass gently and made the liquid dance. "A lot of people don't go there because they're evil as hell."

Bridge stared at the table. "I know I won't be going there…"

"What did you do?" Cora probably shouldn't pry, but she couldn't help it.

Bridge sighed before he spoke. "I was committed to this girl once, but I met this other woman...and I couldn't help myself. She found out in a brutal way, and I felt pretty terrible afterward. But the worst part is...I really don't regret it."

Flare took a drink and chuckled into his glass. "Pig."

Bridge gave him a playful shove. "You're one to talk."

"I don't remember ever committing to someone." Flare set the glass down. "Do you?"

"Well...no." Bridge shrugged.

"My dragon is too picky for something like that." Flare snatched the bottle from the table and poured more scotch.

"You can drink that much?" Even in Vax, she'd never seen the men drink hard liquor so effortlessly. They'd be passed out by now.

"This is a light day." His eyes lit up playfully before he took another drink.

Bridge tapped his glass against Flare's. "We've had much worse nights, my friend."

"You said it." Flare returned the glass to the table, half of its contents still available.

"What do you mean your dragon is too picky for that?" How did that work? Did they have to make a decision together on everything? Did one being have more control than the other?

"When it comes to romance, both the human and the dragon have to agree." Flare leaned back in the seat and stared out the window, watching the torches burn across the street. A man guided his horse past the window. "If I commit to someone for a lifetime, my dragon has to approve. If not…that would give me a headache."

She'd never considered the thought. "That's interesting."

"It's a relationship between three people, not just two." Flare's eyes drooped slightly, showing the effect of the alcohol. "It's a weird ménage à trois."

Bridge laughed into his glass. "For lack of a better phrase…"

Since the wine was gone, she poured herself a glass of scotch and took a drink.

Both men stared at her in surprise. They were frozen in their positions, neither one of them moving.

"What?" Was she being rude for not asking first?

"I've never seen a woman drink scotch." Flare gave her a quizzical expression.

"Well, we do. Our anatomy is almost identical to yours." She rolled her eyes before she poured herself another glass.

"You're going to have more?" Bridge set his glass on the table and watched her with a hanging jaw. "Now you have to marry me."

Cora laughed before she took another drink. "Flare will be the first one to advise you against that."

"This woman is a handful." He leaned toward Bridge. "You don't want to get involved with that."

"Maybe I like a handful." Bridge waggled his eyebrows at her.

Flare nudged him hard in the side, making Bridge gasp aloud. "And a stomachful."

Cora was shown to a private guest room with a bed and a washtub. The second she saw the large bed with clean sheets, she almost fell to her knees in joy. "It's the most beautiful thing I've ever seen."

Bridge chuckled. "Honestly, this place is a dump. But thanks for the compliment. Do you need anything else?"

"No." She approached the bed and felt its softness with her fingertips. "It's perfect."

"Let me know if you need anything else." Bridge gave her a playful wink before he walked out and shut the door behind him.

Cora didn't bother undressing. She pulled back the covers and jumped into the bed, all her muscles screaming in pure joy. Now she didn't have to lie on the hard ground with nasty bugs crawling all over her. She closed her eyes and released a sigh of happiness.

The door flew open, and Flare walked inside. "Up."

"No!"

He shut the door behind him then approached the bed. "Come on. I need to look at your cut."

"It's fine." She gripped the pillow tighter, as if that would make Flare go away.

"And I need you to help me with mine. Come on." He gripped her shoulder and shook her.

"I really hate you sometimes."

"Don't lie." He gave her a smug smile. "You hate me all the time."

She growled before she sat up. "What do you want me to do?"

"Change my bandages. I can't reach the ones on my back."

She didn't have a choice in the matter. The reason he had wounds at all was because of her. "Okay."

Flare walked to the table and placed gauze and ointment on the surface. Then he took a seat in the wooden chair and removed his black t-shirt.

"Whoa…" She held up her hand and quickly looked away.

"I know I'm one fine piece of man, but you need to get used to it."

"That's not what I meant." Sometimes they had a sense of camaraderie, but then he said something rude and destroyed it.

"Then what do you mean?"

She kept her eyes elsewhere as she walked to the table and grabbed the towel. A pail of warm water was beside it, so she dunked the cloth inside. "Just give me some warning before you get naked in front of me."

"Get naked?" His eyes contained the laugh that didn't escape his lips. "Shirtless isn't the same thing as being naked."

"Well, I'm not used to it."

"How is that possible? Don't tell me you've never seen a man without a shirt."

She was embarrassed to admit it out loud, so she concentrated on her work. She pulled the cloth out of the pail and squeezed the excess water from the fabric. Once it was only damp, she set it aside.

"Wow…you've never seen a man without a shirt." He chuckled to himself. "That's unbelievable."

"People in my village are more conservative."

"And boring." His taunts were getting under her skin. And the smug smile on his lips wasn't helping.

"Do you want me to help you or not?"

"Yes, please." He removed the gauze then pivoted his body so she could see the wound along his shoulder blade.

She saw the deep and grotesque cut and actually felt sorry for him. As a dragon, the wound didn't seem so serious. But as a man, it was much different. The wound hadn't healed, and fresh blood still leaked out. It was better than it was before but still excruciating. "The pain must be unbearable…" She grabbed the washcloth and began to wipe away the residue.

"I've had worse." He stared at the opposite wall and didn't tense when she applied pressure to his skin. He didn't seem affected at all.

She wiped away the dried blood and examined the wound for infection. There wasn't any pus in the area, so that was a good sign. By the time she was finished, the cloth was ruby red. "Are you doing okay?"

"I'm fine." If he were in pain, he probably wouldn't admit it anyway.

She stared at the definition of his back and noted the way his shoulder blades curved toward the center of his spine. Different grooves of muscle protruded out, reminding her of chiseled rock in the mountainside. There was so much detail in his skin. It was a work of art.

"What?" It was one of the rare times when he didn't sound so confident.

She cleared her throat then grabbed the gauze. "Nothing." She wrapped the material around his body, crossing it over his ribs on one side and his opposite shoulder. When she touched his dry skin, she noticed how warm it was. She tightened the gauze around his body but inserted two fingers inside the material to make sure it wasn't cutting off his circulation. "It's taking a long time to heal."

"That's a side effect of dark magic."

She rinsed the towel in the warm water then drained it. "How are your other cuts doing?"

"They feel better." He turned in his chair and faced her, the remaining gauze covering the area where his scales had been removed. His prominent chest was directly in her line of sight, along with the tight muscles of his stomach.

Every time she looked at him, she felt uncomfortable. There was something about him that made her feel on edge. Maybe she just needed to accept the fact that different cultures had different ways of doing things. Being shirtless in front of her obviously didn't bother him the way it bothered her.

Cora removed the bandage and cleaned the reddened area. There were small punctures in his side where the scales had been removed. The protrusions were fairly deep but small in comparison to the dragon. She kneeled down and cleaned the wound.

Flare watched her every move, his eyes boring into her. "How does it look?"

"Honestly, terrible."

A snort escaped his lips that sounded like a laugh. It was similar to the chuckle he made as a dragon. "Thanks."

She cleaned the area as best she could before she wrapped the new gauze around this wound. "I'm surprised you haven't died from losing so much blood."

"That's one of the perks of being fused with a dragon. It's pretty damn hard to kill me." He touched the gauze with his palm before he pulled his shirt over his head.

Once he was clothed again, her heart slowed down. "What do we do now?"

"What do you mean?" He rose from the chair and towered over her with his height.

"In general. Now that we're here, what's our next move?"

He crossed his arms over his chest and stared at the pail of bloody water. "Damn, that's gross."

"Don't change the subject." If he planned to continue this journey with her, he needed to be less secretive. "What do I have to do to gain your trust?"

His eyes didn't leave the pail. He examined the dirty cloth beside it, his eyes glossing over with deep thoughts. Flare rubbed his bicep absentmindedly. "Nothing."

"So, you do trust me?"

"No. There's nothing you can do to gain my trust." He turned to her, a hint of sadness in his eyes. "I'm sorry. It's nothing personal."

"Why do you trust Bridge and not me?"

"I've known him for much longer."

"Time isn't an appropriate measurement. Just because Bridge has been trustworthy in the past doesn't mean he'll always be. And just because you haven't known me for years doesn't mean I'm deceitful. You really need to reconsider your philosophy. I trust you because I know I can. I trust my instincts."

"And you shouldn't." His voice came out dark, almost threatening. "I'm not a good man, despite what you may think. All you see is what's on the surface. Underneath flesh and bone, I'm as evil as they come. Don't judge a book by its cover."

Even with the threat in his voice, she wasn't scared. "I don't believe that."

"That doesn't surprise me. I've told you from the beginning what I think of your intellect."

She wasn't offended by the words because she knew he didn't mean them. "Why are you trying to free the dragons if you're so evil? Why would a man do such a thing?"

"Because." He met her gaze with a hard look.

"Because why?" she pressed.

He took a step forward, his face practically touching hers. The power of his body spread through the room. He had strength she couldn't defeat no matter how hard she fought. "All your questions are going to get you killed someday." His brilliant blue eyes were terrifying, despite their obvious beauty. "I suggest you stop prying and keep your head down. That's what survivors do."

# THIRTEEN

When Cora woke up the next morning, the sun was shining through the windows. It was the first time she'd woken up feeling refreshed in nearly a month. The sheets were soft against her skin, and her body was relaxed from the full night of rest she received.

She didn't want to leave the bed.

After lying there for another half hour, she heard her stomach growl. Despite the feast she'd had the night before, she was still starving. Her body clearly hadn't recovered from the state of perpetual hunger during her journey.

She took a bath in the washtub with fresh water she'd found outside the door, then sat at the vanity and fixed her hair. The second she looked at her face, she noticed the slight differences. Her cheeks were more hollow and her neck more slender. The journey had taken body mass that she didn't have to spare to begin with. Her face was weathered and her skin more pigmented. Since discovering she was part elf, she hadn't examined her reflection. Now, she studied the shape of her eyes and the softness of her mouth.

Was it really that obvious?

She combed her hair and dried it with her fingers before venturing downstairs. Hopefully, breakfast would be on the table with some coffee. Having a proper meal was something she'd taken for granted when she was fleeing the Shamans.

She wouldn't make that mistake again.

When she walked into the kitchen, Bridge and Flare were already there. An aged map was spread across the table, the corners frayed from years of use. They were both examining it quietly, their scotches replaced by a morning brew of coffee.

"Morning." She grabbed a plate and piled it with spiced ham, toast, and eggs.

Flare gave her a slight nod while his eyes remained glued to the map.

Bridge acted like he hadn't heard her at all.

Cora took a seat at the table and dug into her meal.

"Don't eat like a pig again." Flare grabbed the map and pulled it away from her side of the table. "We can't damage this."

"Go to hell." She sipped her coffee and devoured her eggs.

Bridge was absorbed in his work, ignoring his breakfast and coffee. "I don't have a clue, man. It should be here."

"It should…" Flare rubbed his chin, his features tense with concentration.

"What are you looking for?" Cora continued to ask questions even though she never got answers. They were bound to give up their secrets eventually.

"A place." Flare sipped his coffee before he returned it to the table.

"What place?" She ate much slower than last time, feeling famished but not starved.

"An important place." Bridge ran his fingers through his light brown hair. "Which doesn't seem to exist…"

"Maybe it doesn't." Flare finally looked up from the map, his eyes falling on Cora. They were glued to her face for a moment, noting the change of her hair and her new clothes.

"Don't say that." Bridge released a depressed sigh. "We can't afford that."

Being ignored was getting old. "If you included me, I might be able to help."

"Doubtful." Flare kept staring at her.

She grew tired of his unblinking stare. Most of the time, he ignored her, but now, he studied her more intently than the map. "What?"

"What?" His word echoed back at her.

"You keep staring at me." Her fork was in her grasp, but she didn't take a bite. "Do I have something on my face?"

Without answering, he looked away.

Bridge glanced at Flare before he examined the map again.

Silence ensued.

She was treated as an outsider, even though she'd proved herself to Flare multiple times. Her impatience was getting the best of her. "Then I'll just sit here and blindly follow orders when they are given."

Flare gave her a thumbs-up. "Perfect."

Her anger overcame her, and she chucked her piece of toast at him. "Note the sarcasm."

Flare caught the bread in his fingers then took a bite. "Duly noted."

She sank into her chair and released an irritated sigh. "You're unbearable."

"I get that a lot." Flare pointed to an island a short distance off the coast of Anastille. "What about here?"

"Slave labor camp." Bridge dismissed the idea like he'd already considered it himself.

Cora's eyes moved to the island Flare had just pointed to. "Slave labor camp?"

"The land is rich in gems." Flare leaned over the table as he searched for another location. "The slaves dig them from the earth before they're deported back to Anastille. It's High Castle's main source of revenue."

It was one of the most disturbing things Cora had ever heard. "So, those slaves live there and work around the clock?"

"Yep." Bridge's voice didn't possess any sympathy. "It's been going on for hundreds of years."

Cora shook her head slightly, even though no one was looking at her. Now she understood why the elves went into hiding. Why would they want to live among humans, an innately selfish and despicable species?

"I don't see any possibilities." Flare leaned back in his chair and severed his focus from the map. "Maybe it really is just a myth, a story to lighten hearts on a particularly miserable day."

"I don't know…" Bridge pulled his gaze away from the map. "There's never been any sign of Aiken, living or dead. We would have heard something by now."

"True." Flare nodded in agreement.

"Who's Aiken?" Cora wasn't sure if she should even bother asking questions anymore.

Bridge eyed Flare, sympathy in his expression. "We can't keep her in the dark about everything."

"Thank you." Cora slammed her fist against the table. "About time someone said it."

Flare's reaction didn't change. "No."

"No?" Cora was approaching a meltdown. She was about to destroy everything in that kitchen, including the two of them. Unsure what lay in the outside world, she'd rather stick with Flare. But if she was going to be treated like a criminal every step of the way, then it wasn't worth it.

She jumped to her feet and placed her hands on her hips. "I've been nothing but a trusted ally. The only reason I got mixed up with the guards in Polox was because I was trying to get you a healing potion. I've proven myself time and time again. If you're going to continue to ostracize me, then there's no reason for me to be here." She stormed off and headed to the doorway.

Flare wore a blank expression, like he didn't believe her charade was true.

She was about to prove just how wrong he was. "Good luck to you and all your endeavors. I sincerely hope we don't meet again." She marched up the stairs and gathered her pack and supplies. Her sword leaned against the wall in the corner. It was the most powerful blade she would ever possess, but it felt wrong to take it, especially when it was made of Flare's scales. Even though it left her feeling ill, she abandoned it and headed to the door.

Neither of the men came after her, and that was perfectly fine with her. She was tired of being treated like a child, when Flare knew exactly how valuable she was. She left the house and slammed the door behind her.

The sky was dark with heavy rain clouds. A storm was coming in and would undoubtedly be a strong one. In the wilderness, she would be soaked to the bone and freezing cold.

But that was better than staying there.

She pulled up her hood then headed to the gate. She hadn't taken ten steps before a firm hand pulled her back.

"Get your ass back inside." Flare's hood was pulled up, but his face was still visible up close.

"Am I your prisoner?"

"No."

"Then let me go." She twisted from his grasp and stepped away.

Flare grabbed her again. "Fine. You win."

"Win what, exactly?"

His face was contorted in a look of pure irritation. Admitting defeat wasn't easy for him, especially when a woman bested him. "I will include you from now on."

"No more secrets?"

He clenched his jaw.

"No more secrets, or I'm gone."

"I'll tell you most of my secrets—but not all of them. That's the best I can give you." His eyes burned with their usual intensity, and the truth rang loud like a bell. This was the best offer he would make. If she didn't take it, he would let her go.

She wanted more than that, to be treated as a partner the way he treated Bridge. But she was only going to get so much from this man. Some secrets were fine. She had a few of her own. How could she expect him to give more than she was willing to give herself? "Deal."

Flare poured a glass of scotch then slid it across the table toward her.

She eyed the glass before she brought it to her lips and took a drink.

"According to legend, myth, folklore—whatever—the remaining free dragons fled Anastille before they could be enslaved. It's unclear where they went, but it must be a distant island. The only other possibility is with the elves, but that seems farfetched. The elves wouldn't grant them asylum, not when their own lives are on the line." Flare held her gaze as he spoke, his glass resting in his fingers.

Despite her calm face, her heart was beating painfully hard. "What about the dwarves? Could they have gone with them?"

"Underground?" Bridge didn't hide his incredulity. "Unlikely."

"Why?" What was so obvious to him but not to her?

"Dragons have a difficult time getting around as it is." Flare's voice didn't contain the same arrogance as it had before. He was talking to her in a different way, treating her as an equal for once. "It's unlikely they could venture underground and live among dwarves. Also, dragons hate being underground. They need to be as close to the open sky as possible—trust me on that one."

Now that she knew the reason, she realized how stupid her guess was. "Makes sense. But how sure are you the dragons escaped to an island?"

"Not sure at all," Bridge answered. "There's no way to know."

Flare took over. "The only evidence we have is Aiken. No one can recount what happened to him. His body was never recovered, and as far as anyone knows, he never fused with a human—no matter how much they tortured him. He was one of the few dragons who was strong enough to resist dark magic."

So, there was hope. "What do you think, Flare?"

"What I think is irrelevant." Flare took a drink of his scotch and closed his eyes as it moved down his throat.

"But as a dragon, you must have some kind of opinion." Cora didn't understand the full effects of fusing with a dragon, but she could only assume his intuition and intelligence were heightened.

Flare's face relaxed as he considered the question. He became quiet, his fingertips resting on his lips. "As a man, I have no inclination either way. Humans tend to make up stories to comfort themselves in times of trial, so these assumptions aren't valid in my eyes. However, the dragon has a different opinion. Knowing Aiken himself, he believes these stories are true."

Her heart thudded against her rib cage with every beat. "Really?"

"That's his opinion." Flare spoke without an ounce of emotion. "And I trust what he says."

"That's great." Her heart did the talking while her mind took a rest. "That means there is hope. If we can find these dragons, we could have an army to take down King Lux."

"Not so fast." Flare held up a finger. "First, we have to figure out where they are. The ocean is a big place."

"But we know it's within flying distance." Cora knew dragons were strong and could travel for leagues, but they couldn't go on forever. "So, it can't be that far away."

Flare chuckled. "You don't understand just how far dragons can travel. Keep in mind, if I don't find the island, I have to turn back…and I doubt I could travel that entire distance without stopping."

She hadn't thought of that. "We could take a ship."

"The only ships available are at the harbors. Guards are watching them, and it wouldn't be an easy task to steal one. Besides, even if we were successful, they would just chase us down and sink our ship." Bridge grabbed the bottle and refilled his glass.

"Talk about a mood kill…" Cora took a drink.

"I've got to be the voice of reason." Bridge eyed Flare. "It's saved his life a few times."

"Well…what should we do?" She asked the question hesitantly because she suspected there wasn't an answer.

Flare rubbed the scruff of his chin before he spoke. "For argument's sake, even if we do find this island and there are enough dragons there that we can somehow convince to fly back to Anastille to help us win back the throne, that still wouldn't be enough. We'd need soldiers, an uprising."

"Wouldn't people volunteer immediately?" Cora knew she would.

"Unlikely," Bridge said. "If they speak out in opposition to the king, they're risking their lives and their families."

She hadn't thought of that either. "Oh…"

"We need more bodies, but it's not clear where to get them." Flare held the glass by the rim and swirled the scotch.

A thought came to her. "What about the slaves? The ones on the island you mentioned? They'd probably jump at the opportunity to fight. They have nothing to lose."

Flare's expression softened as he stared at her. Like clouds parting the sky to reveal the sun, his approval shone through. "That's not a bad idea." He turned to Bridge. "What do you think of that?"

"Not bad at all." Bridge looked at her in a new way.

"Would the dwarves help us? What about the elves?" If they had a chance to rid the evil humans from the land, surely they'd take it.

"No," Flare said with a sigh. "We're on our own."

"The dwarves would never leave their caves," Bridge said. "And the elves will never leave their magical fortress."

"How do you know?" Cora might be ignorant, but if there was even a small chance, they had to try. "Have you ever asked?"

Flare returned his glass to the table. "No. But it would be a waste of time."

"You don't know that." How long had it been since humans communicated with the elves? A lot could change in hundreds of years. "I say we give it a shot."

"They won't speak to us." Bridge shook his head. "They hate humans." He nodded to Flare. "And they hate dragons even more. There's no way in hell they would even hear us out."

Maybe they wouldn't listen to a human or a dragon, but they might listen to someone of their own kind. "I could speak to them."

"You?" Flare didn't keep the surprise out of his voice. "Why?"

"I'm half elf, remember?" She wasn't full-blooded, but she was still their kin. If Flare took one look at her and recognized her bloodline, then the elves would realize the same thing. "It's perfect."

Bridge turned to Flare. "Hey, that's not a bad idea at all. It is perfect, actually."

Flare held his silence.

"All she has to do is speak to them," Bridge said. "Maybe they'll hear her out."

His eyes swelled with darkness. "Or they'll murder her right where she stands."

Cora's blood ran cold.

"Remember, she's an abomination. She has a mixed bloodline." Flare lowered his eyes to the surface of the table. "They might want to annihilate her so she can't ever reproduce and continue this anomaly in their DNA."

Cora swallowed the lump in her throat. "Would they do that?"

"I really don't know," Flare whispered. "But I can't rule out the possibility."

"I wasn't aware they were such a violent species." Whenever people spoke of them, they mentioned their grace and elegance, not their bloodshed.

"Well, they are." Bitterness was in Flare's voice. "While the dragons were being enslaved, they quickly turned their backs and fled into their hiding places. If you ask me, that's just cowardly."

Cora began to realize that Flare had a personal issue with the elves. Perhaps that was why he had been so cold toward her when they first met. Even now, he wasn't exactly warm—and she was only half elf.

She could only deduce that Flare had been alive during that time. He'd witnessed the war himself. He spoke of those times like he was there. But that would have been 422 years ago. Could he really be that old?

Bridge picked up on the rising anger emitting from Flare. "Anyway… I think we should still consider it."

"As do I." Cora refused to believe any species would murder a harmless visitor on their doorstep. Maybe she was an idealist, but it didn't seem practical. "I think we should find this island in the sea and enlist the help of the dragons. Then we should convince both the dwarves and the elves they should join this fight. Once we have those three things, we can rescue the slaves and any free people who may want to join us. Unless we have a formidable army marching behind us, people aren't going to believe us."

"But how do we expect the dwarves and elves to join us if we don't have anyone besides the three of us?" Bridge picked up the bottle of scotch and realized it was already empty. "It's a circle within a circle."

"I don't know. But we have to start somewhere." If they did nothing, the Shamans would hunt her endlessly, the dragons would never have their freedom, and slavery would continue to be as common as the rising sun every morning. Something had to change—now.

Bridge ran his fingers through his hair, his eyes staring at nothing in particular. "Well, where do we start?"

Flare was no longer participating in the conversation. He was closed off and brooding in his own world.

"I think I should travel to the elves and ask for their help. Meanwhile, Flare should search for the island and speak to the dragons. Since he's one of them, there's a good chance they'll listen—"

"Or think it's a trap." Flare finally spoke up but with a pessimistic attitude.

"Then make sure they know it's not a trap." They would accomplish nothing if they gave up before they started.

"You don't understand dragons," Flare said. "They're irritable, stubborn, hostile—"

"They are just like you." Cora gave him a deadpan look. "I know how they are."

Flare clenched his jaw, his typical behavior when he was seething behind his eyes.

Cora ignored his look and continued. "And Bridge can stay here to gather news, or he can venture to the dwarves."

Bride released an uncontrollable laugh. "Me? You think I should venture to the dwarves?"

"Why not?" As far as she could tell, he had a pair of legs and a voice. What more did he need?

"They wouldn't hear me out, some ordinary human. They need an elf or a dragon." Bridge retained his smile like the possibility still amused him. "Not some scholar. I'm more than willing to help but in a way that's actually productive."

"You're a scholar?" Cora became intrigued. Now the maps and books throughout the house made more sense.

"Yes," Bridge answered. "My job is to preserve history in its truest form. It sounds simple, but it's really not. Separating fact from lore is actually very difficult."

Would he know who her parents were? "I believe you."

"I wouldn't want you to be involved anyway." Flare finally broke his impenetrable silence. "It's too dangerous."

"Psh." Bridge brushed it off. "Nothing is too dangerous for me."

"Well, I can't lose another friend. I've lost too many already." When Flare said such things, it showed the man underneath the scales and weapons. He was just a heartbroken man without any hope.

Cora had seen it before.

Bridge patted him on the shoulder. "Thanks, man."

Flare nodded in return.

"So, I can speak to both the elves and the dwarves," Cora volunteered. "And Flare can travel to the island—when we find it."

"That sounds like a good plan," Bridge said. "I'll continue to work on the location."

Flare's eyes met hers, his thoughts hidden deep down inside.

"What do you think?" Cora could tell he was in a vicious mood again. When he was a man, she could read his expressions much easier than when he was a dragon. It was much more difficult for him to hide.

Flare downed the rest of his glass before he inverted it and placed it on the tabletop. He wiped a drop of scotch from the corner of his mouth with his sleeve. "It doesn't look like we have any other choice."

# FOURTEEN

Cora had never been in love before, but she realized she'd fallen deeply into its throes.

The bed made of straw was the most comfortable thing she'd ever slept on. The sheets were soft and cool, keeping her body at the perfect temperature. Never in her life had she slept so well.

It could only be love.

The door to her bedchamber opened, and Flare walked inside.

Jolted by his unexpected presence, she hiked up the sheets over her body and covered herself. "Damn, you scared the shit out of me. What are you doing?"

Flare shut the door then came to the bed, a wicked grin on his lips. He was particularly amused. "You doing something nasty?" He lifted up the sheets and tried to take a peek.

She pulled the sheet back down and gave him a merciless glare. "Excuse me?"

"You know…giving yourself a treat." He winked like an arrogant bastard. "And I bet you were thinking about me."

She still had no idea what he meant. "I assure you, I wasn't doing whatever it is you think I was doing."

"I don't know…people only jump like that when they're hiding something."

"Or maybe I just didn't expect you to walk in here without knocking."

"If you're worried about that, why not just lock the door?"

"There's a lock?" She couldn't find one when she tried to lock it before she went to sleep.

He chuckled. "Let me give you some advice. Always lock the door before you touch yourself."

Touch herself? "Flare, get out of my room. And don't walk in like that again. Knock first."

He cocked his head to the side, his eyes lit up with interest. "You don't know what I'm talking about, do you?"

She wasn't sure if she should admit to it or not. "It's late and I'm tired. Good night."

A chuckle escaped his lips. "I'll take that as a no. And that means you're really missing out."

She lay down again and pulled the sheets to her neck. "I don't really care, Flare."

"I'm talking about masturbation. You've never done it?" He sat at the edge of her bed and leaned over her. "I can teach you. The women tell me they love it." He waggled his eyebrows at her in a sleazy way.

She rolled her eyes and turned on her side so she wouldn't have to look at him. "Goodnight, Flare."

"Come on." He shook her shoulder gently. "Don't be such a prude."

"A prude? I don't even know what that is."

"It's a woman who denies her sexual freedom. And believe me, that's no way to live."

All this talk of sex was making her uncomfortable. "Is there a reason you came in here?"

"Actually, yes." He glanced at the fireplace. "You want me to start a fire for you?"

She wanted to kick him right between the legs. "If I wanted a fire, I would have made one myself. I'm not one of your typical damsels in distress. I'm perfectly capable of doing things on my own."

"Except touching yourself…"

She turned over and smacked him hard in the shoulder. "Get out, Flare. I mean it."

He rubbed the area and chuckled. "You've got one hell of an arm."

"I wonder if your nose will think the same." She pulled her right arm back and aimed.

"Whoa, hold on." He grabbed her arm and pushed it down to the sheets. "I'll play nice."

She lay down again and waited for him to leave. "Will you let me get some sleep now?"

"In a minute. I wanted to talk about something."

"Can't it wait until the morning? You know, when I'm rested and less irritated."

"Less irritated? I think that's arguable."

She prepared her right hook again.

He laughed then pushed her arm down. "Man, you're feisty."

"I just value my sleep."

"Or you're lazy…"

"That's it." She sat up and grabbed him by the front of his shirt. "I'm kicking your ass right now."

"Oh, really?" he asked with a laugh.

"Yes, really." She didn't care that she was just in a t-shirt. She was too pissed to care about being conservative.

Flare gripped both of her wrists then pressed his mouth against hers. Immediately, she stopped moving. His lips were warm and soft, not callused like she assumed they would be. His scent washed over, the distinct smell of man. The scruff along his jaw rubbed against her delicate skin slightly.

The whole thing happened so quickly that Cora could barely process it. She'd never kissed a man before, never come close to it. And now, her first kiss was with an arrogant man who insulted her every chance he got.

She gave him a hard shove. "What the hell are you doing?"

"What?" he asked innocently. "It works on the other girls."

She wiped her mouth with her forearm. "Well, I'm not like the others. Don't do that again."

Now he looked truly offended. "You didn't like it?"

"Why would I?" She was told her first kiss was supposed to be magical. If the chemistry was right, her lips would burn. But that was simply unwelcomed and rushed.

Flare couldn't wrap his mind around what she said. "It's just… They always like it."

She rolled her eyes and got back into bed. "Maybe you aren't as good as you think you are."

"Or maybe there's something wrong with you."

"Doubtful." She lay down again and waited for him to leave. "So…goodnight."

He grabbed a chair from the corner and dragged it to her bedside.

She groaned under her breath and wondered what time it was. She should be enjoying every moment of sleep before she was traveling across the land again. Her body would be pushed to the limit.

"I've been thinking about our conversation earlier, about our plan."

At least it was something relevant. "Okay."

"I'm not sure if it's the best idea for you to see the elves."

"Why not?"

He leaned forward and rested his elbows on his knees. "I don't trust them, Cora."

"You don't trust anyone." The only time she saw him truly relax was around Bridge, his old friend.

"For good reason." His attitude completely changed now that they were being serious. "I know you're strong and capable, but sometimes, that's just not enough. Not every opponent you face can be defeated."

"I'm not going to challenge the elves to combat. I just want to talk."

"Well, maybe they don't."

It really didn't matter what might or might not happen. She still needed to travel to their realm and at least make the attempt. "Not going isn't an option. And you can't send someone else. I'm your best hope."

He massaged the knuckles of his right hand, his eyes following his movements. "You know what I think?"

"Hmm?" The sooner this conversation was over, the sooner she could get to sleep.

"I think your real motivation is your lineage. You hope you'll see your parents again—or at least find out what happened to them." He slowly lifted his head and met her gaze.

She looked away because she couldn't deny the allegation. "I admit I'm curious to see where I come from."

"You're approaching a treasure chest expecting to see gold and jewels inside. But when you open the lid, there will be only cobras." He didn't sugarcoat his thoughts, getting right to the point. "If you were abandoned outside a village that's a week's ride away, it can only mean one thing. For whatever reason, you were not safe in Eden Star."

She didn't want that to be the truth, but she didn't see how she could deny it. Her parents left her in the street because they didn't want her or couldn't keep her. What did she hope to find in Eden Star?

Flare didn't take any joy in being right. The same sadness in her heart shone in his eyes. "I'm sorry."

She knew he meant it, somehow. She was beginning to understand him more than ever before. He was covered in layers, superficial walls to hide who he truly was. But as she peeled them away, she saw the extraordinary man beneath it all. "I know…"

"For what it's worth, I know what it's like to have parents that let you down. I know what it's like to hope for love but only receive disappointment. You aren't alone."

It was the first time he'd voluntarily revealed something personal about himself. When he said he didn't trust anyone, that was a lie. Slowly, like a blooming flower in the spring, he was beginning to trust her.

"I still want to go," she whispered. "Even if I'm only met with disappointment, I have to try. I'm our best chance of convincing them, simply because I share their likeness."

Flare nodded because he couldn't deny that truth. "But you don't have to. If you change your mind, we can figure out another way."

"I won't change my mind." She was certain of that. Whether she met her end or was exiled from Eden Star, that was okay. She knew she would regret it far more if she didn't even try.

Flare didn't try to change her mind again. This time, he let it be. "Your guardian truly loves you."

The thought of Dorian made her heart convulse painfully. She missed his cheerful face, those playful eyes. Even when the rest of the village whispered behind her back, he defended her. And she wasn't even his daughter. "I know he does."

"I could sense it in the air when he was near you. It was powerful, blinding."

"Because of the dragon?"

He nodded. "I'm susceptible to vibrations and emotions. Like I said before, I can't read minds. But I can definitely sense moods."

"That must come in handy."

"Sometimes."

She sat up in bed and pulled the covers with her. It didn't seem like Flare was leaving anytime soon. "Why is this important to you?"

"What?"

"Freeing the dragons. It's a huge undertaking, and it doesn't sound likely that it'll ever work. So, why are you willing to risk everything, including your own freedom, to change things? Couldn't you just find the island and live the rest of your days there? Why fight?"

The expression on his face was strikingly similar to the one the dragon possessed. It was unreadable, like a solid wall. He didn't even blink. All he did was stare, the cogs in his mind turning furiously. "When you're connected to a dragon in this way, you become a single person. I feel what he feels. Seeing the rest of his glorious species used like machines is heartbreaking. It pains him every single day that passes, and for an immortal being, that's a long time. I need to right all the wrongs that were committed—for him."

While that was noble and selfless, it left her confused. "If the dragon wishes to be free, why is he fused at all? Why does he continue to remain connected with you?"

When Flare looked down, it was clear this was a question he didn't want to answer. It crossed the line into personal territory.

"I'm sorry. I wasn't trying to pry."

Instead of him snapping at her or storming off, his voice came out quiet. "I know. Flare and I fused a long time ago. It's been so long now that I don't even remember when it happened."

She hugged her knees to her chest and hung on every word. She knew this information was important, even groundbreaking. He was confiding something deep, something he wouldn't tell anyone else.

"I…" It was the first time he'd ever faltered in his speech. He had the confidence to say what he needed to say without hesitation. But now he wasn't himself. He was practically weak. "When Flare and I fused for the first time…I forced him to do it. I broke him down until he was at his weakest point. Then I infected his mind and made it mine to mold." He wouldn't meet her look, the shame etched into every feature of his face. "I controlled him for years."

Cora squeezed her knees, her hands starting to shake. To hear such horrific words escape his mouth left her speechless. She assumed he was one of the good guys, one of the rare people who actually respected the dragon species. But now she knew he was just another monster.

"One day, I realized just how horrific it was. Being linked to his mind for so long forced me to understand his suffering. He was a captive in his own body, unable to do anything else but pray for the sweet release of death. That was when everything changed. I grew to love the dragon, and somehow, he grew to love me."

She tried to keep her breathing quiet so she wouldn't disrupt him. Every word was vital, and she didn't want to make a sound in case he stopped.

"I decided to free him and unfuse. He deserved to be free after all the things I'd done to him. But when I attempted the transition, Flare wouldn't allow it. He kept me bound there, refusing to let me go."

The dragon didn't want to unfuse? She didn't know such a thing was possible. "Why wouldn't he release you?"

His eyes were glued to the thick blanket on top of the bed. He didn't make eye contact again, too ashamed to face her head on. "Dragons are immortal, while humans are not. This is something you already know. But when you're fused, you retain that immortality. Just as the dragons live forever, so does the human. Since my life-span had come and gone hundreds of years ago, I would die if we unfused. My body would quickly accelerate through the aging process, and then I would become dust in the wind. I accepted that fate freely. It should have come long ago. But my dragon wouldn't allow it."

It was the sweetest and saddest thing she ever heard. "Because he loves you…"

Flare nodded. "He's agreed to release me after I repair all the damage I've caused. Once the dragons are free and the world is as it should be, he'll allow me to go."

Agony ripped through her heart like a knife. "You want to pass on?"

He nodded.

"Why?" She remembered Flare mentioning this in the past. Long life might seem like a blessing in the beginning, but as the years wore on, it became a curse. Elves took their own lives just before they became insane.

"I've done a lot of evil things in my life. Flare isn't the only dragon I've tortured. I was directly responsible for a lot of things that happened during the Great War. In fact, I was instrumental in it. Just because I feel differently now doesn't excuse my previous behavior. I deserve a gruesome death. It's wrong that I'll go so quickly and peacefully."

Without Cora realizing it, her eyes had welled up with tears. The story was heartbreaking to hear. He captured the dragons with his bare hands and imprisoned them, and now he was their savior. "I don't think you deserve death."

"Why not?" he said coldly. "There's not a single person who would agree with you."

"Not even Flare?"

"Person. Not dragon."

"What about Bridge?"

He shook his head. "He doesn't count."

"You may have done terrible things in the past, but you aren't that person anymore. Flare wouldn't love you unless you were a good person."

"He's been with me for too long. Love the one you're with."

"There's more to it than that."

"Maybe you think so." His voice was barely above a whisper. "There's nothing left for me to live for. If I destroy the castles of Anastille and return the power where it belongs, I'll feel better. But that won't heal me."

"Maybe you'll feel differently when that time comes."

"Doubtful. I've felt this way for a hundred years now. I doubt anything will change in the next hundred."

She eyed his hand on his thigh then grabbed it with her own. Even though she wasn't a dragon, she could sense his sorrow. It was heavy like a rain cloud about to pour. She should hate him for what he did, but she simply couldn't. She saw the light shine through him as well as the remorse. "Everyone deserves a second chance."

He eyed their interlocked fingers. "Not me."

"When this is all over, you'll feel differently."

He brushed his thumb across her fingertips. His skin was dry and cracked from gripping the pommel of a sword. His hand was twice the size of hers and twice as warm. "Maybe. Or maybe I'll hate myself even more."

# FIFTEEN

"So, what are we doing?" Bridge stood with his arms across his chest in the entryway.

"You and I are going to the coast." Flare was dressed for the journey. His typical black clothes fit him to a T, and his dark cloak covered his shoulders and chest. He pulled up his hood and obscured his face. "Cora is going to Eden Star."

"I don't know how much help I will be," Bridge said. "If there are beautiful women bathing in the sea, I'll be too distracted to be of much assistance."

Flare chuckled. "I'll make you focus."

"We don't know where this island is," Bridge said. "You want to figure it out when we get there? Sounds reckless."

"We can't hide here forever." Flare's black sword hung at his side. "And we shouldn't waste unnecessary time. I can't stay in one place for too long. They'll track me down eventually."

"Who?" Bridge asked.

Flare shrugged. "Everybody." He pulled a map from his pocket then stared at Cora. "Are you sure you're up for this? Maybe we should escort you there."

"That'll take a whole month out of your journey." He might be a dragon, but that trip would still be exhausting. "And it's unnecessary. I'll be fine."

"I'm not worried about you being fine," Flare said. "I'm just worried you might get lost."

Cora took the map and examined it. "It's pretty straightforward. It's almost a straight shot to the hills."

"Not really." Flare snatched the map then pointed to the left side of a riverbed. "There's an orc clan here. Stay away from them. They may be mindless, but they're strong. They could crush your skull with a simple squeeze."

"Good to know." Cora marked the spot with her pen.

"And don't forget about the poisonous frogs." Bridge pointed farther up the stream to a small pond. "That stuff can kill you instantly."

She wasn't afraid of frogs; that was certain. "Thanks for the heads-up."

"If they come your way, just run." Flare marked the map even though it wasn't necessary. "Even if you stab them with your sword, you risk contracting their poison."

Would she need to stab a tiny frog? "I think there are far more dangerous creatures than a poisonous frog."

"Have you seen them?" Bridge gave her an incredulous look. "They're as big as us. A frog may be a frog, but a gigantic frog is terrifying in my book."

"As big as us?" She didn't know that was possible.

"And they jump high," Flare said. "And I mean, *high*. If you had to pick an enemy, you're better off with the orcs than these guys." He turned back to the map. "Avoid the sandpits here. They'll pull you under and suffocate you."

"That sounds like a terrible death." It was just like drowning.

Flare sucked his inner lip as he moved his gaze to her face. Hesitation shone brighter than the sun. "Maybe I should just come with you. A lot can go wrong on your journey."

"I'll be fine. Really." She could handle herself.

"You almost died last time you went somewhere alone." Flare would never let her live that down.

"I made a mistake, and I won't do it again." How many times did she have to admit he was right? "I'll keep my head down and just focus on getting there. You have my word."

"She seems strong enough," Bridge said. "She'll be alright."

Cora gave him a grateful look. "Thank you."

Flare was still hesitant. "I can't afford to lose you. You're one of the few allies I have."

"You're overthinking it. You're just as likely to come to a terrifying death as I am." He was a dragon after all. The Shamans wanted him more than her.

"I don't know about that…" He closed the map and folded it. "After the sandpits, it should be an easy road."

"How will I know if I've reached their land?" Cora asked.

"They'll see you before you see them," Bridge said. "And they'll approach you or shoot you down where you stand."

That was a little terrifying. "Should I hold up a white flag or something?"

"No," Flare answered. "Just look harmless. Sheath your sword and stash away your bow. It's important not to alarm them."

On the surface, she looked like easy prey, so that shouldn't be hard to accomplish.

"And finally," Flare said, "stay hidden at all times. Don't go into any villages or towns. You understand?"

She hated it when people spoke to her like she was an idiot. "Yes, I understand, asshole."

Bridge chuckled. "Don't use that language with the elves. They won't like it much."

"Well, they aren't going to like me much either." It didn't matter who she was speaking to. If they were rude to her, she'd be rude back. "Where do we meet when we're finished?" They couldn't return to this house.

Flare rubbed his chin as he searched his mind for a good place. "Do you remember the place by the river? Where you healed my wing?"

"Yes." It was close to home.

"Do you know how to get there?"

"Yes." She grabbed the map from his hands. "I can figure it out."

"That will be the rendezvous point," Flare said. "And hopefully, there will be others among us when we do meet."

Dragons, specifically. "Sounds like a plan."

"Alright." Flare watched her with concern in his eyes. "Are you sure you want to do this? If the road gets difficult, you won't be able to change your mind."

"I'm sure." A little danger didn't scare her.

Flare was silent for a few moments, giving her the opportunity to really think it over.

She rolled her eyes. "Let's hit the road. The sun is about to come up."

They snuck out of the city and entered the wilderness. Once they were a league away from unfriendly eyes, they stopped.

Cora pulled out her map. "Alright. I'm headed this way." Her journey would take much longer than Flare's since they were already near the coast. But then again, if he had to sail across the sea, he might be gone for a long time. She folded the map and stuck it in her pocket. "I guess I'll see you guys later." She kept the farewell light because it was too difficult to say how she really felt. Despite his harsh demeanor, Flare had become a close friend. She couldn't return to her village and see her friends and family again, so he was the only comfort she had. Even though she hadn't known Bridge as long, she felt the same way toward him. The possibility of never seeing them again saddened her heart.

"Yes." Bridge gripped both of her shoulders and gave them a gentle squeeze. "Later." He embraced her with a pat on the back. "You better bring us some elven treats when you do."

He was attempting to cheer her up, and she smiled in gratitude. "I'll try."

He gave her another pat before he stepped back.

Flare stared at her without moving, his arms hanging by his sides.

She knew he wouldn't hug her. It simply wasn't something he did. The kiss they'd shared the other night was random and full of lust. She wasn't interested in that. "I'll see you soon."

"Yeah." He gave a slight nod, his face barely visible behind his hood. "I'm sure you will."

Now that she was about to turn around and walk the opposite way, fear gripped her by the throat. She tried to combat it and keep her head held high, but it was a struggle.

Flare was the first one to step back. "Good luck, Cora." He turned around and walked off, Bridge following him a moment later. Their backs receded into the distance, their powerful shoulders slowly disappearing from sight as they departed. When their outlines were no longer visible, she knew they were really gone.

She turned around and stared at the terrain before her feet. The whole world was out there, waiting for her to pass through. The month would be long without any companionship, and the road would be difficult, pushing Cora to her limit.

But that didn't stop her from taking the first step.

# SIXTEEN

Flare and Bridge approached the wooden door and blew out the torches mounted on either side. When darkness blanketed them completely, they picked the lock with a dagger and a nail.

"You're sure this is the place?" Flare worked the lock, trying to find the exact spot to make it click.

"I know where the Grand Library is." Light was unnecessary to see Bridge's exaggerated eye roll. It was clear in his voice.

"Do you think anyone is awake?" Flare's hood was still pulled up as he worked the lock.

"Academics never sleep."

"Then we'll kill the accolades." Problem solved.

"Whoa, hold on." Bridge stopped scanning for the guards and looked at Flare. "We aren't killing anyone."

"Then what else are we supposed to do?"

"Tie them up. Did you think of that? Why do you always resort to killing?"

"Because they'll tell a steward we were here. Idiot."

Bridge's eyes narrowed in the dark. "We'll be long gone by then."

"They'll figure out what we're doing."

"And if we kill them, they'll still figure it out."

Flare couldn't argue with that. "But they won't know for sure."

"Who else would be responsible, other than the dragon they're trying to recapture?" Venom seeped out of Bridge's voice. "Everyone in Anastille must know about it by now."

Flare turned the knife and finally heard the distinct click in the keyhole. "I got it."

"Wait." Bridge grabbed his hand. "No killing, alright? These accolades are just students of history. They've done nothing wrong."

Flare had a much different attitude about right and wrong. "If they're in the way, that's not my problem."

"I'm not going in there unless you promise me. And you know how much you need me."

Bridge's unrealistic morals showed Flare just how ignorant he was. "Fine. We're wasting too much time talking about it." He opened the door and walked inside first. The stone stairway led to the different floors of the library. Low-burning candles illuminated the room, showing the volumes of hardbound books on the mahogany shelves. "Where do we start?"

Bridge walked through the shelves and searched for the map. "I've never been here before. It'll take me some time to figure out."

"Great." Just what he needed. He pulled out his sword and scanned the room, making sure there were no surprises lurking about. He kept his eyes on the stairs and the door, waiting for an assailant to approach.

After twenty minutes of searching, Bridge came back. "It's not here. Next floor."

Flare took the lead and leaped off the stairs without making a sound with his boots. The floor was identical to the previous one with the same number of shelves and books. Tables were dispersed around the room where a few open books lay. The red rug underneath his feet silenced his steps. "Get to work."

Bridge searched the floor, pulling books off the shelves and scanning their pages at a table. He moved quickly, making more noise than he should. Flare focused for the sound of approaching guards. Fortunately, he didn't hear anyone.

"Goddammit." Bridge came to his side, empty-handed. "Nothing."

Flare hadn't gotten his hopes up in the first place. "Let's move." There was one more floor they hadn't explored. Hopefully, they would find what they needed there. They moved past the open windows that displayed the city below. The moon glowed high in the sky and was particularly bright on that summer's eve.

They reached the tallest room of the tower but stopped when they spotted an accolade sitting at a table. His back was to them, and an open book lay on the table's surface. His red robes reached to the floor, and his head was shaved down to the skin.

Flare turned to Bridge and silently asked what they should do.

He mouthed, "Don't kill him."

Flare mouthed back, "Then what am I supposed to do?"

Bridge shrugged. "Knock him out."

That wasn't the worst idea in the world. Flare approached him from behind then gripped his sword by the hilt. With lightning speed, he smashed it against the back of the accolade's skull.

He collapsed onto the table, his face resting in the open pages of the book he was reading.

"Get to work," Flare said. "There may be others."

"Did you have to hit him that hard?" Bridge headed to the shelves and began his search.

"If I'd known how soft you were, I would have suggested that you become a gardener or a seamstress."

Bridge threw a book at his head.

Flare knew it was coming, so he blocked it with his forearm. "That's productive."

Bridge disappeared into the shelves and searched the area.

Flare hoisted himself onto the table beside the unconscious man and rested his sword across his knees. The view from the window was mesmerizing, despite the danger they were in. It was difficult to be worried about anything when he stared at the beaming moon.

"Damn, it's not here."

Flare fought the sorrow in his heart. "You're sure?"

"If it were here, I would have found it."

That map was their greatest hope. Without it, they'd have to figure out everything based on intuition.

Flare glanced at the book the accolade was reading. A map spread across the two pages, and it included the continent of Anastille as well as the surrounding oceans. "Bridge, come here."

"What?" He emerged from the sea of bookcases.

"I think I found it."

"Nice one." He disappeared again.

"I'm being serious. Get over here." He lifted the man's head and pulled the book out. Then he let his face fall against the wood with a dull thud.

Bridge saw what he did and gave him a glare.

"What? He's already going to have a headache when he wakes up anyway." He passed the book along.

Bridge examined the pages with little expectation. He turned the book sideways and had a closer look. When his eyes narrowed and his lips parted, the excitement returned to his face. "This is it."

Flare clapped the unconscious man on the shoulder. "Thanks, buddy."

"This is the map." He turned the book and displayed it to Flare. "See this island here?" He pointed at a small landmass far out in the ocean. "It's not on the newer maps. It's been removed."

"Why would they remove it?"

Bridge shut the book and stored it in his pack. "There's only one explanation."

"And what explanation is that? The preservers of history were careless with details and allowed something as important as an island to disappear from the world map?" That didn't give him much hope in humanity.

"No." Bridge put his hands on his hips, excitement burning in his eyes. "It looks like the dragons still have some allies."

## SEVENTEEN

Cora's only companions were the trees. They swayed in the gentle breeze and sang a quiet song. Sometimes, when the loneliness enveloped her, she placed words with the sounds, making a comforting tune.

It was the first time she'd been alone since she'd met Flare. When they were together, he was irritating, but now that he wasn't around, she realized how much she missed him. She preferred his insults to this silence any day.

She didn't come across anything interesting in her travels. The only other living creatures she saw were birds. They hopped from branch to branch and chirped as she passed. With every passing day, she consulted her map to see how close she was to the elven lands, but then quickly realized she was moving at the pace of a snail.

If only she had a horse. Or better yet, a dragon.

At nighttime, it was difficult to sleep. The sounds of the forest always made her jump out of her dreams. It was difficult to tell if the sounds were natural or a bad omen of her approaching doom.

Whenever she was stirred from her sleep, she opened her eyes and lay absolutely still. After ten minutes had passed, she realized it was just her imagination. Then she fell back asleep.

By the fourth day, she'd run out of water. According to her map, she was close to a stream, and it wasn't the stream of the orc clan or the poisonous frogs. She approached the water's edge and filled her canteen. Since there was no one around, she decided to take a bath.

Being naked in the water reminded her of the time she'd bathed in front of Flare. She hadn't realized he was a man as well as a dragon, and the fact that he'd seen her naked made her cheeks turn blood red.

Was that why he'd kissed her?

Vax was a conservative place. She always wore pants and a long-sleeved tunic to cover her skin. She already had enough advances from men, and she didn't want to encourage more by showing her feminine curves. It was clear that outside of Vax, things were different. Flare and Bridge both spoke of women like they had a lot of experience with them, even though neither was married.

She needed to let go of her former culture and adapt to a new one, at least if she wanted to survive.

After bathing, she changed her clothes then washed the old pair she'd been wearing. Being clean was a necessity. She'd never considered herself to be high-maintenance, but cleanliness was important to her. When the grime piled up, she didn't feel like herself.

When she was finished, she hit the road again, knowing she'd be traveling on foot for a long time. She considered running until she reached Eden Star, but she would have to sleep longer to regain her energy, so it wouldn't really make a difference.

She hunted every few days and cooked the meat over a fire. As soon as the meat was done, she would put out the flames and move on, not wanting to attract visitors. Flare could eat raw meat, but she was certain she'd grow seriously ill if she did that. While on foot, she ate her dinner and kept moving.

By the end of the first week, she'd had enough. Every tree and every hill looked exactly the same. The boulders she passed started to blur together, and she didn't know whether she was traveling in circles or going in the right direction. Every time she consulted the map, she seemed to be on the right track.

But could she ever know for sure?

Maybe she should have allowed Flare and Bridge to accompany her. She could take care of herself, but she wasn't proficient in traveling. All she'd ever done was visit the neighboring towns and villages. Now, she was hiking across the continent with a blind eye.

She rested her head on her pack and tucked the thin blanket around herself, keeping the warm air directly next to her body. She lay between a bush and a tree, using it as cover from anyone who passed.

She lay on her back and looked up at the sky. There wasn't much to see because it was so dark. In the distance, the stars shone high in the sky, twinkling deep into the unknown.

The stars comforted her in a way she couldn't explain. Whenever she couldn't sleep in Vax, she always stared at them through her small window. After a few minutes, their silent song lured her to sleep.

Her eyes grew heavy and started to close. Her heart slowed down, beating at a steady rhythm. Her muscles relaxed from the long journey, and her body welcomed its unconscious state.

But then she saw something.

It happened so quickly, she wasn't sure if it happened at all. A mass passed across the sky, not having any specific shape. It was a shadow, a blackness, that moved with lightning speed.

Her heart stopped beating.

Did she really see that? Was her mind playing tricks on her? Was her fatigue so paramount that she was hallucinating? She lay absolutely still and hardly breathed. She was certain she saw it, whatever it was, and it was bigger than any bird she'd ever come across.

The adrenaline kicked in, and blood pounded in her ears.

She didn't move for her sword or bow because she was too scared to make a single sound. Just the slight rustling of the grass could attract someone—or something.

Her eyes remained wide open, unblinking. She stared at the sky and hoped she didn't see anything else. It was strange how quiet the world became once you really started to listen.

Other than the breeze and the swaying of branches, there was nothing else to focus on.

There was only silence.

And then it happened again.

A black mass flashed across the sky. If it were bright and sparkling, it would have reminded her of a shooting star. Dark as it was, it felt more like a bad omen, a hint at an apocalyptic end to the world.

All Cora heard was the movement of the black body through the air. There was no other sound. Despite her limited visibility, she knew the beings were traveling fast.

There were two of them.

The number resonated in her head like a gong. High-pitched and piercing, alarm shot through her body like a sharp arrow. Perhaps it was paranoia, but she could only think of two other beings that could fly besides dragons.

The Shamans.

She didn't get any sleep that night.

Too afraid to close her eyes for long, she hardly blinked. Evil was directly on her tail. They must have tracked her down to this location. She avoided making footprints in the dirt and only made fires during the day for just a few minutes, but maybe that wasn't enough precaution.

Perhaps they had other ways of tracking her.

Did they realize Flare went a different way? In her eyes, Flare was a much more important target. But if one of them had to be captured, it should be her. A dragon was far more important than she, a stupid girl.

She shouldn't have stabbed the Shaman in the first place. Sometimes, she had unrealistic views of her own strength. And that could have gotten her killed. But if she hadn't intervened, that boy would have been turned to dust.

So, could she really regret it?

Could she make it to the elves and avoid being captured? After she was in their realm, she wouldn't have to worry about the Shamans anymore. While most of the trail was covered with trees, some of the journey brought her directly across a desert.

There would be no way for her to hide.

When the sun rose the following morning, she consulted her map. The brush was denser near the river, right past the orc clan and the poisonous frogs Flare had advised her to stay away from. It was the best terrain to remain hidden from the skies.

Her choices were limited. She might be able to avoid the Shamans by taking the path near the river, but she might become dinner for the orcs in the process. Or even worse, she could be poisoned by the frogs.

What was worse?

The Shamans sent a chill up her spine. When she battled the first one, she'd barely escaped with her life. Their use of magic was unparalleled by her bow or her sword. She couldn't see their faces, but her imagination was far worse than the real thing. Whatever was behind that hood was foul and evil.

It didn't take her long to come to a decision.

"Orcs and frogs, here I come."

She moved across the forest floor, careful not to make a sound. She bypassed the fallen leaves and twigs and stuck to the firm earth. Her eyes constantly scanned the world around her, making sure she hadn't been spotted. She was near the orc settlement.

She could smell it.

When she heard voices, she retreated into a bush and concentrated on the noises.

A guttural sound filled her ears. An image of a dragon munching down on a raw bear came to mind. The sound of cracking bones and severed tendons was something she'd never forget. That type of carnal sound, of a predator eating prey, was the first thing she thought of.

She crawled farther toward the end of the forest and watched the river. Massive black orcs gathered around the stream, refilling their water sacks and washing their thick hides. She'd never seen an orc, but they were just as terrifying as she once imagined.

Thick black hair covered their bodies, and their faces were gray like stone. Their features were concave rather than convex, and their noses were pushed in like someone had punched them too hard. Their mouths were lipless with just an opening that showed expansive teeth. Eyes as big and round as an owl's made them seem like monsters.

Cora definitely didn't want to have a rendezvous with them if she could avoid it.

She retreated farther into the trees and made her progress noiselessly. While Flare insisted the frogs were worse than the orcs, she found that unlikely. Orcs were aggressive and massive beasts. The muscles of their arms and legs could snap her to pieces. No matter how poisonous, the frogs were far less terrifying opponents.

Three days had come and gone, and she hadn't spotted the Shamans again. Hopefully, they'd moved on and lost her trail, but she suspected that was just hopeful thinking. The annoying tug in her heart said she would see them again, as much as she wished that weren't the case.

She didn't see the orcs again as she continued, but she found evidence of their passing. Heavy footprints were in the mud, their feet the size of her torso. Branches had been pushed aside or even broken in their path. When Flare was in his dragon state, he moved around the environment rather than destroying it. But these orcs didn't seem to care.

She stayed along the river until the trees began to change. Their leaves took on a lighter shade, not as vibrant and green as before. Even though the river was nearby, it didn't seem like vegetation in the area was getting enough water. The desert was just a few more days' travel, so the climate was beginning to change.

Since the Shamans hadn't made an appearance in many days, she decided to get some sleep. For all she knew, the shadows weren't Shamans at all. Maybe they were large birds. With her limited knowledge of the outside world, she couldn't provide an accurate guess.

Her thoughts and vision were starting to blur, so the second she rested her head on her pack, she fell asleep. When she'd lived in Vax, she had to lie still for nearly an hour before sleep finally took her. Now that struggle was nonexistent.

Dreams came and went. Some were about the Shamans, their gloved hands reaching for her throat. Sometimes, Dorian's face came to her mind, the blinding pain in his eyes when they said farewell to each other. And then other times, she saw a pair of black eyes drilling into her own. They ripped into her, stripping every layer and every limb. They stared right into her soul, not allowing her to hide anywhere else. The irises were black as coal, and the distant colors surrounding them were orange and red, the beginning of a blazing fire. Not once did they blink, not willing to give her a single moment of liberation.

Cora tossed and turned, running from something she couldn't escape. Doors appeared on her journey, but every time she walked through one, she was met with the same raging eyes. It was vivid and real. She could smell the smoke in the air and feel the burn in her lungs. Her leg muscles ached from the distance she'd run. It was worse than any nightmare she'd ever experienced.

It was a night terror.

The eyes squinted, turning vengeful. "I. See. You."

She continued her journey up the river and tried not to think of the dream she couldn't forget. Nightmares such as those had never plagued her in Vax. Now, they were coming nearly every night. She was chased by a pair of unforgiving eyes.

They never allowed her to escape, subjecting her to the torture of a complex cage.

She'd never told Flare about it, but now she wished she had. Maybe he might know something about it. Did he have dreams? Did he have nightmares such as that? She wished she knew.

Her water canteen was depleted. It'd been empty for nearly a day. If the desert was on the horizon, then she desperately needed to refill it before the barren stretch ahead. If not, she wouldn't make it. Cora could survive stab wounds, nightmares, and even orc attacks, but she couldn't survive dehydration. It was the one thing that connected every living thing. Without water, they all would perish.

She approached the edge of the forest and crouched behind a boulder. The stream was quiet, and the water was hardly moving. The distant sound of the running water was soothing to her ears. The noises of nature made her forget the danger that loomed behind every corner.

Instead of running out immediately, she waited. She listened for the sound of a crying orc or the bellow of a frog. Nothing out of the ordinary played against her ears, and there wasn't a creature in sight. The riverbed was filled with lily pads that gently floated across the water. The surface sparkled under the sunlight, making it glimmer like flecks of gold.

She grabbed her canteen then approached the river, still cautious in her movements. If she were going to be ambushed, it would happen right then and there. Her knees hit the soft grass, and she crouched down in preparation to fill her bottle made from the stomach of a bear.

Still nothing.

She leaned down and scooped the moving water into the bottle. It was cool to the touch and soft, immediately reminding her of bathwater. It removed the dirt from her fingertips and the grime under her nails.

When the canteen was full, she took a deep drink. She didn't realize just how dry her mouth was until the liquid ran down her throat. After consuming the entire bottle, she still felt parched. Her skin was pale and unusually tight. When she touched the flesh of her forearms, she saw the distinct change in color, something Dorian taught her a long time ago. She filled her canteen again and drank the contents. It was important to consume as much water as possible before continuing forward. Water wouldn't always be so accessible.

A strange tingle prickled her skin. The hair on the back of her neck became rigid and stiff. Even though she was warm, her forearms freckled with bumps. Her body suddenly chilled despite the summer day.

It was like an itch she couldn't scratch. She knew something was wrong in the clearing, but she couldn't distinguish what it was. Just like the black eyes in her dream, something was drilling into her.

Her eyes left the stream and looked across the water. Staring at her with menace was a green tree frog. But it was no ordinary frog. This wasn't the kind that sat in your palm while you played outside. It wasn't cute, as the girls would claim.

It was threatening.

Red eyes sat atop its head, and they were trained on Cora. The plump lips of its mouth were trembling, but not in a fearful way. The anger over her presence shook his entire body, and he couldn't contain it. There wasn't a single doubt in Cora's mind that he wanted to murder her.

She discreetly replaced the lid to her canteen and shoved it into her pack, not taking her eyes off the frog that seemed determined to kill her and feed her to his tadpoles.

She slowly rose to her feet and took a step back. "I just wanted some water…"

Its lips stopped trembling but widened in a grimace. Teeth sharper than her dagger emerged, pristine white and lethal. A roar fit for a bear came from its throat, echoing in the clearing.

"Aren't you supposed to say ribbit, ribbit?"

The amphibian was nearly twice her height, and the power in its hind legs was noticeable in the distinct muscles that formed its size. It crouched hard into the ground then pushed off the surface, flying all the way across the riverbed and directly onto the opposite bank.

"Shit, Flare wasn't kidding." She took off at a sprint and ran for the trees.

The sound of its hops thudded behind her, shaking the ground with every landing.

Of all the ways she thought she would die, she never thought she would be killed by a tree frog.

She couldn't wield her sword because she might contract the poison from her blade. Coming into contact with it would end her life immediately. How did you kill something without touching it?

She wanted to smack herself upside the head.

She armored her bow and yanked the arrow out of her quiver as fast as possible. The arrow fit against the string, and she pulled her arm back in preparation for the shot. If she missed, she wouldn't get another chance. She would be frog food.

She skidded to a halt on the grass and turned around. Her arms scraped against the dirt and caused a painful burn. A cry escaped her clenched jaw, but she didn't lose her focus. The evil frog prepared its hind legs for a final leap, the pounce of death.

She released the arrow and watched it penetrate the monster right between the eyes. The slime covering its skin splashed out as the arrow dug deep inside its skull. The redness in his eyes died like a blown-out candle, and he fell forward into an ungraceful roll, stopping just a few feet from Cora.

A stitch burned in her side, and adrenaline was still heavy in her blood. Her heart was about to give out from both the effort and the fear. She was as careful as possible, but an enormous beast had still managed to sneak up on her.

She placed her bow across her back then lay on the grass, recovering from the near-death experience. Once her breathing had returned to normal, she walked to the frog and looked down at its corpse.

The arrow protruded out of its skull, the red feather tip moving slightly in the breeze. She knew she should leave the arrow behind because it was infected with deadly poison, but she couldn't spare it. One arrow might make all the difference when it came to life and death.

She slowly pulled the arrow from the skull, doing her best not to flick bits of poison onto her clothes or skin. The moist slime covering it had a shadowed tint, emitting a sign of danger to anyone who looked at it.

The arrow contained bits of frog brains, so Cora rubbed it off on the lush grass. The stench burned her nose, causing her to grimace and feel nauseated. "Yuck." She wrapped the arrow with a clean cloth before she returned it to her quiver. If the poison spread to the remaining arrows, she wouldn't be able to touch any of them—at least not without dying herself.

The familiar feeling of being watched fell on her shoulders, and she looked up to see a gathering of tree frogs near the bank. They were all different colors, some pastel blue while others were pink. Their skin shone from a layer of poison their bodies constantly produced. It gleamed in the sunlight, acting as a warning to anyone with eyes. Their eyes were all the same color—fiery red.

She didn't have enough arrows.

Their demeanor wasn't threatening like the other frog she'd annihilated. They crouched to get a better look at her, but none of them chased her down. Quiet ribbits escaped their throats, speaking to one another in their own language. They cocked their heads from left to right, moving like curious birds.

"Okay…"

Even though there were more of them than there were of her, they stayed back. Fear might have kept them in place. Or maybe it was something else entirely. Cora didn't stick around to find out.

She took off.

The trees thinned, and the underbrush became nonexistent. Vegetation was scarce, and the stream curved around and headed in the opposite direction, originating in the mountains.

Now, all that was left was the desert.

She didn't know how long the sand would last. She could barely see the mountains on the other side. No living creature could cross the stretch unless they had a wagon full of water barrels.

Could she make it?

She only had a single canteen, and there was no way it would last, not under direct sunlight. Her only option was to eat food dense with water along the way.

But could anything survive out there?

She decided to camp out in the trees for the day until the sun went down. It would be better to travel in the dark, to decrease water evaporation, than to travel under the blistering sun.

Her heart hadn't slowed down after the attack with the frog. With one obstacle completed, there was another one to replace it. She would never admit it out loud, but she missed Flare. He always knew where to go and how to do things. He'd probably have a solution for the desert problem if he were there.

But she needed to figure it out on her own.

When the sun sank behind the mountains, she made her move. She didn't need a torch to guide her because there was nothing in her path anyway. All she needed to do was walk as far as possible until the sun rose the next day. She'd bury herself in the sand for protection from the sun until the night returned.

The sand moved under her boots with every step she took. It was unique in its composition, nothing like stone or dirt. If she distributed her weight in the wrong way, the sand would slip from underneath her feet.

The desert was more silent than the forest because there were no trees to sway in the wind and no birds to chirp to the moon. It was a wasteland of nothingness.

When she heard a sound, she stopped in her tracks. It was familiar—something she'd heard just the day before.

Ribbit.

She looked over her shoulder but only saw a black wall. She couldn't even see the tip of her nose because it was so dark. When she held her hands in front of her face, there was nothing there.

Ribbit.

She heard it again, and this time, she knew it was real. Only one thing would make that noise.

The poisonous frogs.

They were following her out into the desert, risking their own lives just to claim hers. Would she be able to stop and sleep on the way? Or would she be chased the entire time?

Why didn't she steal a horse? She wouldn't make the same mistake twice. If the opportunity to acquire a horse presented itself, she would take it.

Ribbit, ribbit.

"Ugh." She had no chance of survival now. How could she hit her mark when she couldn't see the ground beneath her feet? Her only option was to run and hope she made it to the other side before they made it to her.

The sky turned pink with the expectant sunrise. The air temperature picked up slightly, already warming even though the sun hadn't yet arrived. Cora needed to sleep and get out of the deadly rays. Every drop of moisture in her body was vital, and she couldn't afford to lose a single ounce.

Or she might die.

The sound of the frogs had died away, but that didn't mean they'd retreated back to the river. She glanced over her shoulder in the hope of seeing nothing but a dry desert, but instead saw them lined up together, their throats protruding out while they breathed.

"Dammit."

She put her hands on her hips and tried to appear as menacing as possible. "Shoo!" She held up her sword and pointed it to the sky.

They didn't move forward or backward. They kept their position in line, their red eyes reflecting the approaching sunlight. There was an invisible line none of them would cross. The frog she had killed didn't hide the fact that he sought murder. But with these guys, it was hard to tell.

"Show's over," she called. "There's nothing to see."

In sync, they started to ribbit. Their deep bellows reached her even across the desert. Instead of sounding like a song, it felt like an alarm. They hopped in place but didn't leap forward.

"Weirdos…" She turned around and prepared to continue forward.

High in the sky were two distinct black shapes. They were headed right toward her, the sun shining behind them. Winged steeds that resembled horses flew elegantly across the sun, despite their blackness. As soon as the sun peeked over the mountains, they spotted her.

The ribbits increased in volume, growing more frantic. Were they trying to warn her?

The assailants drew near, and their identity was unmistakable. Black leather pants clung to their legs, and their black tunics contained the same shine of the fabric. Black greaves led to black gloves. The dark tunics covered their chests and hid their faces in shadow.

The Shamans.

Her first instinct was to run, but there was nowhere to hide. If she retreated, she'd be swallowed by a sea of dangerous frogs. Even if they weren't there, she wouldn't get far.

She had to fight.

Knowing she was stepping into a futile fight was disheartening. All she could hope to do was cause the worst pain imaginable before they put her in her grave. She armed her bow and drew the first arrow her fingers touched. The cloth covering the poisonous tip fell to the ground at her feet.

Cora didn't know if the poison would be effective against these unnatural creatures. She suspected it wouldn't have any effect at all but hoped it would burn like hell.

She aimed for the Shaman on the left and released.

The arrow launched and flew through the air with incredible speed. It punctured the Shaman in the center of his chest, dangerously close to where his heart would be if he had one, and caused the Shaman to falter in his saddle.

He tipped over and fell twenty feet to the ground, his body making a loud thump when he hit the hard earth.

Cora held her breath as she waited for the Shaman to stir. A simple arrow couldn't have taken him down, but her heart hoped for a miracle.

He didn't move.

The second Shaman released a loud cry, a piercing noise that made her grit her teeth in protest. The sound came straight from the underworld. It released a second cry, and Cora covered her ears because it was too painful to hear.

It swooped down from the sky and landed beside its fallen comrade. The Shaman felt his chest and shook him violently. A series of clicks and guttural sounds emitted from the shadowed hood.

It was the creepiest thing she'd ever seen.

The Shaman released his brethren then slowly turned his head toward her. He stared her down from inside his dark hood. Invisible eyes bored into hers and burned of death.

Slowly, Cora lifted her bow again.

Another ear-splitting scream erupted from deep within his hood before he jumped to his feet.

She pulled an arrow from the quiver and placed it hard against the string. She didn't have another poisonous arrow, but her heart felt lighter knowing they could be killed after all.

He raised his palm then unleashed his power.

"Agh!" Cora dropped her weapon and fell to her knees. The pressure in her skull made her writhe in agony. Everything was caving in, forcing her head to explode. She couldn't think about anything other than the pain. Death was preferable to the torture she felt, and she'd only endured it for a few seconds.

He marched forward with his palm still raised and gave her another dose.

She fell to her back and rolled around in the dust, flapping her hands as she pointlessly tried to avoid it. The pain was coming from inside her body, not the outside. There was nothing to fight. All she could do was suffer.

The Shaman approached her, his boots grinding against the sand, and he stopped when he was just above her. He pushed his hand toward her, increasing the force of the torture.

"Stop!" Her back arched toward the sky.

The Shaman inched his hand toward her face, the black glove reeking ominously of death.

"Agh!"

When his palm touched her face, she was about to lose her mind. Her brain was boiling, rotting in her skull. Lightning bolts echoed inside her head. All she knew was excruciating pain. Blades stabbed every inch of her all at the same time. She would do anything to make it stop—anything at all.

And then the world went black.

# EIGHTEEN

Thud. Thud. Thud.

Her head pounded with a migraine more explosive than a bubbling volcano. It was fiery and hot, and the constant pulse was enough to drive anyone to pure madness. The throbbing was the worst part. It pressed against both of her temples like the blood was trying to find a way out of her skull.

It was as if someone had stepped on her head with a boot made of jagged nails.

Slowly, the previous events came back to her mind. She could think more clearly now that her skull wasn't being burned to coal. The Shaman had placed his hand over her face and gave her a jolt that almost killed her.

But she wasn't dead—not yet anyway.

She opened her eyes slightly, wanting to see the world without telling anyone she was awake. Her eyes moved to a tiny window near the ceiling. Black bars intersected it even though it was too small to climb through.

Her wrists were bound together. She could feel the burn of the rope every time she moved. Without any further information, she knew she'd been tied up for some time.

Her back lay against cold stone. Judging by the placement of the window and the throbbing pain in her back, she was lying on the floor in a cell. The oil in her hair told her she hadn't been bathed or taken care of in any regard. Her mouth was parched and dry, and her tongue felt like cotton picked right from the plant.

Her eyes opened wider, and she examined her holding cell. The small room was constructed of blue stone. It reflected a metallic sheen that glinted in the dying light from the window. Her best guess told her it was the end of the day.

The wooden door was blood red with a sliding window near the top. Black bars, similar to the ones on the window, separated their prisoner from the water. She stared at her cell and knew there was no way for her to escape.

It was hopeless.

The door opened, and a man wearing a guard's uniform walked inside. Without a helmet, his face was visible. He looked to be a few years older than her, but the look in his eyes said he was much fouler. "You've been out for a while."

She wouldn't give in to his taunts. He was a cat playing with his food, picking it apart until there was hardly anything left, before he finally ate it. "That's what happens when someone boils your brain." She stared at the ceiling and tried to forget about the throbbing sensation in her skull.

He smiled, but it was grotesque. "The steward was very happy to hear of your visit. He's been waiting for you to wake up."

"Well, today's his lucky day." Her bound hands rested on her stomach. She was already bored of this man and the conversation.

"I'm Rune, by the way. It's a pleasure to meet you—a real pleasure."

The way he said those words rubbed her the wrong way. She knew a creep when she saw one. "I'm sure you already know who I am."

"Cora." He said her name slowly, like he was savoring each syllable. "Yes."

"So…why haven't you killed me yet?" She had no idea where she was or the terrain of the fortress. Even if she wanted to escape, she had no idea where to go. Death was the only option at that point.

"Kill you?" That disgusting smile spread across his lips. "Why on earth would we do that?"

"Because I killed one of your hounds." And she'd liked it. Too bad she hadn't killed the other one.

"Oh yes. Shadow wasn't happy about that."

"Shadow?" She couldn't restrain herself from laughing. "That's really his name? That's the lamest thing I've ever heard."

His eyebrows furrowed, the first sign of irritation. "That's the name we've given him—because we can't pronounce his real one."

She chuckled again. "You couldn't do better than that?"

Striking like a snake, he slapped her hard across the face.

She turned with the hit but didn't react. In fact, the smile was still on her lips. "That's the best you can do? A little girl could slap harder than that."

He slapped her again, using his entire body to gain momentum.

Again, she didn't react. Maybe if she pissed him off enough, he would kill her. "Wuss…"

He gripped her by the throat and squeezed. Her air supply was immediately cut off, and she was thankful for it. If he held her long enough, she would choke to death. It would end quickly.

But he released her. "Shadow isn't happy you killed his twin brother. In fact, he tried to kill you because of it."

"When?" All he did was hold her down and torture her.

"The Skull Crusher." His eyes glinted ominously. "No one ever survives that move. But somehow, you did. Very strange…" Like she was an intriguing specimen, he watched her with interest.

He'd tried to kill her? And she survived? She kept her mouth shut because she refused to say the wrong thing. Questions came to mind, but they never passed over her tongue.

"And we're very interested in finding out what kind of powers you have."

"Powers?" she asked. "I have none."

"Really?" He cocked his head to the side, his eyes narrowing on her face. "A hybrid—half human and half elf. I've never seen that before."

"It's pretty straightforward. A human and an elf got it on—and had me. Surely, you could have connected those dots on your own."

Instead of choking her again, he smiled. "I know you don't think I'm very bright, but I'm smart enough to know when I'm being manipulated. I'm not killing you—at least not yet."

Disappointment washed over her like an incoming tide.

"But there is one thing you can do to speed up the process."

She kept her mouth shut.

"Tell us where the dragon is."

Alarm bells rang in her heart, and her breathing increased on its own. She kept the reaction hidden as much as possible but was unsure if she mastered it. She'd assumed she was being hunted for attacking the Shaman. But somehow, they knew about her relationship with Flare.

"I was hoping that would be your answer." He gave her a grin that showed all of his unnaturally white teeth. "It'll be more fun this way." His eyes roamed over her body, noting her hips and settling on her legs. "And we'll have some fun when we need a break from the torture."

It was the first time she'd felt fear. She accepted pain freely, knowing she could handle it. She even accepted death, knowing it was going to come sooner or later. But this was something on a different level. It was emotional and intimate.

She kept her face relaxed and hid the fear deep down below. The second he recognized she was in distress, he would prey on it. He would abandon the torture and stick to that instead.

And that was worse than death.

Rune brought a tray of food. "Lunchtime." He set the tray on the floor beside her. A glass of water sat beside a plate of chicken, potatoes, and greens. "I know you must be starving."

That was an understatement.

What she really needed was water. She was severely dehydrated, and that wasn't helping her headache. Her lower back hurt because her kidneys were shutting down, and her skin was beginning to shrivel. It looked like she'd lost five pounds in just a few days.

"Go on. Eat." He sat beside her with no intention of leaving.

If she refused to eat, she would die. Her stomach gnawed at her like a dog chewing on a bone. All she could think about was devouring the delicious meal set before her. The glass of water had her name written all over it.

But she wouldn't allow herself to do it.

"Why are you so intent on dying?" He laughed like the situation was a joking matter. "Come on, darling. Just sit up and eat."

"The sooner I die, the sooner I don't have to look at you."

"Did you have a bad childhood or something?" He nudged her in the side. "You need to lighten up."

"I'm not hungry."

He cupped his hand to his ear. "Then why do I hear your stomach rumbling?"

She grabbed the tray and flipped it over. She was surprised how weak she was. It took much more energy and strength to execute the simple move than it normally would have. The plate crashed to the floor and shattered into three pieces. The glass of water cracked, and the vital liquid spread across the stone floor. Cora lay back and looked at the ceiling as if nothing had happened at all.

Rune stared at the mess and sighed. "You really shouldn't have done that…"

She tilted her chin up, exposing her throat to him.

The humor in his voice disappeared entirely. All that was left was an icy wind. "This is what's going to happen. If you don't eat, I'm going to shove everything down your throat. And believe me, it'll hurt. So, you can be a big girl and do it on your own. Or I can do it for you. What's it gonna be?"

The sincerity of his threat was unmistakable. She sat up then picked the food off the floor. Her wrists were still bound together, and that made eating awkward. She knew she was truly starving because she'd never had a meal that tasted so good. In that moment, she felt like a king.

Darkness still burned in his eyes. "Good choice."

Adorned in red robes with gold stitching, a man entered her cell. His sleeves extended past his hands, almost touching the stone floor. He was a man marked by time, the premature lines of aging embedded into his skin. His face was weathered like he'd spent too many days in the sun.

Cora's eyes immediately went to his. The blue crystals were strikingly similar to another pair she'd already seen. Flecks of white and gray filled the irises, which were startling in their complexity.

As he entered the room, the air changed. It became heavy with suffering. Power rang in the air, hinting at all the things he could do with a simple snap of his fingers.

She knew he was the steward even without being introduced. "Good evening, Your Highness." It was easy to insult him with just her tone. They wouldn't grant her any mercy, so she refused to be cooperative in any fashion. She didn't possess idealistic hopes and dreams. They would torture her relentlessly until they got what they wanted.

And then they would kill her.

She wouldn't give up any information about Flare. It didn't matter what they did to her. There was no torture strong enough for her to betray her loyalty to her closest friend.

"Good evening, Cora." He stood beside her and folded his arms together, his billowing robes hiding his skin.

She leaned against the wall, her wrists red and irritated from constantly rubbing against the harsh rope. Her knees were pulled to her chest. Her untidy hair hadn't been brushed or washed in nearly a week. "What can I do for you? Or did you just come for the scenery?"

His smile almost looked like a sneer. The black mustache above his lips gave him a constant demeanor of irritation. "Rune painted a perfect picture of you."

"Thanks…I guess." She held his gaze, showing him just how unaffected she was by his clothes and jewels.

"You know why you're here."

She shrugged. "I suppose."

"It's very important that I find this dragon you encountered. You know where he is, and you're going to tell me."

"I am?" She raised an eyebrow as she looked at him. "Why would I tell you the whereabouts of someone I don't know?"

"Don't be coy. It's a waste of time."

"I don't know where he is." It was easy to lie to someone she didn't have any respect for. "And if I did, I still wouldn't tell you. You may as well prepare to torture me to death. Because this conversation is also a waste of time."

His eyes darkened in nature, becoming sinister and a little terrifying. "So be it." He turned around, his robes twisting in a spectacular way, and marched out of her cell.

"Yes. So be it."

Rune entered the cell, smiling as usual. He took a seat beside her, getting too close for comfort. "So, is there anything you'd like to tell me?"

"Not really." The ropes that bound her wrists together had become frayed from being tied around her for so long. She was dirty to the point where she was uncomfortable in her own skin.

"Are you sure?"

"Yep." She just wanted to get it over with.

"You don't want to tell me how you defied the Skull Crusher?"

"Nope. I don't even know the answer to that one."

His smile only widened. "Where's the dragon?"

"Don't know."

"Where did you get that sword?"

She'd known that would come up eventually. "It was a gift."

"From a dragon?" he pressed.

"Maybe. Maybe not."

"And how was it made? Who created such a blade?"

Normally, she would be irritated that he assumed only someone else could have created the weapon. But now, she thought it was amusing. "Your guess is as good as mine."

"Who are your parents?"

"I wish I knew." She knew she would never find the answer to that question.

He rested the back of his head against the stone chamber, an empathetic sigh escaping his lips. "You know what happens now, Cora."

"Why don't we stop talking about it and just get it done?"

"You know what I think?"

She shook her head.

"I think you're all talk. The second you're in that chair, you'll crumble like all the rest."

She hoped he wasn't right.

"I've seen mothers betray their own children. I've seen fathers send their own sons to the grave. I've seen the closest of friends throw each other to the dogs. You won't be any different, Cora."

She tested the tightness of her ropes in the hope they'd become loose enough to rip apart.

"You never have to find out if you just talk to me."

"Rune."

He turned his head her way. "Hmm?"

She held his gaze without blinking, seeing the brilliant green eyes he didn't deserve to have. "We can't run away from our destiny. You believe that, right?"

"Actually, I do." He smiled in expectation.

"Good." She threw her arms over his head then pulled the frayed rope against his neck, choking him and burning his skin at the same time. "Then you knew this was coming." She wrapped her legs around his waist and held him still as he tried to fight her off. He gripped the rope and tried to pull it away, but her hold was too strong. "It was nice knowing you, Rune."

The door opened, and one of the guards came inside. Once he saw the commotion, he rushed to Rune's aid.

Cora held on, knowing she only needed a few more seconds.

The guard pulled her off, punching her right in the nose to get her to back off. The hit stung and brought tears to her eyes, but she still fought him off.

Rune slipped away then rolled over as he coughed violently. He gripped his throat then heaved as he tried to catch his breath.

The guard held her back, positioning her hands tightly in his grasp. "You alright, sir?"

Rune kept coughing, still trying to recover.

Cora spat on his face. "Just a few more seconds and you would have been worm food."

He wiped the spit from his face then sat up, an unmistakable threat in his eyes. "Take her to the chamber. Now."

The guard yanked her to her feet, forcing her to get up even though she fought against him. "Being choked doesn't feel good, does it?"

Rune rose to his feet, still rubbing his neck. "Darling, you're going to regret that."

The guard dragged her to the door, bringing her directly past Rune. "Believe me, nothing could make me regret that."

# NINETEEN

Rune tightened the leather belt around her, restricting her arms directly against her sides. He did the same to her legs, making her a human pin. A malicious smile spread across his lips as he walked past her, enjoying every second of what would come next. Once he was behind her, he pressed his lips to her ear. "Are you sure you don't want to tell me where the dragon is?"

A pool of freezing water was at her feet. Bits of ice floated across the surface, almost freezing completely on top. Steam rose in small tendrils, evaporating in just seconds.

"Cora?"

"I don't know what you're talking about." While she feared the torture about to commence, she feared for Flare's safety more. He was the only hope for returning power to the rightful beings. If she gave him away, all hope would be lost.

Rune sighed before he pushed her into the water.

Face first, she fell into the pool and immediately began to sink. The cold pierced her like a hundred blades of ice. Her lungs froze in place, unaccustomed to such extreme temperatures. She wanted to scream but somehow fought the urge.

Futilely, she tried to get loose from the straps binding her in place. They kept her body absolutely still, eliminating any opportunity to swim away. She continued to hold her breath and wait to be pulled up for air, but the rescue never came. Her lungs started to scream, and she couldn't hold her breath for a second longer. Automatically, her mouth opened for air, and the water flooded in.

She was dragged back onto the platform, gasping for breath. The dry air was harsh against her frozen, wet skin. She lay back and stared at the ceiling, not truly seeing anything. Everything was blurred. All she could think about was breathing.

Rune kneeled next to her until his face was close to hers. "Now, I'm sure you don't want to do that again. Why don't you just tell me what I want to know? This can end right now if you just speak up."

The idea of going back into that water sent chills up her spine. Her lungs wouldn't be able to handle it again, and her entire body would give way. Just when she was on the verge of death, she would be violently pulled back to life. It was too much for anyone to bear. "I don't know where he is."

He shook his head in disappointment. "Wrong answer."


Just when she fell asleep, she was awoken once more.

"Where is he?"

Her eyelids were heavy with an invisible weight. They couldn't remain open, no matter how much she tried. Three days had come and gone, and she hadn't gotten even an hour of rest.

Rune wouldn't allow it.

"Tell me what I want to know, and you can sleep as long as you want."

When they'd threatened to torture her, she'd assumed blades and fire would be involved, something more physically painful. Everything they'd been doing was more mentally and physically exerting than bloody—but it was still effective.

"Where is he?"

"Who?"

"The dragon."

She closed her eyes.

He shook her again. "Cora, answer me."

"I don't know…"

"Yes, you do." He slapped her across the face. "Now, tell me."

"No." It didn't matter what they did or said; she refused to give in.

"Goddammit." He gripped her shoulders and shook her violently.

She closed her eyes again.

He smacked her head against the tile. "Cora, tell me."

She mustered the energy to spit in his face.

He slammed her head hard against the stone, making her black out immediately.

When her eyes opened, she had no sense of time. How many days had come and gone, she didn't know. How long had she been a prisoner of the steward? Time blurred together, and she couldn't figure out how long she'd been there. The window in her cell was the only measurement she had. At least she could tell when it was daylight.

Rune was hovering above her, giving his grotesque smile for her private enjoyment. "You were out for a long time."

"I was hoping I was dead." Her voice was lifeless because she truly didn't care about anything anymore. As far as she was concerned, her life was already gone.

"No, not yet," he said with a disappointed sigh. "Unfortunately."

She turned her head the opposite way so she wouldn't have to look at him anymore.

"You were so sleep deprived, you blacked out. I've never seen that before." He sat beside her on the floor, leaning over her so she could see her facial expressions reflected in his eyes.

"Sounds like a logical response to me."

"Most people die."

"Too bad I'm not most people." She wasn't sure if she believed in the afterlife—and even if it were real, she doubted her soul would make it there. Despite that knowledge, she still wanted to die. It was the only option she had at that point.

"You're strange."

Unable to form a response to that, she remained silent.

"I've never seen a woman so focused. They usually break faster than the men."

"Strange isn't the right word to describe it."

"I wonder if it's because you're part elf."

She stared at the blue tile that constructed the wall of her cell. The color was unusual. She wondered if the rest of the castle was made of the same stone. In Vax, all they used was wood.

"Do you know where their hidden realm is?"

"No." That was the truth, but she knew he wouldn't believe her.

"Really?" Incredulity was in his voice. "You're one of them but have never visited their land?"

"I've never seen one of my own kind—at least, not that I can remember."

"Again, strange." He shook his head.

She slowly turned her head his way, loathing burning in her eyes. "You need to expand your vocabulary."

"You need to shut that pretty mouth of yours." His eyes trailed over her face, resting on her full lips. The intent was written as clear as a message on the wall. "I don't know if it's the elf or human in you that gets me going…but something does."

Terror returned in full force. Being frozen and suffocated at the same time was preferable to what he had in mind. Sleep deprivation was a different form of torture, one that made her brain pulse in agony. She couldn't think straight because her dreams fused too well with reality. What was real and what wasn't? But she would take that any day over what he had planned.

Rune moved his hand to her thigh and reached for the top of her pants.

She was weak from insufficient calories, and her body was broken from all the trials it had endured, but her instincts immediately kicked into gear. She kicked him as hard as she could in the side of the neck.

Rune flopped down onto the tile, groaning and rubbing his neck at the same time. He lay still, fighting the pain that burned his every nerve ending. The fact that he didn't get up and smack her around told Cora she'd really hit him where it hurt.

"Bitch." He kept rubbing his neck, his face contorted in insufferable agony.

"That's what my friends call me." If she pushed him hard enough, it would ignite the blood rage. All he'd want to do was hurt her, cause her as much agony as possible.

Which worked for her.

He slowly sat up, the flames of the world burning in his eyes. "You cracked my neck."

"Sorry. I meant to break it." There would be no remorse on her end.

"You'll regret that, elf." He slowly rose to his feet, gripping his neck like his head might roll off.

"You've said that twice now, but still haven't made good on your word."

He walked to the door, moving his upper body as little as possible. "I will this time. Consider it a promise."

## TWENTY

The door flew open, and Rune walked inside with two guards. Vengeance was as clear in his eyes as the sun on a cloudless day. His neck appeared to be restored to its previous capacity, but Rune hadn't forgotten the pain it caused him. This time, he might kill her.

"So glad you could join me." Bored by him as she always was, her voice came out hollow.

"Grab her." Rune unbuttoned his jacket then threw it on the floor.

Cora panicked. "I don't think so." She kicked one guy in the ankle and made him buckle to his knee. When the adrenaline kicked in, she had bursts of newfound energy. She jumped to her feet and kneed the other guard right in the groin. "I hope you've already had your children." She kneed him again for good measure.

Rune gritted his teeth and spoke under his breath. "Absolutely ridiculous. She's a goddamn woman."

"Just a woman?" Cora grabbed the guard cupping his balls and shoved him into Rune. They both fell to the floor in an ungraceful pile.

That was when she noticed the door.

It was open.

She could escape.

This was her chance.

She punched the guard next to her before she jumped over the tangled mass of Rune and the other guard.

"No!" Rune shoved his comrade off. "Don't let her get away!"

She sprinted as hard as she could, ignoring the blinding pain in her legs and everywhere else. Her lungs burned because they couldn't hold the same amount of oxygen as they used to. Nothing worked the way it once did.

But that didn't matter.

She had to get out of there. Failure wasn't an option. It was either succeed or die.

"Get her!" Rune's voice echoed down the hallway. Torches lit the walkway, and the blue stone stretched deep into the castle. When a guard approached at the very end of the hall, she darted to the left.

"Run." She coached herself to keep going, to resist the fatigue and pain. "Come on."

She grabbed a torch off the wall with her bound hands and kept running. She had no idea where she was going, whether she was up high near the top or in a dungeon near the bottom. She found a window and peered into the night.

She was at the top.

She kept going and tried to find stairs. She was even willing to jump out of a window. Her feet thudded against the stone floor, and her breathing echoed in the small enclosure.

"Let her escape, and I'll kill all of your children." Rune's voice erupted from behind her. "I'm not kidding."

She pushed herself harder and kept going.

The tower bells started to ring, piercing her ears. She was directly beneath one at the top of the castle. When she finally found a circular stairway, she took the steps two at a time.

Guards emerged from the bottom of the stairwell, torches and swords in hand. When they spotted her at the top, they stopped, momentarily appearing to be just as frightened as she was.

"Damn." She turned around and retreated.

"There!" Rune and his guards were closing in on her from the way she'd come. "I'm going to gut you like a fish."

Panic rose in her throat, and so did the tears. She didn't fear the oncoming punishment but rather the confinement she would be returned to. She could taste the freedom on her tongue.

Now it was about to be taken away again.

She was grabbed by the neck from behind, and her airway was immediately restricted. Instinctively, she shoved the torch behind her and pressed the flames into the guard's face.

"Agh!" He fell back, gripping his skull as his face was charred. He toppled down the stairs, taking a few guards with him.

Her hope resurged.

She headed back down the stairs. When she reached the bottom, she jumped over the guards and sprinted once more. She was one level down and only had a few more to go. Before she turned the corner, an external force pressed against her skull. A wall of solid marble slammed against her, forcing her to stay in place, no matter how hard she tried to move. Her skull began to feel hot, burning to ash.

She clenched her jaw and tried not to scream. The pain was excruciating, just as it had been the last time. Unable to move or even think, she was forced to remain still. Slowly, Shadow appeared out of the darkness, his palm raised directly at her.

The Shaman.

Cora had never felt so much hatred in her entire life. This foul creature had put her in this dungeon. He was a coward, hiding behind magic to do what he wanted. If only she'd had a second poisoned arrow, she could have taken him down as well.

His magical strength kept her in place, but somehow, she found the ability to move her lips. "I'm glad I killed your brother. And I would do it again in a heartbeat."

His hand shook before he made a fist.

She fell to the floor as her body gave out. Her skull was being pressed in on all sides. At any moment, it would be crushed, and her brain would boil out of her ears.

"Enough." Rune gripped her by the arms and yanked her to her feet. "I've got it from here."

Shadow kept his hand raised, exerting his full force to snap the life right out of her.

Cora screamed so loud she couldn't hear anything else.

"Stop." Rune's voice carried all of his authority. "I need her alive."

Hesitantly, Shadow dropped his hand. His hood faced her for a few more seconds before he abruptly turned on his heel and left. Just as his name suggested, he disappeared into the darkness.

Cora's head dropped forward when the torture stopped.

"You're going to get the beating of a lifetime." He gripped her by the hair and dragged her up the stairs. When she didn't move fast enough, he shoved her. "You really thought you'd get out of here? Stupid girl."

She threw her foot back and kicked him.

Rune caught her leg then shoved her hard against the floor. "When will you ever learn?" He grabbed her by the back of the neck and dragged her to her feet once more.

The last thing Cora wanted was to return to that cell. She had no idea how much time had passed or how long she would be confined to the prison. If they refused to kill her until she talked, then she would be there for a very long time.

The thought made her want to collapse.

Windows were etched into the stone wall, bigger than the one she had in her solitary cell. It was at least twenty feet down to the bottom, and the fall would surely kill her. The second her body hit the pavement, that would be the end.

She went for it.

Elbowing Rune in the nose, she dashed to the window.

"No, you don't." He wiped the blood from his nose then snatched her just as she crawled onto the windowsill. "You don't get that luxury." He wrapped his arm around her throat and constricted her air as he dragged her back to her cell. Without enough oxygen, she constantly gasped for breath.

Rune returned her to the cell and dropped her. "Let's not repeat that. Maybe it was fun for you, but it gave us a headache." He rolled up his sleeves then cracked his knuckles. "Hold her."

Cora didn't care about anything anymore. The fight inside her had vanished like a blown-out candle. Nothing mattered at that point. She was an empty vessel, devoid of anything—even a soul.

The guards held her upright and forced her face upward, making it visible to Rune.

He massaged his knuckles with an eager look on his face, the blood lust heavy in his eyes. Then he prepared his right hook and slammed his fist into her face, making blood fly from her mouth.

She felt the pain but didn't concentrate on it.

Rune hit her again, punching her right in the ribs. A distinct crack sounded in the cell. "Looks like I broke a few."

Cora didn't make a sound. She refused to give him any kind of satisfaction.

Rune beat her like a punching bag, laying blows across her face and body. Blood oozed from every opening and dripped down her skin. Bones were cracked and muscle was torn. Her heartbeat grew fainter with every second.

*Death, come for me.*

## TWENTY-ONE

"If we steal a ship, we'll have to move quickly." Bridge stood beside Flare in the shadow of the outpost building. Massive ships bobbed in the harbor, riding the tide as it moved in and out. The moon was bright overhead, reflecting off the black water.

Flare scanned the harbor, noting the guards on the tops of the walls surrounding the city. "Even if I kill these guys, it'll only buy us a day. The ocean is a big place, but they'll find us eventually."

"Then what do you propose?" Bridge leaned against the wall and remained hidden in the shadows. "Give up?"

"I said no such thing." Flare's eyes were glued to the wandering guard. He held a crossbow in his hands as he paced his station. "But this plan might not work. If they chase us and we never find the island, we'll be food for the sharks."

"I guess."

"Besides, it'll be difficult to commandeer a ship of that size. We'll need more than two men."

"We can steal a smaller boat."

Flare pondered their next step quietly. His arms were crossed over his chest as he thought through their next move. "We can buy a smaller ship and leave without any problems."

Bridge shook his head like the idea was preposterous. "We don't have any gold."

"No." Flare pulled up his hood so his face was hidden. "But we can steal some."

---

Bridge walked up to the guard with an empty bottle of rum in his hand. "Eh, sir. Did you see a hot little number come this way?" He slurred his speech and staggered in a drunken stupor. "Because I've been looking for her." He held up his bottle. "And when I find her…" He staggered again.

The guard didn't draw his weapon or seem suspicious at all. "Sounds like you can't hold on to your woman."

"Who can?" Bridge threw his arms down. "Just when you get a hold of them, they slip away." He staggered on the cobblestone road and fell to the ground. "Woe is me."

"You alright?" The guard hunched down then grabbed him by the arm. "You should head on home. The streets aren't safe for an intoxicated man."

Flare emerged from the shadows then slit open the guard's coin purse. He shoved all the gold into his pockets then returned to his hiding place in the darkness. He released a quiet pigeon's coo.

"You're right." Bridge immediately got to his feet when he heard the signal. "I really should lie down… Have a good evening, Your Highness." He held up the bottle as he moved down the street.

When he was out of sight, he turned into the alleyway. "You there?"

Flare emerged from the other side. "I got it."

"How much do we have now?"

"Two hundred gold coins."

Bridge's eyes widened. "Why did I ever become a historian? It pays nothing compared to that."

"Picking pockets is no treat. I just make it look easy." Flare had learned the trade a long time ago, and with his dragon companion, he was able to move silently.

"It looks like we have more than enough for a boat," Bridge said. "Let's head to the boat master at the harbor. I'm sure he'll hand one over without asking any questions for a price like that."

Only suspicious people operated under cover of darkness. "We'll wait until morning."

"What do we do until then?"

"Sleep." Flare moved to the ground and leaned his back against the wall. "I'll keep the first watch."

Bridge settled down on the ground. "I hate sleeping on stone. I miss my bed."

Flare chuckled. "You remind me of Cora." His thoughts were on her constantly, hoping she made it to her destination without any problems. She was a strong woman who could handle herself, but sometimes, the paranoia would sink in. As much as he hated to admit it, he cared for her.

He never wanted something bad to happen to her.

After the boat master was paid, they headed down the dock until they reached their medium-sized ship. The sun had barely crested the horizon, and the guards were switching shifts.

"It already has fishing poles, so we'll be able to find lunch on the journey." Bridge explored the inside of it, checking the integrity of the masts and the wheel. Fifteen people could fit inside the boat easily, but only one man was needed to operate it. "There's some water stowed under here, but we'll have to collect rainwater on the way."

Flare hopped inside and drew up the masts. "It's perfect. It'll get us there in one piece."

"And hopefully back in one piece." Bridge untied the massive boat rope from the dock so they could shove off. "You know, if you weren't a dragon, I never would have agreed to this."

Flare chuckled. "I get that a lot—" He stopped in midsentence when a peculiar sound came to his mind. Twisted and warped, the broken voice was full of heartache—and hopelessness.

*Death, come for me.*

Bridge turned to Flare when he didn't finish his words. "You alright?"

Flare heard the words again, sounding more feminine and familiar.

*Death, come for me.*

He'd heard that voice before, but he couldn't identify it.

Bridge studied Flare with concern. "Flare—"

Flare held up his hand. "Silence." He looked out to the horizon, feeling something deep in his core. There was a connection there, to something or someone. It reminded him of his relationship with the dragon, their ability to communicate with thoughts and feelings.

He closed his eyes and concentrated.

A man's face emerged in his sea of vision, dressed in blood-red clothing. He was a soldier of the Steward of Easton. That was unmistakable. He was beating someone, on the verge of killing them. "Tell me what I want to know, Cora. The torture will stop."

Blood pounded in Flare's ears, and his entire body tensed with rage. His hands formed fists that cut into his skin. Every vein in his body expanded as adrenaline coursed through him. Bloody rage blurred his vision, making him see red spots in place of the blue sky. While the world was silent, a war raged inside him. Pain seared across his skin, and his heart turned black.

Instantly, he transformed into his dragon counterpart, becoming ten times bigger and stronger. His wings opened violently, prepared to carry him wherever he needed to go. His wing was still sore from the injury, but Flare didn't notice it.

The dragon's voice came into his head. *She hurts.*

*Yes.*

The same rage burned inside the beast. *She cries.*

*Yes.*

*She must be saved.*

*Yes.*

Bridge rolled to the side of the boat as it prepared to sink under the weight. "What the hell are you doing?" He gripped the edge so he wouldn't fall into the water.

*Sail to the hideaway.* Both dragon and man spoke. *I will meet you there.*

Flare leaped up into the sky and used his powerful wings to propel himself high into the air. Keeping his identity a secret was negligible to the pain he felt in his heart. With a blood-curdling scream, he roared across the city, terrifying everything and everyone who heard it.

Then he flew to Easton, prepared to burn it to the ground.

## TWENTY-TWO

Days passed without meaning.

Cora hurt everywhere. Two of her ribs were broken, her wrist was sprained, and dried blood caked her face. She wasn't given the luxury of bathing. She was barely allowed to relieve herself.

She was still alive, but that wasn't a good thing.

Just when Cora thought she was weak enough to pass into the void, she held on. Her spirit was gone and so was her hope, but somehow, she persevered. Every time she knocked on death's door, death didn't answer.

Where was he?

When the physical beating didn't make a difference, they returned to the drowning chamber. When that didn't work, Rune shoved bamboo sticks under her fingernails. No matter how excruciating it was, she never mentioned Flare's name.

They didn't intend to kill her, but it would happen eventually. Her body would give out somewhere down the road. She kept hoping for that day, praying for the sweet escape of something that most people fled from.

Heavy footsteps sounded outside her cell. The movement was slow, like the person had all the time in the world to get where they needed to go. "Has she said anything?" The powerful voice of the steward leaked through the bars of her chamber. He kept his voice low, barely above a whisper.

But Cora heard it.

"No." Aggravated, Rune spat out his answer. "But she will."

"It's been weeks."

It'd been weeks? The knowledge only made Cora more depressed. Her captivity felt like an eternity, not a few weeks.

"She'll crack, Your Highness." Despite Rune's determination to make it happen, he didn't sound confident.

"She's stronger than that." Awe was in his voice, but in a sinister way. "She's part elf?"

"Yes."

"I haven't seen an elf in a very long time."

Cora remembered what Flare had said about the history of Anastille. The elves fled into their realm once the battle started to take a turn for the worse. If the steward had seen one before, that could only mean he was alive 400 years ago.

And it would mean he was fused with a dragon.

She swallowed the lump in her throat at the realization. He had the power to infiltrate her mind and detect her moods. If he opened his mind to hers and she accidentally allowed him to enter, he could manipulate her into getting the information he needed.

Now she was terrified.

"She's not so special," Rune said. "She's a pain in the ass, that's it."

The steward chuckled in a condescending way. "You say that because she bested you—a woman."

Rune held his tongue.

"I will have a visit with her."

"What if it doesn't work?"

The steward was quiet for so long it wasn't clear if he was going to say anything at all. "Then we'll flog her."

Cora knew how painful that would be, but she preferred it over a mental battle.

"Hopefully, it won't come to that." Rune approached the door before he opened it. "Darling, you have a visitor. Please give him your respect. This isn't a man you want to piss off."

She pretended like she hadn't been eavesdropping. "Oh, goody."

The steward walked into the room, his hands buried in the sleeves of his robe. "Hello, Cora. You don't look too well."

"Yeah, I've seen better days." She sat up and leaned against the wall. The slight movement made her ribs scream in protest. They dug into her stomach at an odd angle. Her appetite had evaporated since the injury occurred.

"You know, we could clean you up and treat you much better. But you have to do something for us first."

Rune carried a chair into the room and placed it on the stone floor.

Without looking at him, the steward took a seat. "Let's talk as friends for a moment. Forget Rune. Forget your injuries."

"Like that's so easy to forget." Her temper flared up uncontrollably. To belittle her pain like it was nothing was insulting. This guy obviously had never had a bad day in his life.

The steward continued on like she hadn't just snapped. "That sword is truly marvelous. Where did you get it?"

She held his gaze defiantly, her lips pressed tightly together.

"Is the blade made of dragon scales?"

She crossed her arms over her chest and got comfortable since they would be there for a while.

The steward cocked his head, similar to the way Rune did. "You've held your silence for so long, I'm not surprised you won't answer my question. But for your sake, I wish you would."

"I also wish you would stop talking. It's annoying."

His eyes narrowed on her face. "I'm about to do something you aren't going to like."

"It's okay. I'm used to it."

"Very well." His eyes bored into hers, crystal-blue and shiny. Then his voice sounded deep inside her head, similar to Flare's when he was a dragon. *Tell me about the sword.*

If she hadn't experienced this already, she would have been thrown off. *Your voice is more annoying when it's inside my head.*

The steward's eyes widened even farther, clearly surprised she knew how to communicate so easily. *Tell me where the dragon is.*

*Let me think about it. Hmm…nope.*

Now his blue eyes turned ice-cold. *You will tell me what I want to know, child.* A foreign pressure exerted on her skull, similar to what the Shaman had done. But it was just a push, like something heavy was leaning right against her brain. Despite her weakness, she could fight it.

She held his gaze the entire time, not giving any indication of a struggle. Her mind was her own, and she wouldn't allow it to be infiltrated, not when Flare's safety depended on it. The steward would see his plan to sail to the lost island of the dragons. That secret had to be kept at all costs.

Sweat trickled down his forehead, and his face turned beet red in concentration. Drops absorbed into his mustache then fell to the floor. His hands started to shake from the exertion.

She didn't break a sweat.

The steward abruptly withdrew then rose to his feet. Now he gave her a new look, a derisive sneer on his lips. She was officially his enemy, someone he had to annihilate. "Will you die to keep your secrets?"

That answer was simple. "A million times over."

"Then you will be flogged to death in the courtyard—where the entire city can watch. And you will be naked." He turned on his heel, and his robes billowed around him in a glorious way. The gold stitching reflected the minimal light in the cell and glowed on its own. He walked out and shut the door behind him, the massive lock clicking into place.

His final words played in her mind repeatedly. Stripped naked, she would be flogged for everyone's entertainment. Her bare skin would be on display, and all her respect, vanity, and privacy would be deprived of her. In her final moments of life, she would be seen as a reckless whore.

And then she would die.

Steel cuffs were tight around her wrists. The chain connecting them together was much stronger than the rope she'd had before. There was no way she would get out of this one, not when she was chained to two other guards.

The city square was filled with people on all sides. A sea of faces stretched far into the distance, flooding the streets and alleyways. They'd all come to stare at the strange creature before them, the hybrid.

She fought against the fear in her chest, knowing it wouldn't make this moment any easier for herself. Now that she had to be naked in front of thousands of strangers, she realized just how good she'd had it in Vax. No one had ever seen her naked body before. She was conservative when it came to her appearance.

Now, she would be on display.

They marched her to the pole in the center of the square. It was made of steel and was buried deep into the ground. There was no hope of her ever pulling it out. The screams and yells from the crowd became louder as she approached the last place she would ever stand as a living person.

The two guards removed their chains then hooked them to the metal clip several feet above the ground. It forced her arms up, making her stand on her tiptoes just to reach. The brown robe she wore swayed in the slight breeze.

One guard untied the strap around her neck, and the robe slid down her body to her feet. Every inch of her skin was revealed to anyone who wished to look. Her breasts hung from her chest, her nipples hard from the breeze, and her ass was directly facing the man who would whip her to death.

She was humiliated.

All she could do was stare at the pole in front of her and concentrate on the faceless metal. She tuned out all the yells erupting around her. The material from the robe touched her feet, and she took comfort from the warm fabric.

If this were how she was going to die, she would leave this earth with her head held high. It was difficult to be proud when she was naked, but it wasn't her choice. Her freedom had been stripped away from her. All she could do was make the best of it.

Rune stood fifteen feet behind her. "This is your last chance, Cora." He threw the whip against the stone at his feet, making a loud cracking noise. "This will be a bloodbath." He cracked the whip again, intimidating her with the sound.

"Just get on with it." Her voice was lifeless. Death was near, but it was also far away. She had to get through the pain and the humiliation first.

"I was hoping you'd say that." He prepared himself, holding the grip of the whip. He aimed before he threw his entire body into the action, striking her across the back so hard, blood splattered into the air.

Cora wanted to cry out. The pain was tenfold what she'd anticipated it to be. Her delicate skin was ripped from her body and thrown to the ground. Warm blood oozed from her wounds, trailing to the small of her back and then her ass.

"I'm sure you don't want more than one."

She stared at the pole and tried to block out everything else. The sting of her back was excruciating, but she tried to forget about it. If she didn't, she would succumb to her distant tears.

She refused to give him any satisfaction.

"Does your arm hurt?" she asked. "Why have you stopped?"

People in the crowd murmured quietly to themselves, their words indecipherable.

Rune couldn't mask the irritation in his voice. He wanted tears of pain, a confession, some sign of weakness.

But he wouldn't get any of those things.

"That was just one, darling. You have a lot more to go."

"Do you talk just so you can listen to yourself?" If she pissed him off enough, he wouldn't drag it out. He would lose his control and go about it quickly, trying to cause her as much pain as possible. Also, humiliating him in front of the steward was an extra perk.

"Bitch." He murmured it under his breath, but she could still hear it. He aimed before he struck her across the back, tearing off new skin as well as hitting the previous wound.

Her back convulsed automatically, but she didn't cry out. She bit her inner cheek until she drew blood.

Rune struck her again and again. With every new wound, blood dripped out, soaking the skin that remained and creeping down her thighs. It pooled at her feet and made the stone slippery.

With every crack of the whip, he hit her harder, trying to outdo himself. It was a sick game to him, trying to hit the same spot more than once and then trying to hit some place new. He whipped her across the ass, and that almost made her scream because it was so unexpected.

Minutes passed, and he kept going. More blood pooled at her feet, and her strength dissipated. She could barely hold herself up anymore, so she dangled by her wrists. She was losing her grasp on reality, her mind becoming foggy from the pain and lack of blood.

Her heart began to slow, finally shutting down.

She was almost there.

The suffering would end soon.

All she had to do was wait for it to happen.

Rune struck her again and admired his handiwork. "I can hardly see your back anymore, darling."

She wanted to respond with a smartass comment but didn't have the strength.

"Have you nothing to say?" His joy was unmistakable. "Cat got your tongue?"

She was on the verge of the end. Balancing on the edge of a knife, she was about to tip over and plunge into the abyss. But she wanted to have the last word before that happened. "You hit like a girl."

Rune didn't respond, letting his whip do all the talking. He struck her across the back again, hitting her with as much force as possible. He made a series of quick strikes, flogging her to the extreme.

Her back spasmed, and her body grew limp. She could hardly feel anything anymore. There was nothing left to feel.

She wasn't sure if it was real, but she thought she heard the mighty roar of a majestic creature. It was more powerful than an orc and more sinister than a Shaman. It sounded like a dragon's fierce battle cry.

"*Rawr!*"

The crowd fell quiet before a collective scream emerged.

*Cora, I'm here.* Flare's voice played in her head.

But was it real?

The ground trembled underneath her feet as something landed beside her. It was heavy enough to shake the entire world. *Hold on.* Massive jaws wrapped around the pole, and effortlessly, it was ripped from the ground. Her chain slipped from underneath and came loose. Unable to hold herself up, she collapsed.

The steward's calm voice billowed from his seat behind Rune. "Nephew, how nice of you to drop by."

Flare released another mighty roar and chased Rune down. Cora's red sword hung at Rune's waist, bright and shiny under the morning sun. Flare snatched Rune by the arm and threw him down to the ground. Then his massive jaws took the sword off his hip.

"Ah!" Rune crawled away and hid under the steward's seat.

Cora could barely hold on to consciousness. She wasn't sure if any of this was real. Was this a dying vision? Something to comfort her as she slipped away? Did she imagine Flare because his presence subdued her?

The dragon walked to her before he gently cradled her in his massive claws. He was careful not to injure her further, but that was impossible. Arrows were released and punctured his sides. Smoke billowed from his nose, the fires of his rage about to be unleashed.

She stared up at the dragon's face, wishing it were real. "Is that you?"

*Yes.*

In her final moments, there was only one thing she wanted. "Kill them…kill them all."

*I can't.*

"Why?" Her eyes grew heavy.

He opened his wings and launched into the air. *Because I have to save you.*

## TWENTY-THREE

She fell unconscious until she felt the familiar touch of grass beneath her body. The smell came into her nose and reminded her of summer. The scent of salt was in the air, the same scent she'd noticed when they visited Polox.

She was on her stomach, and she felt hot blood all over her body. The feeling was unmistakable. It was heavier than water and had a metallic scent to it. When it dripped into her mouth, it tasted like a gold coin.

*Lie still.*

There was little else she could do.

Flare hovered above her and didn't move.

"I can't…"

*Shh.* A liquid drop fell on her back, splattering like a heavy raindrop. The touch burned her skin painfully, making it sizzle like acid. But then the pain suddenly numbed.

More drops fell and splashed onto her back, burning in the same way before everything went numb. She didn't feel the drops anywhere else, only her back and her ass.

"What are you doing?"

*Rest.* Flare continued dropping the moisture directly onto her torn flesh. It went on for several minutes before finally ending. Then the burning sensation went away and so did the pain—at least, the worst of it.

"Flare?" A sound erupted behind her, the grass and trees moving as something passed.

When Flare spoke again, his voice was different. It didn't sound in her mind anymore, just her ears. "You'll be alright, Cora." He placed a canteen against her skin, collecting some of the liquid that had been dropped. "You're safe now."

"What are you doing?" She tried to turn over, but she couldn't. Her body was completely unresponsive now.

"Healing you." He grabbed her by the shoulder and gently lifted her up, careful not to touch her wounds.

She watched him stick two fingers inside his canteen, soaking his fingertips in a clear liquid. Then he wiped it across her face, moving over her bruised brows and swollen eyes. He smeared it across her lips and applied it to all her cuts.

When she looked into his eyes, she saw the coat of moisture that had developed. A red tint was deep in his irises, and he looked different than he had the last time she saw him. Now, he looked devastated—broken.

"Drink this." He held out the canteen.

"You just wiped that on my face."

"Drink it." He brought it to her lips and supported the back of her head. "It's dragon tears."

"What?" She remembered the potion she'd spotted in the shop in Polox. And she remembered everything Flare told her about it. "Where did you get them?"

He focused on the canteen and didn't make eye contact with her. "The sooner you drink this, the better you'll feel. You need to get some rest, and you won't be able to if you feel like shit." He pressed the mouth of the canteen to her lips and forced the liquid down her throat. "And they're mine."

She swallowed as much as she could and tried not to cringe at the taste. It was liquid sulfur and ash. Her stomach wanted to throw it back up, but she somehow mastered it. She drank every drop until the canteen was empty.

Flare set it aside then examined her face once more. "I know it tastes terrible, but you won't regret it later."

She looked into his eyes and saw the distant tears that still shone. He'd shed those tears for her—and that touched her in a way nothing else ever had. She didn't even care that she was naked because his actions made her forget about it entirely.

Flare never looked at her body once. He removed his jacket and covered her with it, hiding her torso and legs under the voluminous material. "I'll get you something else to wear. But this will do for now."

She wrapped it around her body and noticed the pain was diminishing with every passing second. She was woozy from losing so much blood, but she felt better now compared to when she was chained to that pole. "How did you know?"

He rested her head on his pack. "Sleep now. I'll answer your questions when you wake up."

"But won't they be searching for us?"

"They won't find us here." He ran his fingers gently through her hair and began to lull her to sleep. He stared at her with the crystal eyes she'd seen before, but on a different man. She remembered what the steward had said, that Flare was his nephew. Flare had deeper ties to the kingdom than she realized, and now she understood why he wanted to keep it a secret. If she'd known from the beginning, she never would have trusted him.

Flare continued to watch her until her eyes could no longer stay open. His protection allowed her to drift off into a true sleep. She wasn't afraid of what might happen to her when her eyes were closed. She knew the dragon would guard her against any enemy.

Even when her eyes were closed, she knew he was still staring at her. The dragon watched over her as well as the man. Together, they formed an impenetrable line of defense. She never allowed anyone to look after her, but in this instance, she gladly accepted it.

And she fell asleep.

When she woke up, she was inside a cave.

The smooth walls led to a ceiling twenty feet above her head. There wasn't a grain of sand anywhere in sight. Everything was made of solid stone. A fire burned gently a few feet away, and she was still bundled up in Flare's large black jacket.

She sat up and looked around, wondering where she was and how she'd gotten there. There was light at the end of the tunnel where the entrance stood. Flare must have left to take care of something. Just when she was about to get up, a man's silhouette approached her.

Her entire body was still in agony after her captivity. Her back ached every time she moved, but it was the first time she'd felt decent in a while. She could sleep without fear of what might happen, and her body could finally relax.

Flare approached the fire with a deer over his shoulder. He set it on the ground then pulled out his cleaning knife. Without looking at her, he got to work. He skinned the hide quickly then gutted the animal.

She ran her fingers through her hair and noted the dirt, oil, and sweat that had built up. She knew she looked like hell, so heinous that hell would actually spit her back out.

Flare placed the meat on a wooden stick then situated it over the fire so it cooked evenly. When he was finished with everything else, he took the remaining pieces and discarded them outside the cave.

The meat started to sizzle and cook, and that was when Cora realized just how hungry she was. She was never given enough food in Easton, always on the verge of starvation, and water was a rare commodity as well.

Flare returned with clean hands then held out his canteen to her.

She took it quickly then drank as much as she could. Her throat absorbed the liquid but was still dry. Her tongue felt as though it had become a permanent cotton ball. Rushing to feel hydrated, she drank as quickly as possible, the water running down her throat. She had the manners of an animal but couldn't care less at the moment.

Flare watched the fire.

She set the empty canteen on the ground then wiped her lips with her forearm.

"You want more?" He didn't take his eyes off the flames. When one side of the meat became charred, he rotated the spit.

"I'm okay. Thank you." She felt her stomach growl as she watched the meat become hot and juicy.

Flare must have heard it because he said, "It's almost done."

She should've felt ashamed of her savage nature, but she simply couldn't. Her body had been pushed to the limit, and she wasn't sure how she'd survived the ordeal.

When the meat was done, he removed it from the stick and dropped it onto a flat piece of bark. He slid it across the ground toward her, giving her all of it.

"What about you?"

"I already ate."

She didn't hesitate as she stuffed herself full. It was the tastiest meal she'd ever had in her life. Her mouth couldn't chew fast enough, and no matter how much food her stomach got, it wasn't enough.

Flare took out his dagger and played with it in his hands. He sharpened it with a rock and made the metal sing with every swipe.

She ate everything in front of her and felt her stomach bulge out with fullness. It was the first time she'd felt satiated in weeks. Forsaking all manners, she sucked her fingertips for every drop of juice.

"You want more?"

"No. I'm full." She pushed away the makeshift plate and suddenly felt tired again.

Flare pulled an outfit from his pack and tossed it on the ground beside her. "I got you some clothes. Just a few feet from the cave is a cove. You can bathe there."

She could bathe? It was a luxury she'd never truly appreciated before she started this journey. The idea of feeling clean almost made her cry. The constant grime in her hair was giving her a headache from the extra weight. "Thank you so much." She appreciated Flare's friendship even more. Not only did he save her life, but now he was taking care of her. She gathered the clothes then left the cave.

When she reached the water's edge, she glanced behind her to see if Flare had followed her. He was nowhere in sight, so she assumed he was giving her some privacy. But since he'd seen her naked twice now, she didn't see why it mattered anyway. Being stripped down and flogged in a town square made her care less about nudity.

She dropped the jacket then walked into the water. It was surprisingly warm, not chilling like the ocean usually was. She swam around then scrubbed the dirt from her scalp. As the grime left her skin and hair, she felt better. Her wounds didn't sting when submerged in the water. Actually, it was soothing.

She was out there for nearly an hour, enjoying the water and the way it made her feel. Having freedom was a pleasure she would never take for granted again. Although, she shouldn't have allowed herself to be captured in the first place. From now on, she needed to make better decisions and not be as reckless.

When she finished, she dried off and examined the clothes he'd gotten for her. They were women's clothes, deep-brown pants the color of tree trunks and a long-sleeved green shirt. It was perfect for camouflage. There were also feminine undergarments, and she blushed slightly, knowing he'd picked those out for her.

Clean and dry, she felt like a new person.

She entered the cave with his jacket over her arm. The fire was still burning low, practically dying embers now that the fat from the deer meat had been cooked. Distant crackling echoed in the enclosure. "Thanks for letting me wear this." She placed it beside him. "It probably smells a little bit…" She would have cleaned it down by the water, but she wasn't sure if that was what he wanted. It was always smart to ask first.

"I'm sure it's fine." He continued to sharpen his blade.

She didn't know where to begin. How could she thank someone who did so much for her? "Thanks for everything, Flare. Not just rescuing me, but for taking care of me while I've been…indisposed."

"No need to thank me." His demeanor was different. Instead of wearing a sarcastic smile and carrying himself like he owned the world and everything in it, he was somber. Excitement no longer burned in his eyes. In fact, he seemed sad. "You would have done the same for me."

She knew that was true. "I hope you weren't injured."

"Just a few scratches. Nothing major."

She pulled her knees to her chest and moved her damp hair over one shoulder, letting it dry by the fire. "How did you know where I was? How did you know I was captured?" Did he intercept a message from somewhere down the road? Did he happen to be in Easton when she was being flogged?

"I heard you." His eyes were still focused on his dagger, endlessly sharpening it.

"Heard me?"

"I heard your thoughts." He swallowed the lump in his throat and paused the dagger's movement. "Death, come for me."

The blood drained from her face.

He cleared his throat. "And then I saw what Rune was doing to you, through your eyes. Our minds were linked together. When I saw the color of his robes, I knew where you were."

"But…how?" She hadn't tried to communicate with him. She didn't even know she could do that.

"I'm not sure. Our minds have spoken before. Maybe it's easy for them to connect."

"But we were so far apart. Is that normal?"

"No. I've never done something like that in my lifetime."

"Then how did it happen?"

Flare shrugged. "I don't know. Maybe you were in such distress, it projected outward. Perhaps I'm not the only dragon who heard it. But when I did, I had to come to your rescue."

"I didn't do it on purpose," she whispered. "I would never want you to risk your life for me."

"I know, Cora. But I'm glad I heard your call anyway." He dropped the rock then examined his blade in the firelight. "What did they want from you?"

"You." They'd wanted Flare's location more than anything else. "They wanted to know if I was in contact with the elves. How the sword was made. Where they could find you. Pretty much everything."

"And what did you tell them?" There was no disapproval in his voice. It didn't seem like he cared if she'd given up his plans or his whereabouts.

"Nothing."

He abandoned his dagger and looked her in the eye. "Cora, I don't think less of you for giving them information. You were being tortured to death. Truly, I understand."

"I really didn't tell them anything."

His eyes scanned the bruises on her face, and the memory of her scarred back glimmered in his eyes. "You didn't?"

"No. It wasn't an option. You are the only hope this continent has for returning to its former glory. If I gave you up, that would be the end. And I couldn't tell them about the secret island where the dragons were located. I just couldn't."

An unfamiliar look spread across his face, and he stared at her with new eyes. He cleared his throat like something had been caught deep inside his chest. For a moment, he looked down and broke their eye contact. "I don't know what to say…"

"Nothing needs to be said."

"Most people would have cracked. Actually, all people. I know how they torture their prisoners."

"I was only there for a few weeks…"

"They crack after the first day. I doubt even I would keep my secrets."

"You would." She knew he would. If there was anyone who could withstand the pain, it was Flare.

He pressed his lips tightly together then bit his inner cheek. "I knew you were someone worthwhile the moment we met. Actually, I was a little afraid of you. It was impossible to trust someone so unnaturally gifted. But now…I realize how much I underestimated you." Compliments didn't escape his lips very often, so she understood just how much they meant.

"If I were gifted, I wouldn't have been captured in the first place."

"You figured out how to kill the Shamans. And you even killed one yourself. Never in a million years would I have figured that out."

"It was just luck."

"Don't be coy." His words erupted viciously. "There's something special about you. I know it. You know it."

She held his gaze before the intensity became too much. She shifted her attention to the fire, finding it easier to watch the flames dance to silent music. The tension felt heavy on their shoulders, the awkwardness loud on their ears. "You haven't visited the island yet?"

"I was about to depart when I heard your voice."

"Where's Bridge?"

"He's traveling to a hideaway up north. I told him I would meet him there."

She was relieved he was okay. "What now?"

"You need to rest. Then we'll get moving again."

"Where are we moving to? The whole realm must be chasing us by now."

"I'll escort you to Eden Star."

Even if they flew, it would take forever. "I can go on my own. You need to meet up with Bridge."

He gave her the coldest look she'd ever seen.

She knew it would be stupid to argue with him. "Never mind. Will we fly?" Would he allow her to ride him?

"No. We'll walk."

"What?" she blurted. "That will take an entire month."

"It's much easier to spot a dragon from the skies. And that's exactly where everyone will be looking."

She couldn't deny the argument, even though she wished she could. It made even more sense for her to travel alone, but suggesting the idea would ignite his temper.

"When you're strong again, we'll get moving."

"I can manage now." She couldn't run, but she could at least walk. Time was of the essence.

"You need at least a few days. If you don't give your body enough time to recover, you won't be able to defend yourself. While I'm powerful, I can't protect you and fight off everything at the same time. I need your skills."

Giving her a sense of purpose was enough to make her give in. "Okay."

The cove they'd settled in was beautiful beyond understanding. It was peaceful and quiet, exactly what she needed.

"Do you want to talk about it?"

She knew what he was referring to but ignored the question.

"It can be therapeutic."

"Honestly, I'd rather just forget about it." She lay down on the hard stone and rested her head on his pack. The red sword sat a few feet away, glimmering in the firelight.

"I'm here if you ever change your mind."

"I know." She listened to the flames simmer down to red coals. "Flare?"

"Hmm?"

"Your dragon tears—"

"I don't want to discuss it." His voice cut her off like a steel blade. Invisible walls erupted around him, blocking him off from her completely.

She knew she'd broached a sore subject, something he wasn't ready to talk about out loud. If he accepted her silence, then she needed to accept his. "Did the tears close the wounds on my back?" Since she couldn't see behind her, she had no idea how it looked.

"Yes. It stopped the bleeding. If you'd lost any more blood, you would have died."

"Does that mean my back looks the way it used to?" She was never vain about her looks, but she hoped her back wouldn't be permanently disfigured by the whip that slashed it open.

He bowed his head slightly. "No. You have scars."

"Oh. Will they go away?"

"No. I'm sorry."

She pulled her arms to her chest and cradled herself, feeling a new kind of pain.

"My tears can fix almost any injury. It repaired your ribs when you drank it, and it sealed the wounds all over your body. But it can't remove the superficial aspects of healing."

"I see…"

He watched her with sad eyes.

"And there's nothing I can do? There's not a potion of some sort?"

He shook his head.

"How does it look?"

He lowered his gaze. "Your scars look exactly the way they felt when you received them."

Now her captivity would never be forgotten. She would have to carry a reminder of what she went through—every day until she died.

She looked down into the pool of ice, her arms pinned to her sides. Rune walked around her, a sinister smile on his lips. "Tell me what I want to know."

Her eyes were on the frigid liquid, remembering exactly how it shocked her lungs and forced her to breathe a gulp of water.

"Cat got your tongue?" He shoved her hard.

She fell into the water and immediately panicked. She flapped her arms around and tried to get away. She tried to breathe but wasn't getting any air. The agony drowned her, and she sank to the bottom of a dark chasm.

"Cora." Flare shook her shoulders firmly. "Come on. Get out of there."

When her eyes opened, she jolted upright and smacked Flare away from her. She scooted back and tried to catch her breath, the dream still playing in her mind. It started to fade like a wisp of smoke, floating higher and higher until it disappeared.

"It was a dream." Flare didn't come closer to her. "It wasn't real. Just a dream."

She stared into Flare's face and found comfort. If she was with him, she was safe. She wasn't in Easton. She was in the same cave she fell asleep in. Rune was nowhere to be found.

She was safe.

"I'm sorry I hurt you."

"Hurt me?" His old smile stretched across his lips. "You could never hurt me."

She leaned against the wall and caught her breath, noting the large flames in the fire. He must have added wood throughout the night. "I didn't mean to startle you."

"You can't startle me either." He patted his pack then made a clicking noise with his tongue. "Come back to bed. The nightmare is over."

"Don't call me like a dog."

"What? You don't like dogs?"

She knew he was trying to cheer her up, but this time, it wouldn't work.

"Who the hell doesn't like dogs?" He shook his head. "I always knew you were peculiar."

She returned to the pack and positioned herself to go back to sleep. But she didn't think she could rest, even if she tried. That nightmare haunted her. The last thing she wanted was to experience it again. She purposely kept her eyes open just to avoid it.

Flare's voice turned gentle. "Dreams can't hurt you, Cora."

"I respectfully disagree."

"Well, I can keep them away for you—if you wish."

"Keep them away?" She looked up at him, unsure of his meaning.

"My dragon can. They have special powers when it comes to the mind. He can wrap a cocoon around your thoughts and stop the bad ones from entering when you're asleep. It stops the nightmares."

"Really?"

He nodded. "When I sleep, he keeps a lookout. He can't necessarily see, but he can sense things. That's why it's impossible to sneak up on me, even when I'm not conscious."

Now she wished she had a dragon of her own.

"You want to give it a try?"

"How does it work?"

"He wraps the cocoon around both of us. Basically, you have to let him enter your mind. I understand if that's something you're uncomfortable with. He can accidentally see things you may not want him to see."

She didn't have many secrets, and even if she did, she didn't mind sharing them if she never had to experience another night terror. "Okay."

"You're sure?"

She nodded.

He moved to her place near the fire then lay beside her.

"What are you doing?"

"We have to be close to each other in order for it to work." He lay on his back and closed his eyes, his arm touching hers. "Is this okay?"

Actually, his proximity was soothing. "Yeah."

"Close your eyes."

She did as he asked.

Within a few minutes, she felt a thin blanket cover her thoughts. The sensation was odd. It felt like cobwebs had scattered throughout her mind, gently masking some things, while allowing other memories to come through. The dragon had entered her subconscious, but he didn't make his presence known. He was a quiet visitor, a mouse running around in the house.

She dreamed of her home, Dorian, and the funny conversations she'd had with Flare and Bridge. It was soothing and restful. The night passed without any incident, and when the sun rose the following morning, she didn't want to wake up.

## TWENTY-FOUR

"Can you show me my back?"

Flare handed her a mug of tea before he gave her a quizzical expression. "What do you mean?"

"I want to see it, but I can't bend that way. So, can you show me?"

"One, I don't see how I can do that. Two, why do you want to see it?" He sipped his tea and rested his arms on his knees.

"I just do." She wanted to understand how bad the damage was. What would people see when they looked at her? She needed to know. "You said I sent you an image of Rune when I was being tortured. Can't you send me an image of my back in the same way?"

"I suppose I could try. But I really don't think you want to see it."

"If I don't, I'll always wonder."

He sighed like the idea repulsed him. "Fine." He pivoted his body toward her so he could face her head on.

She turned around then lifted up her shirt, exposing her bare back to him. She felt his stare bore into her skin, heating the tender scars. Her arms rested in front of her chest, keeping them from view.

Then an image emerged directly in her brain. The image of her back appeared crystal clear. Every crack and scar were highlighted from the flames of the fire. There were so many lashes that the skin didn't look like skin at all, just a patchwork of marks. The groove of her spine was indecipherable in the mess. Even her shoulders held the abrasions. It didn't look like skin anymore.

It didn't look like anything.

Her eyes welled up with tears at the sight. Unable to handle it anymore, she pulled down her shirt and ended the image altogether. She kept her back to him because she didn't want to face him. He would think less of her for caring so much. The delicate skin that she carried all her life had been taken away from her. Now, she had to bear the marks of a ruthless man.

Like he'd once owned her.

She watched the sun set into the ocean. Her feet were buried in the sand, and her knees were pulled to her chest. Lost in quiet solitude, she kept to herself most of the day. Flare stayed inside the cave and never emerged.

"Do you mind if I join you?" Appearing out of nowhere, Flare stood beside her. His approach wasn't picked up by her ears. His boots didn't make a sound as they dug into the sand.

"No."

He sat beside her, keeping a foot between them. "Do you think you're ready to leave?"

She would never completely heal from the trauma, but she had to hold her head high and move on. Moping around in self-pity wouldn't get her anywhere. All she had to do was remain fully clothed, and no one would know what had befallen her. "Yes."

"You're sure?"

She nodded. "I've rested long enough. And you've stuffed me like a swine."

He chuckled in a throaty way. "You're the one who ate like a pig. I just hunted and prepared the food." He nudged her in the side playfully, reminding her of the relationship she had with her three adoptive brothers. He teased her, but he was also there for her.

"Yeah…I guess I did overeat a little."

"You're almost back to your former weight. But you're missing some muscle. You'll gain it back once we start moving."

"I hope so." She needed her strength. Being thin and bony wasn't her preference. She didn't have as much energy as before. It didn't matter how much meat she ate; she needed to get moving if she wanted to rebuild lost muscle.

"Don't worry about it." Flare watched the sun until it completely disappeared beyond the horizon. The sky turned pink and orange, the last few rays of light streaking across the sky.

"I'm sorry about yesterday." She'd avoided him ever since that painful conversation. "I know it's stupid to care about something so superficial."

"It's not stupid." His sincerity shone through. "Someone mutilated you, changed your appearance. It would bother anyone."

She cared a great deal about his opinion, but she wasn't sure when that had begun. When they'd met, she didn't care for him. But somewhere along the road, that had changed. "I guess I'm embarrassed by those hideous scars. I can never show anyone."

"Embarrassed?" He turned away from the setting sun and watched her. "You should never be embarrassed by what happened to you. You survived unspeakable torture. They pressured you to give up your secrets, but you never did. Even when they flogged you buck naked in front of thousands of people, you still didn't give them what they wanted. If anything, you should be proud."

The blue color of his eyes was usually bright like a summer day, but now, it had darkened to the color of the ocean. "I know I am. You're the strongest woman I've ever known." He rested his arms across his knees. "Actually, I take that back. You're the strongest *person* I've ever known."

Without realizing it, the corners of her lips lifted into a smile. It was the first time she'd felt some form of happiness in a long time. Flare always made her feel good about herself, even between the insults. "Thank you."

He faced the ocean again, his eyes on the darkening sky.

Silently, she sat beside him and stared straight ahead. Unstoppable tears formed in her eyes, and one escaped down her cheek. She wanted to wipe it away, but she knew it would draw Flare's attention.

So she let it drip to her chin before it fell to the sand.

"Are you sure you're ready for this?" Flare stood with his pack over his shoulders, his blade hanging from his hip.

"Yes."

"Because I'm not going to slow down for you. I expect you to keep up and give it your all. We have a lot of ground to cover. So, if you need a few more days, you'd better speak now."

Cora appreciated the fact that he didn't treat her like a sad pity story. He expected her to overcome her pain and push on like a warrior. He didn't cut her any slack because he shouldn't. "I'll be fine."

He searched her gaze for sincerity.

"If I felt otherwise, I would tell you."

That seemed to be enough to assure him because he turned around and began the hike. He moved uphill, walking quickly as if the steep hill had no effect on him.

She took a deep breath then followed close behind him.

"How long will Bridge wait for you?" She matched his stride now that they were on flat land. They stayed away from the trail and moved between the trees, relying on the cover of their leaves.

"Until I get there."

"But you'll have been traveling for two months."

"He'll wait." He said it with the utmost confidence. "If I say I'll be somewhere, I'll be there."

"Does he have enough supplies?"

"Plenty. Honestly, it's probably a vacation for him." His hood was pulled up, and his face was hidden with the exception of his chin. He'd shaved by a pond earlier that morning, and now his face was clean of whiskers. His lips were more noticeable without the distraction of facial hair, and they looked soft.

"How do you know where you're going all the time?"

"I have a good sense of direction. And I've been around a long time."

She knew he was old, but he never gave her a real number. "Have you been everywhere in Anastille?"

"Pretty much. Except Eden Star. They don't let our kind pass."

"Because they hate you? From the war?"

He chuckled sarcastically. "Hate is an understatement. We're absolutely vile to them."

"Do you think they'll feel the same toward me?"

"It's possible. Actually, it's probable. But you're the one who seems confident they'll accept you with loving arms."

"I'm sure when they meet us, they'll drop their prejudice. We're obviously not a threat to them."

"They'll always be prejudiced against me." His statement lingered on for minutes.

She didn't voice the question in her mind because she knew she wouldn't get an answer. "During wartime, there are casualties on both sides. A lot of elves may have died, but so did humans. We've both lost people."

"They don't see it that way."

"Why?"

"They just don't." It was clear he was hiding something. He didn't make eye contact with her, like that would open the gateway to spilling every detail.

Cora tried not to be offended by his secrecy because he'd saved her from a bloody death. His secrets were his own business and had nothing to do with her. But she hoped one day he would take down a few walls and let her in—completely. "Maybe we can repair what happened in the past."

"Doubtful." Every stride of his was equal to two of hers. She had to walk twice as fast to keep up with him. "For humans, it only takes a few decades to move on from a big event. And that's because our life-spans are so short. When the older generations pass away, new ones emerge. And over time, all the hostility and prejudice slowly die down because the newer generations weren't around to experience it. But with elves…all the survivors are alive. And they never forget. To them, the war happened just yesterday."

Now she understood the situation a little better. "I see."

"So, don't have unrealistic expectations. If they agree to meet you, that's a miracle in itself."

She gripped the straps of the new pack he'd given her and stared at the scenery as they walked. "Do you think we can stop by the poisonous frogs on the way?"

"Why?"

"To create another venomous arrow."

"That's out of our way. We'll have to double the length of the journey to make it happen. And neither one of us has time for that."

Perhaps on her way back, she would make a stop.

"But I think it's worth doing eventually," he said. "I would love the opportunity to kill a Shaman. I'm just not as good an archer as you." He glanced at her with a smile on his lips.

"I've never seen you shoot an arrow."

"I'm pretty good. Not an expert like you, though."

"I miss my bow…" All of her things had been left behind in Easton. The only thing she got to keep was her sword, which was probably the most valuable thing she owned anyway.

"We'll get you another one."

"But I prefer to make my own. I do a better job."

He chuckled. "Cocky, are we?"

"I'm just being honest."

"Maybe the elves will let you use their forges. I can only imagine what you could create with their tools."

Excitement coursed through her at the thought.

When she opened her eyes the following morning, she looked directly into two enormous yellow eyes.

Startled, she jolted upright.

*Do not be scared. It is I.*

Her heart was pounding hard in her chest, and it took her nearly thirty seconds to calm down again. "You scared the crap out of me. You should have told me you were morphing into a dragon." Looking at a winged beast first thing in the morning wasn't a pleasant way to wake up.

*He was tired, so we made the change late last night.*

Cora was confused by the choice of words. "He?"

*The man you know as Flare.*

"As in, he's not here right now?" Weren't they together at all times? Or something like that…

*No. We disconnected.*

"Oh… Any reason why?"

*He needed to rest. But don't worry, I'll look after you.*

In that moment, she realized something. "Is this the first time I've ever spoken to you, and only you?"

*Yes. For the most part.*

Wow. That meant she was speaking to a real dragon. Flare wasn't present, and it was just the two of them. "Well, it's an honor to formally meet you, Flare."

The dragon released a quiet snort that sounded like a sigh. *It's nice to meet you too, Pretty.*

Both of her eyebrows rose up. "Pretty?"

*You're pretty like treasure. That's what I call you when I speak to him.*

It was a compliment, but it took her a moment to accept it in that way. "Well, thank you."

The dragon rose to its full height and surveyed the clearing they'd spent the night in. *Are you ready to continue your journey?*

She fixed her hair before she stood up and gathered her pack. "Do you know the way?"

Now an irritated snort came out. *Yes. This was my land long before it was yours.*

Cora realized her serious misstep. "Sorry…I didn't mean it offensively."

*I know. You're lucky.* The dragon turned and continued on their path, its massive claws moving slowly. Its large size made it difficult for it to walk quickly. It was clearly meant to fly, not travel on foot.

"Did you eat breakfast?"

*Two deer. They were delicious.*

Cora pulled out a sack of nuts and snacked on those. "Thank you for saving me a few weeks ago. Without the two of you, I would be dead right now."

*You're welcome, Pretty.*

It was much easier to keep pace with the dragon than the human. She could actually walk at a leisurely speed and breathe through her nose instead of gasping for air through her mouth.

*He and I don't agree on a lot of things, but we agreed on that immediately.*

Cora looked down and kept eating her nuts.

*You care for him a great deal.* The dragon didn't ask a question, but it was implied. He watched her out of the corner of his eye, the yellow iris glaringly obvious.

"Of course I do. He's my friend." Without him, she would be wandering Anastille alone. She would have been captured by the Shamans long ago and surely would be dead right now. He gave her a purpose, something she desperately needed now that she couldn't return home.

*You care for him more than that.*

Cora closed her sack of nuts and looked up at the dragon, unsure of his meaning. "Sorry?"

*I've been inside your head. I see the way you see him.*

Cora still didn't know what he was talking about. "I didn't care for him much in the beginning because he was so rude. But the more I got to know him, the more I realized it was just a cold projection he emitted. He's caring, passionate, and thoughtful, just like everyone else. Actually, even more so. I've come to long for his companionship, to feel at peace when I'm in his presence. I've even come to trust him—with more than just my life."

The dragon's claws thudded hard against the ground with every step they took. To anyone nearby, they probably assumed a herd of wild horses was passing. *He's very fond of you.*

"He is?" She smiled at the thought. "I thought he hated me most of the time—at least when we first met."

*No. I remember what he thought the first time he met you.*

Cora didn't ask because she understood how Flare was. He didn't answer questions when they were asked. He only gave information willingly when he wanted to.

*You were the most beautiful woman he'd ever seen.*

Cora gripped her sack awkwardly and spilled the nuts onto the ground. She panicked and squatted to pick them up, but she moved too quickly and tripped over herself, rolling onto the grass in an ungraceful way.

The dragon stopped and eyed her with an amused look.

Cora quickly stood up and pretended it never happened. "Just tripped on a rock…"

*Sure, Pretty.*

Even though she'd been completely naked in front of thousands of people, she blushed. She examined the passing trees so the dragon couldn't see her face.

*I think you feel the same way.*

She tried to dissipate the tension with a joke. "No, I don't think he's the most beautiful woman I've ever seen."

Flare made an irritated snort. *You know what I mean.*

She returned the nuts to her pack and changed the subject. "What was it like before the humans came to your land? Were there more of you?" The history of Anastille was fascinating, especially from a dragon's point of view.

Flare stared straight ahead, his long neck supporting his massive head. The curvature of his face was fixed with jagged points, extra protection to go along with his hard scales. *You're both strange. Neither one of you will admit how you truly feel, even though you know exactly what's in your heart.*

Now that she knew the dragon personally, she wasn't so scared of him. But she would never forget how she felt when she first saw him. She thought she was going to lose her lunch. Now she was scared of his prominent intelligence and intuition. A being so old was bound to be wise, but not like this.

Flare turned his head slightly and eyed her down below him. He shook his head slightly, full of disappointment at Cora's silence. *Anastille was a much different place before the humans arrived at our shore.*

She breathed a sigh of relief now that the subject had been dropped.

*We had a government, but it was rarely used. There were no such things as castles or homes. Dragons lived freely, roaming the countryside or infesting the enormous caverns of the mountains. We rarely stayed in one place for too long. The dwarves and the elves coexisted with us peacefully. An unspoken rule was forged between us. We didn't eat their kind as long as they didn't hunt ours. And it worked.*

Cora hung on every word, fascinated by a world different from the one they lived in now.

*When the humans arrived, we thought they were harmless creatures. Small and weak, they didn't pose a threat to us. We took pity on them and allocated a small amount of land they could inhabit. The dwarves and elves strongly advised against it, sensing humans were greedy and reckless. But we lacked the same wisdom to see it for ourselves. Quickly, they populated exponentially, and soon they were a force to be reckoned with. That's when King Lux made his move.*

She gripped the straps of her pack as she walked, too enthralled in the story to pay attention to her surroundings. She stopped searching for enemies and obstacles, only caring about the history of the past.

*King Lux and his two brothers forced a fuse between a few of the dragons, using their dark magic to manipulate them in grotesque ways. Then they forced other dragons to fuse with other members of their species. The remaining dragons started the Great War, killing any human who got in our way. But we failed to win—because we refused to kill our own kind. It's our one rule.*

"You couldn't kill King Lux and his brothers?"

*When they're fused, you can't kill the human without killing the dragon.*

Now she understood the problem.

*In retrospect, we should have done whatever was necessary. Those dragons have been slaves for years. Death is preferable to that. Their power has led to the enslavement of every living dragon. Not a single free dragon remains in Anastille—besides me.*

"What about the dragons hiding away on that island?"

*It could be a myth.*

"What if it's not?"

*It would be the greatest hope we could ever ask for.*

"Do you think you would know any of the dragons there?"

*Yes. There weren't very many of us to begin with.*

"I hope we find them. I'm sure it would be nice to have friends of your own kind."

*Yes, it would.*

"When did you and Flare meet?" She had many questions, and there wasn't enough time in the day to answer them all.

A snort that sounded like a chuckle erupted. *He warned me you were nosy.*

"I'm not being nosy. I'm just curious."

*I can't share secrets that don't belong to me. I'm sorry.*

"Oh…" She stared at the grass beneath her feet. "I wasn't trying to pry."

*I know, Pretty. I told him he should just tell you. He's afraid.*

"Afraid of what?"

*That you won't look at him the same way.*

"But he already told me he forced you to fuse with him. I didn't think less of him then, and that's one of the most inhumane things I've ever heard of."

Flare reached his neck down, then gave her an affectionate tap with his nose. *Thank you, Pretty.*

The tap was gentle but almost knocked her over. "It's how I feel."

*He can't forgive himself, so he assumes no one else can either. He hoards his secrets like treasure.*

"He thinks I won't forgive him?" She wasn't perfect either. She'd done things she regretted—a hundred times.

Flare nodded.

"He's sensitive, huh?"

The dragon released a laugh that shot a stream of fire out of his nose. It almost hit a tree and burned it to the ground.

*Pretty, you're so funny. That's why I like you. You'll put anyone in their place—it doesn't matter who it is.*

"Except you. I wouldn't want to become lunch."

The dragon laughed again, releasing more fire. *I don't eat my own treasure.*

They settled down for the night in an enclosure of trees.

Cora yawned before she situated herself on the grass. She pulled a blanket out of her pack and stuffed it around her body to remain warm. It was usually hot during the day, but in the evening, it cooled down to a low temperature. "Good night, Flare."

*Good night, Pretty.* The dragon walked to her then formed a circle from its nose to its tail. He surrounded her on all sides then placed his open wing above Cora, boxing her inside a protective fort. *Now you'll be warm and safe.*

It was dark inside the enclosure, but the moon shone through the webbed wing. She'd never taken the time to truly examine the dragon before. Now she noticed the horns that jutted out from the bones of his wings. While the material was thin, the endless veins hinted at their strength. Her eyes remained open for a long time, just observing the strange beauty of a dragon wing.

*Pretty, he's coming back. Just wanted to let you know.*

"Thanks."

The dragon fell silent and didn't speak again. Several minutes passed, and Cora kept examining the wing that protected her from the sky. She'd never felt so safe in her life, even when she was living in Vax.

*Were you nice to my dragon today?* While the voice sounded identical to the one she just heard, it was clear it belonged to someone else.

"Of course. I prefer him to you."

*Bridge says the same thing.*

"Maybe you should work on your insufferable personality, then."

*Insufferable? I know I'm rough around the edges, but I wouldn't take it that far. I did save you, remember?*

"Flare did too, *remember?*"

*I saved you from the guards in Polox. He had nothing to do with that one.*

She was tired and ready for sleep. "Why don't you disconnect again? I can't keep my eyes open."

*Someone has to keep a lookout.*

She rolled onto her side and got comfortable. "Good night."

He didn't say anything for a long time. *Sweet dreams.* The familiar cobweb spread around her mind, keeping the bad thoughts out and the good ones in. Beautiful images of rainbows and oceans came to her, soothing and warm. Her dreams were truly sweet now, sweeter than any she'd ever had.

## TWENTY-FIVE

"Up." He gripped her by both shoulders and shook her.

"Muh." She turned on her side and clung to her blanket, ignoring the sunlight spilling across her eyelids.

"I've let you sleep long enough." His deep voice was full of irritation, like usual.

She returned to her semi-dream state, seeing a waterfall just up ahead.

"Cora." He shook her again.

She threw her leg back and kicked him.

"Ouch." He faltered and rubbed his shin. "Goddammit, you're a brat."

"Few more minutes…"

Flare walked to his pack then pulled out his canteen. He removed the cap then splashed water across her face.

She jolted upright at the cold liquid. "Ugh!"

"Now you'll get up when I tell you to get up." He returned the cap to the top.

She snatched it from his hands then threw the remaining water all over him. "Ass."

"Whoa, don't waste it." He yanked it from her hands. "When did you become so lazy?"

"I'm not lazy. I'm tired."

"Same thing." He stuffed the canteen back into his bag so she wouldn't take it again.

She wiped the water from her face with her shirt then got up. Ever since she'd started to dream well, she wanted to sleep all the time. It was the most relaxing sleep she'd ever experienced. Having a dragon guard her dreams was just one of the many perks of having one as a friend.

"Let's get moving."

"We should hunt. I haven't eaten in a while."

"No hunting today." He set off at a quick pace.

"What? Why not?" She hated being told what to do. It was her biggest pet peeve.

"Because I said so."

"What kind of reason is that?" She walked behind him and tried to catch up.

"There are orcs nearby. We don't want to cross paths with them. We'd be able to take them out easily, but it's always simpler just to avoid them."

"Oh…"

"Unless you want to hunt orc. But let me warn you, they taste like piss."

"You've eaten one before?" She caught up to him and walked beside him.

"Unfortunately."

"Why were you eating an orc?"

"It was in the heat of battle. I meant to grab him by the jaws and toss him aside, but I accidentally swallowed him."

"Gross…"

He shrugged. "But I was full for a long time. They have a lot of protein."

She would rather starve than eat an orc.

"We have a lot of ground to cover. Can you run?"

"Run?" she asked. "Of course, I can run."

"I mean for long distances."

She'd never tried before. "Probably."

"Probably? Or yes?"

"Yes."

"Good. We need to make better time." He set off at a jog with his back perfectly upright. His breathing didn't change at all, even though his activity did.

Cora jogged beside him and tried to keep up with him. Her body still hurt from the torture in Easton, but she refused to tell him that. The pain was only as strong as she allowed it to be. If she tuned it out, she would be fine.

"Are you okay?"

She gave the only answer she was willing to give. "I'm fine."

The following weeks became repetitive and exhausting. Cora always considered herself to be athletic, but running twenty miles a day pushed her to a new limit. Not once did she complain, but her body screamed at her every second.

As soon as they set up camp for the night, she fell asleep the moment her back hit the ground. Flare always protected her dreams and allowed her to rest peacefully the entire night. But the second the sun peeked over the horizon, she was jolted awake again.

Her body changed in subtle ways, until one day, she realized how different it was. Her legs were muscular and slim, and her calf muscles were powerful. The small amount of girth around her waist had disappeared, and her small breasts were even smaller. The muscles of her biceps were more prominent, and she could see them without even flexing.

The pain from her imprisonment faded away with every passing day, but the trauma still haunted her from time to time. It didn't matter how strong she became. No amount of physical exertion would ever repair her back. It would always be scarred and grotesque.

Flare stopped running when the trees thinned out. His breathing was regular like he hadn't just been running all day, and his body looked exactly the same as it had before.

She knew where they were without him having to tell her. "This is as far as I got last time." The desert was just up ahead, expansive and vast. It was difficult to tell exactly how far away it was with the naked eye.

"You'll make it across this time." He dropped his pack then placed his hands on his hips as he examined the terrain. "It looks pretty dry out there, drier than usual."

"It's unbearable when the sun is out."

"Yeah, I know." He sat in the shade of a tree and relaxed his arms on his knees. "We'll rest now and cross at nightfall."

Her canteen was almost empty. Maybe he could survive without water because of the dragon aspect of his being, but she certainly couldn't. "Shouldn't we retrieve water first?"

"We'll be fine."

"Uh…no, we won't." She shook her canteen in front of him, telling him how low it was.

"We can get water from the cacti."

"What if there aren't any cacti?"

"Then we'll fly at nightfall. Some things can see us, but not many. It's a risk I'll take, but only if I must."

"And what would I do? Run?"

"What?" He gave her a confused expression. "No. You would ride me."

"You would let me?" Dragons didn't seem like the kind of creatures to allow that. They weren't horses.

"You wouldn't be a rider. I would just give you a lift. Very different."

"Wow…then I hope there aren't any cacti."

He grinned from ear to ear. "My dragon loves your admiration."

She remembered everything the dragon had said to her when Flare wasn't around, especially the comment about her appearance when they'd first met. When she felt the color rise to her cheeks, she fought it back. "What could see us in the dark?"

"Shamans."

She hoped she wouldn't run into him again, at least not when she didn't have any frog poison. With his dark powers, it would be hard just to shoot an arrow if she even had one. When the mind was attacked in such a way, it was impossible to do anything. She wondered if Flare could even handle it. "Has the Shaman ever done the Skull Crusher on you?"

"No. If he did, I'd be dead right now."

"Even though you're fused with a dragon?"

He shrugged. "I'm not sure if that would make a difference. I've never seen a Shaman act out against a human fused with a dragon. It would be considered treason if they did."

"I wonder if it would have the same effect on you."

"It probably would. It's the only reason King Lux fears them. He understands what they can do."

"What would you do if we saw them?"

He grabbed a stalk of grass and played with it in his fingertips. "Tell you to run while I fought him off."

"But wouldn't he kill you?"

"No." He didn't give any explanation for his assumption.

"Why wouldn't he do that?" Was she missing something?

"He needs me alive." Flare turned away like he didn't want to discuss it anymore, but he didn't snap at her like he normally would.

She dropped the subject since there was nowhere else for it to go. "Can I sleep?"

"You should. I'll keep watch."

She settled down under the shade of the tree and rested her head on her pack. "What if we flew low to the ground across the desert? Do you think that could work?"

Flare twisted the stalk with his fingertips.

"Even if we're walking, if there's someone watching the desert, they'll see us anyway. If we fly, we'll get across quicker and limit the possibility of being seen."

"Or you're looking for an excuse to ride." He shot her a playful grin.

"I'm just being pragmatic. The desert is a dangerous place, and no one can cross it. If we get far enough away, no one will dare to follow us. They'll give up and wait for us to come back."

"I suppose you're right."

She had only been in the desert for a day, and that was enough for her. Even when she was cloaked and hidden, the water evaporated from her skin, and she was immediately parched. Weak or not, she simply wasn't capable of handling that type of environment. While being captured by the Shaman wasn't her plan, it probably saved her life. In her heart, she suspected she wouldn't have made it across. "Does that mean we'll fly?"

He stared across the vast desert, where the sand was white-hot and steaming. He chewed on the end of the stalk before he tossed it aside. "Your dream is about to come true."

She crawled up the beast, gripping its massive horns for leverage, and then made her way to the top. She slid down his back until she sat in the crook of his neck. Unsure what else to do, she wrapped her arms around his throat. "Is this okay?"

*Yes. You have a good grip?*

"I think so."

*Alright. Hold on.*

She tensed at his words and felt the dragon's body move as it squatted down, its powerful legs recoiling and preparing for launch. His wings opened, ready to feel the air directly underneath the webbing. His back lifted with a heavy breath, moving her slowly.

And then he took off.

With a single beat of his wings, he was in the air. He flew ten feet above the ground before he opened his wings wide and glided back down to the earth.

"Oh my god! This is so cool!"

Flare chuckled inside her head. *I thought you would like it.*

The dragon hovered just feet above the ground, beating its powerful wings as it flew deep into the darkness. The path couldn't be seen because it was a moonless night. They moved forward and hoped they wouldn't collide with anything large.

Cora felt the wind smack her in the face and move through her hair. The air was surprisingly cold and harsh. Her nose and eyes immediately felt dry, and the air moved down her throat automatically. In light of what she was doing, she ignored all the discomforts.

*You okay back there?*

"Yes. I've never felt so alive."

*It's addictive.*

Even though she couldn't see anything in front of her, she enjoyed the ride. She could only imagine how amazing it would be to fly up in the sky on a summer day. Being so high in the sky with the world below you must be the greatest thrill anyone could imagine. "How far is it to the other side?"

*Two days.*

"With rest?"

*Two days without stopping.*

"You don't plan to stop?"

*No. We need to get there as soon as possible.*

"You think that's wise?"

*Wise?* A laugh echoed in her mind. *You should know me by now. I'm never wise.*

Just as Flare recommended, they didn't stop. The dragon's wings beat hard as they crossed the vast desert. When the sun came, it shone ruthlessly on their skin. At least the dragon had thick scales to protect its hide. Cora pulled up her hood and kept her skin covered as much as possible. They were only halfway there, and she was thirsty.

*Get some sleep.*

"Are you sure?" How could she rest when Flare was working so hard to get them both across the desert?

*Yes. You'll hunt for me when we get there.*

"With what? I don't have a bow."

*You have a sword, don't you?*

She'd never hunted with a blade, but it couldn't be that hard. "Okay." She pulled a rope out of her pack and tied herself to the dragon's neck. If she slipped, she wouldn't fall.

*Good night.*

"Let me know if you need anything."

*Dragons don't need anything but wings.*

The days passed achingly slow. By the time they spotted the other side of the desert, it felt like an eternity had passed. Cora constantly glanced over her shoulder to make sure they weren't being followed, and as far as she could tell, they weren't.

Flare's speed slowed down considerably in the last stretch. He was thirsty, hungry, and exhausted.

"Almost there." She patted his back for comfort.

*My wings are tired.* His speech was slower, telling her she was speaking to the dragon.

Cora had come to differentiate between the two. Now she understood who was speaking without having to ask. "You're almost there. You're doing great."

*My scales are so dirty. It disgusts me.*

"I'll wash them for you."

*No, I'll do it. They must be perfect.*

Cora didn't take offense because she understood the dragon's vanity. They prized their appearance more than anything. "I don't think anyone followed us."

*Neither do I.*

They approached the end of the desert and spotted the green trees. The tall mountains were just behind it, glorious and strong. It was the first time they saw any abundant life in days. It made Cora never want to cross the desert and return to the heartland of Anastille. "I see shade."

The dragon finally crossed the line where the desert ended and entered the greenery of the forest. But he didn't stop there. He kept going, knowing exactly where water was located.

She spotted the lake from the sky, seeing it glimmer under the sunlight. "I'm so thirsty right now."

*I'm in desperate need of a bath.* The dragon headed straight for the water without stopping on land.

Cora didn't want to get her clothes dirty, but she was so dry and cracked, she didn't care. She wanted to be in the water, to remember what moisture felt like.

The dragon dove headfirst into the water, taking Cora with him.

The second the water washed over her face, she felt better. It was cool and crisp and even more refreshing than she hoped it would be. She loosened the rope holding her to the dragon and swam to the top.

She breached the surface then floated on her back, letting her clothes soak and become full of water. Her hair floated around her scalp, drifting just as she did. Relaxation washed over her before she pulled her canteen out of her pack and filled it with water. While swimming in place, she drank as much as her body could handle.

The dragon hadn't resurfaced yet, probably exploring some underwater cave.

Cora swam to shore then sat on the sand. She drank her water quietly, enjoying the scenery and the feeling of accomplishment. They crossed the desert without dying or being followed. Now, it was time to relax.

Flare broke the surface of the water, his head emerging first. His scales looked even more marvelous when wet. They shone even brighter in the sunlight. He scooped water into his mouth then drank from the lake, gently gliding at the same time.

"Your scales look like they are sparkling."

The dragon held his head proudly, his nose slightly pointed up. *I know.*

She tried not to laugh. "They look really nice."

*I know that too.*

Cora kept drinking from her canteen and watched the dragon walk out of the water. "Would you like me to hunt now?"

The dragon lay on the sand and immediately closed his eyes. *Bear, please. Two if you can manage it.*

Cora grabbed her sword from her pack and headed into the trees. "I can try, but I suspect I won't even return with one."

## TWENTY-SIX

Flare started the fire then sat back as the meat cooked on the stick.

"Do you think it's smart to have a fire?" Maybe they were difficult to see in the dark, but a large fire wasn't.

"The world is much different on this side of the desert. No one will bother us."

"Why is it different?"

He pulled back his hood then grabbed his razor from his pack. "There's no one here. The dwarves are hidden away in the mountains, and the elves are secluded in their valleys. We're alone."

"King Lux's rule doesn't extend to this place?"

"Technically, yes. How do you control something you're so far away from?" He wiped plant cream on his face then shaved without looking at his reflection. The scrape of the blade moved against his skin but never made a cut. "He could cross the desert if he really wanted to, but why attempt to conquer beings that don't disturb you anyway? Besides, King Lux understands both the elves and dwarves are terrifying species. He wouldn't go to war with them again unless he had no other choice."

Cora couldn't help but piece the puzzle together. He spoke of King Lux like he was acquainted with him personally, and the Steward of Easton was his uncle. Flare had to be close to King Lux in some way. "You speak of him like you know him." She gently prodded him, hoping he would confess his secrets now that they were so close to the elves. He might not get another opportunity.

He stopped shaving, even though half of his face was covered in cream. He watched her across the fire, his blue eyes keeping his secrets locked up tight.

She didn't press it further because she knew it was pointless.

"King Lux is my father."

Even though she suspected some type of familiar relationship, she hadn't been expecting that. She tried to hide her reaction but failed. She was astonished—and a little disturbed.

Flare shaved the other side of his face, pretending he hadn't just said something groundbreaking. He wiped away the spots that remained then washed off his razor. "I ruled beneath him and alongside him for a very long time." He stared at the blade in his hands, turning it slowly. "For hundreds of years, actually. He was the one who broke in to my dragon's mind and forced him to fuse with me. After that, I took complete control. He'd been training me to replace him in the event he perished. And I was the perfect candidate."

Cora did her best to remain calm, to act like nothing had changed between them. While this knowledge changed the way she saw him, she remembered he'd left High Castle for a reason. She remembered he was running from the king, not toward him.

"I didn't question anything for years. As far as I was concerned, the dragons were solely made to serve us. They gave us unspeakable power. We're the only ones worthy to control it. Flare was under my dominion for a long time, and no matter how much he fought me, I pushed him down. I tortured other dragons when they refused to cooperate. I killed a lot of people who didn't deserve to die. I was a monster—just like my father."

His eyes reflected the flames of the fire, and deep within them was the weight of the pain he carried. It was mixed with remorse and guilt. "My father and I were close—inseparable. But as the years passed, I became more in tune with my dragon. A bond started to form, and love started to grow. I reached a point where I couldn't bear to hurt him any longer, and when I was asked, I refused to hurt another dragon. It was the vilest cruelty, and I adamantly refused to do it."

She pulled her knees to her chest and hugged them tightly.

"I started to question everything. I reexamined the Great War and realized the destruction we caused. The dragons granted us mercy, but the second they turned their backs, we stabbed them in the dark. How could I ever have been proud to be my father's son? He took the world by force, not respect. He destroyed an entire species of dragons for his own gain. He chased away the other species that had been here longer than man has even existed."

She could feel the pain oozing from his skin. The air around him was filled with sorrow.

"And then my father killed my mother." His voice broke at the end, emotion burning deep inside his throat. "They had a fight, like they always did, and Dad lost his temper, like he always did. That time, he took it too far. And that's when I left." His gaze grew hollow as he stared at the campfire. "I promised to avenge my mother. I promised to avenge everything that happened to Flare. And I promised to take my own life when I was finished. I intend to keep all of those promises."

His final words shattered her resolve. Sitting across the fire and pretending his story didn't affect her was impossible. She'd never heard a man speak of so much agony or known one who harbored so much insufferable pain. It was much worse than any torture she ever experienced.

Cora came to his side of the fire and sat down beside him. She didn't know how to comfort her friend with words. What did you say to someone who had lost so much? How did you comfort someone weighed down by guilt?

She moved her arm through his then found his hand. She gripped it tightly, silently telling him she was there—that she would always be there.

He stared at their joined hands then brushed his fingers past hers.

"Flare, it'll get better. It may not happen for a long time, even decades, but it will happen someday."

"No."

She flinched at his rejection. "You have to believe."

"No…my name isn't Flare." He turned his head toward hers, his nose just inches from hers. "It's Rush."

Cora replayed his words endlessly in her mind. Even though she anticipated that kind of revelation at some point, she hadn't been expecting it now. It was hard to swallow. There were two different versions of him; the one she knew now and the one from the past.

"We're getting close now." He walked slightly ahead through the trees.

"How do you know?"

"I've been here before."

"You've been in Eden Star?"

"Not inside it. They would never allow me to pass. But I know the entrance is somewhere nearby. They'll come to us before we ever figure it out. They have eyes all over the forest."

"Is there anything I should know beforehand?"

He slowed his pace and walked beside her, his words coming out as a whisper. "What they don't say is more important than what they do say. You'll have to rely on your intuition if you ever want to integrate with them. If they accept you, don't expect them to be kind to you. You'll be the black sheep among their people."

"You make a lot of assumptions for never having been in Eden Star."

He gave her a cold look. "I knew the elves before the war. I understand how they are."

She'd provoked him unintentionally, so she looked away to dispel the tension.

His gaze bored into her. "You don't look at me the same anymore."

"That's not true." She immediately turned back to him and looked him in the eye. "I admit it was a lot to take in, but I trust the man I know. You made a mistake, as we all have."

"Not just one mistake," he said coldly. "But several. And my remorse doesn't justify what I did. Saying I'm sorry isn't going to cut it."

"If you restore the dragons to their former glory, you'll be vindicated."

"It'll take a lot more than that." He was cold and unforgiving, even to himself. It was like he loathed every fiber of his being.

"I think you're the most admirable man I've ever met."

He stopped in his tracks.

"You saved me from the guards in Polox. You gave me your scales to make a powerful blade. You took me under your wing even when you didn't trust me. When the Shaman captured me, you risked your life to save me. Maybe your heart wasn't in the right place long ago, but it is now. We can't live in the past forever, but we can move forward."

Instead of being inspired or moved, he looked fiercer. His blue eyes were strikingly similar to razor-sharp icicles. "I don't think all the dragons I've broken would agree with you. I don't think all the mothers whose sons I've killed would agree with you. And I don't think the elves would agree after I killed Tiberius Riverglade, their king."

They camped in the forest without a fire. The branches swayed quietly on the trees, singing a quiet song. Cora lay on her back beside Rush, looking up at the stars as they peeked through the lush leaves.

Rush advised against a fire so they wouldn't draw attention to themselves. It was better to approach the elves in the daylight, when their faces were clearly visible, than in the dark when their appearance was more formidable.

Rush still wore his hood, trying to hide his visage as much as possible. Both of his hands were tucked behind his head, and his ankles were crossed. His black clothing camouflaged him into the darkness.

Cora didn't know what to say now that she knew everything about Rush. His past was darker than the night sky, and his soul seemed to be tarnished beyond repair. Maybe there was no hope for him.

"Why aren't you sleeping?" Without looking directly at her, he knew she was awake.

"The sky is so pretty. I don't want to close my eyes."

"Hopefully, you'll be staring at it a lot more." He moved one hand to his stomach and rested it there.

"What's our plan?"

"Meaning?"

"How long should I stay? Where should I meet you when I'm done? Or will we be able to communicate with our minds like before?"

"No. We won't be able to communicate. The ability becomes weaker when the distance increases. Also, the elves protect their realm with spells. I doubt I could project my mind to yours even if I were standing right outside."

"Spells?"

"Yes. Elves use magic."

"I never knew that."

"That's why King Lux fears them so much. They guard their secrets jealously. He might be able to break in to the mind of a dragon, but he would never be able to get an elf to reveal the secrets of magic."

"I wonder if they'll teach me."

"Don't count on it." He crossed his arms over his chest and continued to look up at the sky. "After I leave, assuming they let me go, I'll find the lost island. If that goes well and I return with an army, I'll send a messenger to you. Hopefully, you can convince the elves to join the fight by then."

"But how will that work?"

"What do you mean?"

"You said dragons won't kill other dragons. So, how do you expect to overthrow King Lux?"

He breathed a deep sigh that almost sounded painful. "I haven't gotten that far in my plan. But we may have to make an exception to that rule. If it were me, I would completely understand if they had to take my life. Desperate times call for desperate measures."

Cora hoped it wouldn't come to that. "Keep working on something. I'll try to think of a solution on my end."

"Will do."

"And that's it? We march on High Castle?"

"We hit them hard and fast. Hopefully, we don't have to bring the armies or the citizens into it. And the two stewards won't have enough time to come to his aid if it's by surprise."

"The other steward is also your uncle?"

He nodded. "You can't pick your family, right?"

She grabbed his hand and gave it an affectionate squeeze. "Actually, you can."

Rush moved past a large branch then approached a glade of trees. The trunks were massive and tall, bigger than any of the others across the desert. He looked high into the sky and stared at the leafy canopy before he stopped in the center.

She came up behind him, unsure what the holdup was. "What is it?"

He slowly turned around, his eyes scanning from left to right. "They know we're here."

She looked around, expecting to see someone jump out. "How do you know?"

"I can sense it. They're scared and fearless at the same time."

"Then what do we do?"

He stepped closer to her and kept his voice at a whisper. "This is your last chance, Cora. If you don't want to do this, there's still time to escape. We can fly away."

She knew she had to try. A lot more than just her life was on the line.

"If you want to stay, this is where I leave you."

"You won't be here when they arrive?"

"No. They'll kill me—as they should."

Now that she knew what crime he'd committed, she understood.

"I'm going to ask you again." He looked her hard in the eye. "Do you want to do this?"

Coming to a foreign place with strange people was terrifying for anyone. She didn't expect this journey to be easy, and there was a good chance they would never accept her. But she refused to believe the Great War made her people barbaric and cold. The least they could do was listen to her then release her. She had to believe that. If that weren't the case, then there was no hope for Anastille anyway. "Yes."

His eyes contracted slightly, reacting discreetly to her decision. "You're one brave woman, Cora."

"I know where I get it from." She didn't know how much longer they had, but she suspected it wasn't long.

A slight smile upturned his lips, reaching his eyes more than his mouth.

"I'll talk to you later." She didn't want to say goodbye because goodbyes were too difficult. Somehow, saying goodbye to Rush was harder than saying goodbye to Dorian.

Despite Rush's crimes, she trusted him more than anyone and saw the light in his soul.

"Yeah." He swallowed the lump in his throat. "Later."

She wanted to close her eyes so she didn't have to watch him walk away. But she also didn't want to miss his departure, knowing she would treasure the memory for comfort while she was alone in this strange land.

He sighed like there was something else he wanted to say but dreaded actually saying it. "Look, I know the last kiss wasn't that great. Women usually like it, but for whatever reason, it wasn't my best work. Maybe I drank a little too much… I don't know."

Her lips immediately widened in a smile, and her heart formed wings and began to fly like a hummingbird.

"I swear. I can do a much better job than that. I just need one more chance." He stared at her expectantly, waiting for her permission.

"Then give me your best shot." Just like every other woman, she was attracted to his hard jaw and perfect cheekbones. His lips were full and soft, she already knew from experience, but she wanted to feel them again. Last time, there wasn't a spark, but she hadn't really given it a chance. She remembered the way his chest looked when he was shirtless, and she treasured all the teasing and taunting he directed at her. The dragon's words came back to her mind, telling her she felt something in the same way Rush did.

Rush smiled as he stared at her lips. His arm snaked around her waist, and he leaned down, taking his time in his descent. He pulled her closer to him, preparing her for his touch.

His mouth slowly pressed against hers, and his warm breath fell on her skin. His hand automatically tightened around her waist, squeezing the fabric of her shirt.

Her heart raced with a deadly speed. Blood pounded in her ears, and she was suddenly aware of her body, the feel of his arm under her fingertips, and the feel of his mouth on hers. She had to stand on her tiptoes so he didn't lean as far, but she hardly noticed what she was doing.

Rush slowly moved his mouth against hers, their lips dancing together. One hand snaked into her hair and fisted it tightly as he kept her close to his chest. Every time he breathed, air entered her lungs, giving her a sensation she'd never felt before.

She squeezed both of his arms as she moved her mouth with his. She'd never kissed a man before, so she copied what he did, moving her mouth in a similar way.

He sucked her bottom lip gently before he pulled away, his face still hovering near hers.

Her entire body felt hot and cold at the same time. Her heart didn't slow down even though the kiss was finished. She didn't release her grip on his biceps, comforted by the touch.

His eyes were on hers, taking in every reaction. "How was that?"

"Uh, yeah." She cleared her throat.

He grinned from ear to ear. "I can never have all of you. But I'll treasure this piece for as long as I live."

Her mind was still in a whirlwind from the kiss. A flood of emotions rolled through her, and all she could think about was having that kiss again—and again.

Rush glanced at the trees before he turned back to her. "I really have to go. They're close."

Now she wanted him to leave even less.

He cupped her face and kissed her forehead. "We will see each other again." He backed up with his eyes still trained on her. With a final look of sadness, he turned around and disappeared into the trees.

She remained in place, unable to turn around and face whatever was coming. All she could think about was the loss of her friend, her confidant, and now someone who meant something more.

"Turn around." A deep voice sounded in her ear. It was both magical and musical.

She was too distracted by Rush to care about anything else. She slowly turned around, her arms by her sides.

A fair man with a bow trained on her emerged from the trees. His arrow was prepared to pierce her right through the heart. When he got a look at her face, his aim wavered slightly. He stopped in his tracks as he stared at her, watching her like she might not be real. "Who are you?"

"Cora."

Two other elves emerged from the tree line and flanked her on both sides. They removed her pack as well as her sword.

She didn't fight it because she'd expected it to happen.

"You're coming with us." The lead elf motioned for the other two to follow him.

They didn't threaten or shoot her on sight, and that was a good sign. They didn't even touch her. All they did was stare at her as they silently commanded her to begin walking.

Once she took the first step, a voice sounded in her ear. *I'm always with you, Cora. Even if you can't see me.*

# AFTERWORD

If you enjoyed this book and would like to know if/when I publish others like it, please feel free to **join my mailing list here**.

Printed in Dunstable, United Kingdom